CRUSHING CRYSTAL

Books by Evan Marshall

MISSING MARLENE

HANGING HANNAH

STABBING STEPHANIE

ICING IVY

TOASTING TINA

CRUSHING CRYSTAL

Published by Kensington Publishing Corporation

A Jane Stuart and Winky Mystery

CRUSHING CRYSTAL

EVAN MARSHALL

KENSINGTON BOOKS
www.kensingtonbooks.com

KENSINGTON BOOKS are published by

Kensington Publishing Corp.
850 Third Avenue
New York, NY 10022

All Kensington titles, imprints and distributed lines are available at special quantity discounts for bulk purchases for sales promotion, premiums, fund-raising, educational or institutional use.

Special book excerpts or customized printings can also be created to fit specific needs. For details, write or phone the office of the Kensington Special Sales Manager: Kensington Publishing Corp., 850 Third Avenue, New York, NY, 10022. Attn. Special Sales Department. Phone: 1-800-221-2647.

Kensington and the K logo Reg. U.S. Pat. & TM Off.

Library of Congress Card Catalogue Number: 2004105347
ISBN 0-7582-0228-8

First Printing: November 2004
10 9 8 7 6 5 4 3 2 1

Printed in the United States of America

To Lennie Alickman

Acknowledgments

Once again I would like to thank my talented and supportive editor, John Scognamiglio. I am also grateful to everyone at Kensington Publishing Corporation for all the hard work they do on behalf of my books.

Thanks also to Maureen Walters, my agent at Curtis Brown Ltd., for looking out for my best interests so effectively.

As always, I owe a big thank-you to my family and friends for their continuing love and encouragement. A writer couldn't ask for a better fan club.

Chapter 1

J ane let the heavy carton in her arms slide to the floor with a loud thump, then fell back against the doorjamb. Across the living room, Crystal looked up from the tea she was pouring and smiled sweetly. "Is that the last of them, Jane?"

"No, more coming," Jane said, breathing heavily. How she longed to tell Crystal to get up off her sizable backside and help. But she knew it would do no good. As if Crystal had read Jane's mind, her dark, round face grew wistful.

"I feel awful not helping, but I don't dare risk an asthma attack." She picked up one of the china cups from the coffee table. "Tea?"

Jane forced a smile. "No, thanks." With her foot, she slid the carton to the right, where the other cartons she and Florence had carried up were stacked. Then she left the apartment and took the elevator back downstairs. As she emerged into the lobby, Florence entered from the street, carrying a carton.

"Hold the elevator, please, missus," she said, and huffed and puffed past Jane. Once inside the elevator, she set down the carton. Sweat shone on her pretty light brown face, despite the mid-October chill outside. "I can't thank you enough for your help. I know how you feel about my sister."

Jane couldn't deny it. Crystal Ryerson made her crazy. On the other hand, Crystal had been living with Jane, Jane's eleven-year-old son Nicholas, and Florence, their housekeeper, for the past two weeks. Two weeks of putting up with the most maddening, meddling know-it-all whom Jane had ever met. And now Crystal was leaving, moving to her own apartment. Jane had been only too happy to help.

She gave Florence a warm grin. "Hey, kin is kin, right?"

"Right," Florence replied, nodding, and Jane let the elevator doors slide shut.

There were only four more cartons in the back of the U-Haul Mini Mover truck Crystal had rented. Jane grabbed one and headed back into the four-story brick building.

Twenty minutes later, all the boxes had been carried in, and Jane and Florence stood breathing heavily in Crystal's living room. Crystal, still sitting on the sofa, idly flipped through a copy of *The National Enquirer.* "Oh," she said, looking up brightly. "All done? Now come and have your tea."

Jane and Florence sat down in armchairs facing the sofa. It occurred to Jane that she and Florence were fortunate that Crystal had taken a furnished apartment. Then again, Crystal hadn't had much choice. Her separation six months ago from her husband, Dennis Ryerson, had been swift and bitter. By Crystal's account, Crystal and Dennis had had a fight to end all fights, and Crystal had stormed out. Jane secretly wondered if in reality Dennis had thrown her out, fed up with her loud, bossy ways. At any rate, Crystal said she'd been lucky even to get her clothes and belongings out of the house.

Florence poured tea for Jane and herself. "This is so nice," she said with her lilting Trinidadian accent, looking around the sunny little room. "Isn't it, Crystal? A new start for you." Her gaze traveled over the tea things and she frowned. "No Equal or Splenda?"

Crystal looked scandalized. "Of course not! I've told you, those things give you brain cancer. Use sugar."

"Actually," Florence said pleasantly, "I was reading an article about artificial sweeteners the other day in *Ladies' Home Journal,* and the scientists say there's no clear evidence of that. Cyclamate, on the other hand . . ." But she didn't bother finishing. Crystal was glaring at her, eyes slitted. Florence forced an artificial smile. "I guess I'll use sugar."

"Of course you will," Crystal said with a slow nod, sliding the sugar bowl toward her. "Now, what were we saying?"

"A new start for you," Jane said in a dull monotone.

Crystal smiled sadly. "I hope so. You've both been so kind to me, and I do like New Jersey so much more than Florida. But this job . . ." She shook her head sadly. "I don't know."

Four months after Crystal and Dennis separated, Florence heard of an opening at the Shady Hills Public Library for an assistant director. Crystal, who was unhappy in her job as assistant librarian in an elementary school, eagerly flew from Florida to Shady Hills to interview with the library director and, to her delight, got the job. She was to start two weeks before she could move into the apartment she'd rented, and Jane felt she had no choice but to invite her to live at her house in the interim.

"Isn't the job going well?" Florence asked.

"The *job* is fine," Crystal replied, black eyes flashing. "It's that insufferable woman I've got to work with. She won't listen to reason!"

Crystal was referring to Mindy Carter, the library's director. Ever since Mindy had arrived in Shady Hills six months earlier, Jane had found her sweet and easygoing. But apparently she was not so easygoing that she would bend to Crystal's bossing. "It's all about compromise, right?" Jane said brightly. "Working together."

"Not always." Crystal set down her teacup with a bang, sloshing tea onto the coffee table. But she took no notice. "Not when someone's ideas are old-fashioned and just plain wrong. As I said"—she cast a fatalistic gaze downward—"I don't know how this will all work out."

Jane glanced down at her tea. When she looked up, Florence was staring at her. She gave her head a quick jerk toward the door to signal it was time to go.

Jane couldn't have agreed more. "Well!" she said, setting down her tea and rising. "I really should get to the office."

"Yes, of course you should, missus," Florence said, standing. "My sister and I are so grateful for your help."

"Yes, Jane," Crystal said, staying put. "Thank you. I can't imagine how I'll get on without you all." She picked up *The National Enquirer* and resumed browsing, then looked up. "Oh, I almost forgot. Dinner tonight?"

Florence's smile froze. "Uh . . ."

"Sure," Jane said, figuring if she could stand two weeks of dinners with Crystal, she could stand yet another dinner. If necessary, she would speak to Florence about weaning Crystal away.

"See you tonight, then," Crystal said without looking up, and Florence and Jane hurried out.

In the elevator, Florence said, "Don't worry, missus, I'll speak to her about coming over so much."

Jane only smiled. She loved Florence like family, and would do anything to help her, but she wasn't about to lie and say Crystal was welcome anytime, because in truth Jane had begun to find her company unbearable.

They emerged from the building into the cold sunshine.

Across the street at the edge of the pavement ran a low railing, beyond which the ground fell steeply away, affording a view of thickly wooded hills in golds and oranges that were almost painfully bright.

"Beautiful, isn't it?" Jane said. She loved this town, had grown to love it more and more over the eleven years since she and her late husband, Kenneth, had moved both their home and their literary agency here from New York City. Four years earlier, when Kenneth died—hit by a truck in New York City—Jane had thought she couldn't go on. But she had gone on, of course. Pain softened over time. And life was good now. She had Nick and Florence and two affectionate cats, lots of dear friends, a home she loved, and a thriving business. Yes, life was very good indeed.

"Missus?" Florence said softly.

"Hm?" Jane turned, feeling as if she'd been a million miles away. "Sorry. Daydreaming."

"I just wanted to say I'll return the truck."

"Thanks. See you tonight." Jane got into her car, a sleek, silver three-year-old Jaguar XJR she had bought the previous month. Waving as she passed Florence, she headed down Fremont Lane toward Fenwyck, which would take her toward the heart of town.

When Jane arrived at the office, Daniel was standing on his desk, attaching the end of a string of artificial fall leaves to the wall.

"Well, well!" she said, and he jumped, nearly falling off the edge of the desk. "Sorry!" She hurried over to help. She held up the other end of the string of leaves. "Where are you going to put this end?"

He gazed downward, a frown of concentration on his handsome dark face. Dear sweet Daniel, so serious and careful about everything he did. "I think right up here," he said, indicating a spot at the same level as the other end, about five feet away. From the pocket of his gray flannel slacks he took an adhesive strip, peeled off the backing, and fastened the leaves securely to the wall. Then he stepped back, careful not to fall, and regarded his handiwork.

"I'm impressed," Jane said. "I don't believe you've ever put up decorations before. What's next? A costume on Halloween?"

He hopped down from the desk. "Not a chance. This is it for now. Ginny's been decorating the apartment with Indian corn and gourds. I guess she got me into the spirit."

Jane smiled. Ginny Williams, her best friend, was Daniel's significant live-in other. Jane would never have guessed that two such different people—lighthearted, often silly Ginny and solemn, serious Daniel—could be attracted to each other, but almost a year earlier, not long after Daniel had tragically lost his new wife, these two wonderful people had come together.

Daniel sat down behind his desk, putting his blotter and papers back in place. He turned to his computer monitor, ready to work, then spun abruptly to face Jane and frowned. "Why are you wearing sweats?"

"Am I?" she answered, wide-eyed, then laughed. "Florence and I were helping Crystal move into her new apartment." She lifted the shopping bag in her hand. "Got my work duds right here."

He nodded, turning back to his keyboard. "Bet you're not sorry to see her go."

"No, that I'm not," she admitted, setting her briefcase on the credenza in the reception room. Opening it, she removed a stack of book proposals she'd read the night before. One of them she set aside. She'd liked what she read and would ask the author to send her the complete manuscript. The rest of the proposals she placed atop a stack of material already awaiting rejection letters.

Before heading into her office, she popped into the bathroom to change into slacks, blouse, and low heels. She put her sweats in the shopping bag to take home at the end of the day.

Stepping into her office, she stopped at the sight of the work pile in the center of her desk. It had grown considerably since the day before. "What have you added?" she called out to Daniel.

"A bunch of contracts came this morning," he answered through the intercom. Daniel did not like to yell.

She nodded, settling into her chair. The pile was always there—Daniel had long ago given up trying to organize Jane, especially when she insisted she worked most efficiently this way—but she couldn't recall that it had ever been quite this high before. With a shrug and a sigh of resignation, she gently lifted a contract from the top—an agreement from Kensington for three Regency romances by Elaine Lawler—leaned back in her chair, and began to read.

From the reception area came the sound of the street door opening and then slamming shut.

"Is she here?" It was a woman's voice, deep and throaty.

"Yes," came Daniel's response, "but— Mrs. Lovesey!"

The door of Jane's office burst inward with a crash. Framed in the doorway was Myrtle Lovesey, a woman Jane knew but not well. She was tall and strikingly thin, with a raw bony face from which exceptionally pale blue eyes shone fiercely, and a short cap of wavy white hair. In one hand she clutched an enormous brown handbag. She glared at Jane, who couldn't for the life of her figure out what this woman was doing here.

"Mrs. Lovesey, what on earth is the matter?"

For a moment Mrs. Lovesey chewed on the inside of her lower lip. Then her nostrils flared and she took two steps into the room. "Mrs. Stuart," she said in her hoarse, almost manly voice, "I need to talk to you about that—that woman—" But she couldn't go on because she had burst into tears. She fished in her bag for a wad of crumpled tissues, which she pressed to each of her eyes.

Jane jumped up and hurried over to the older woman. "Mrs. Lovesey," she said, guiding her to the chair facing her desk, "what is it? What's happened?"

Myrtle dropped into the chair and sniffed hard. "Mrs. Stuart, it's that woman, Crystal Ryerson. I didn't know who else to talk to."

Crystal. A feeling of dread came over Jane. It was Myrtle, a real estate agent and apartment broker who ran an agency across the green called The Home Place, who had helped Crystal find her apartment. Could Myrtle's distress be somehow related? It must be, but how?

"Why don't you just tell me what's the matter?" Jane suggested gently, returning to her chair. "Would you like some tea?"

"No, thank you." For a moment Mrs. Lovesey stared at Jane, as if deciding how best to begin. "Mrs. Stuart," she said at last, "Crystal Ryerson has done an awful thing. I know she's no relation of yours—I know she's your housekeeper's sister—but I felt that since she was staying with you, and you're a responsible person in town"—with one hand she vaguely indicated the office, the shelves lined with books Jane's agency had handled—"and a mother yourself, that maybe you could help me."

"Just tell me what she's done, Mrs. Lovesey."

"Call me Myrtle." She swallowed. "While I was showing apartments to Mrs. Ryerson, I made a terrible mistake. She and I got to talking about our lives—she told me about separating from her husband, moving up here for the library job—and I guess I got to thinking she was someone I could talk to, someone I could confide in."

Boy, did you think wrong, Jane thought, dreading the rest of the story.

"Anyways, I told her about my daughter." Myrtle tilted her head a little to the side and gave Jane a sad smile. "I don't know you very well, Mrs. Stuart."

"Jane."

"Jane. Your late husband's cousin Stephanie—may she rest in peace—I helped her find her apartment last year, but otherwise you and I have never had any contact. So I assume you don't know about my daughter."

Jane shook her head.

"Vivian, she's twenty-eight now. When she was growing up, she was one of the wild kids in Shady Hills. You and your husband moved here—what?—eleven years ago?"

"That's right."

"Then you might remember hearing talk about my Vivian. She would have been seventeen when you moved here, but then again, you probably didn't hear much about the high school."

"No," Jane admitted.

"Vivian got in a lot of trouble. She was arrested a number of times for drunken driving. She was part of a group that did some vandalism out at the old Porter place on Highland. Anyway, my late husband Eric and me, we had a rough time with her."

Myrtle took a deep breath and cast her gaze about the room. "Long story short, Vivian never graduated high school. She got involved with drugs—heavily involved. She ran away. Eric and me, we didn't hear from her for a full year." Tears sprang to those stark blue eyes. "Then she came back and it broke our hearts. She was so down, she couldn't have gone any lower. She begged us to help her. She couldn't get off the drugs—it was heroin she was on." She pursed her lips as if to keep from crying, then nodded. "We got her into a treatment center. You know, where they do the methadone. Vivian spent a month there, and after that she seemed like a new person, happy for the first time in years, looking forward to the future."

Myrtle's gaze dropped to her lap. She shook her head. "But she went back on," she said, her eyes still lowered. "We lost her again for a while . . . and then one day she was back, asking Eric and me for help. So we tried the treatment center again. It worked, and this time Vivian *stayed* clean. That was almost ten years ago."

Jane nodded encouragingly. What did this have to do with Crystal?

"Vivian's been working at The Home Depot in East Hanover for the past four years. She's working her way up—she has a desk job in the office now. She likes it there. The work is good and the people are nice to her.

"She met a fella there. They started going out, and they were going to get married. Vivian got pregnant. Then she and this man, Brendan his name is, they had a big fight. I think it was because Vivian told him about the drugs. I don't know for sure. Anyways, they broke up, but Vivian had the baby. Emily—that's my granddaughter—she'll be two next month." Myrtle clutched her wad of tissues in both hands and leaned forward beseechingly. "Vivian's a good mother, Jane, she truly is. She's just . . . had some problems. She's been depressed—you know, about breaking up with Brendan and all. I explained this to Mrs. Ryerson."

"Yes?" Jane encouraged her softly.

Myrtle let her hands drop to her lap. "I told Mrs. Ryerson that Vivian's had some more problems lately. You know, with drugs. She's been taking pain pills, Vicodin and such. She's already told me she's going to get some help for it—most likely at the same treatment center she already went to. I'll take care of Emily, of course."

Jane could stand it no longer. "Mrs. Lovesey—Myrtle, please. What exactly did Crystal do?"

"She called DYFS on us. You know, the Department of Youth and Social Services. She reported Vivian. *And she's never even met her.*"

"Oh good heavens," Jane said under her breath.

"She did. Called them right up and made a formal report. Told them Vivian is an unfit mother who's fighting a longtime drug addiction, and that Emily should be taken away from her."

With these words, Myrtle burst into tears, taking great gasps of air and floundering around in her great handbag for more tissues but coming up empty-handed. Jane quickly passed her a box of Kleenex from the top of her desk.

"Thanks. Can you believe she did that? Meddled in our lives like that? Not to mention betraying my confidence. I thought I could *trust* her."

Jane's heart went out to this woman who had been through so much. "But what can I do?" she asked. "Why haven't you spoken to Crystal herself?"

Myrtle scrunched up her face. "It wouldn't do any good coming from me, you must see that. Someone who would do a thing like that isn't going to *un*do it just because I tell her Vivian and me are upset."

She shook her head. "It's got to come from someone she'll listen to. I bet she'd listen to you." She looked into Jane's eyes. "I want you to tell Mrs. Ryerson to call DYFS and take back what she said. Say it was a mistake, that she—she got it wrong. If she doesn't, they're going to send out a social worker. Someone's already called Vivian, a woman who wants to come out a week from today. She told her that Crystal Ryerson had reported her. Vivian told her she didn't know anyone by that name, but the woman said she still had to check it out.

"You know what's gonna happen when she comes. If Vivian so much as looks at her the wrong way, she's going to take little Emily away. They won't give her to me, you know. If they take her away, they'll put her in a foster home while they work on adopting her out. I know this, because—well, I'll confide in *you*, Mrs. Stuart, because I know I can—I almost lost Vivian when I was first married to Eric. I had a drinking problem—*have* a drinking problem. I'm an alcoholic. A recovering alcoholic, but an alcoholic just the same. When I was about Vivian's age, someone called DYFS on me and I nearly lost her."

Suddenly she jumped to her feet. "No one's going to do that to my Vivian. She's getting the help she needs, she's *not* an unfit mother, and *none of this*"—she pounded her fist on Jane's desk, making the heap of papers wobble perilously—"is any of Crystal Ryerson's business!"

Gazing up at this poor woman, Jane wondered what she could possibly achieve with the smugly confident and headstrong Crystal, but she wasn't about to tell Myrtle Lovesey that. "Of course I'll speak to her. I'm so terribly sorry."

"Thank you. I knew you'd understand. Because if . . ." Myrtle stopped, clearly having thought better of what she'd been about to say. "Thank you." Then she slowly rose, turned, and walked stiffly from the room. Jane heard the agency's front door open and close.

Daniel's face appeared in Jane's doorway, eyes wide, brows raised inquiringly.

"Don't ask," she told him, exhaustion washing over her as she realized she'd have to speak to Crystal tonight.

Somehow Jane got through Elaine Lawler's contract, though reading and marking it up took at least twice as long as it usually did. She couldn't stop thinking about Crystal. How *dare* she do that to Myrtle's daughter? What business was it of hers? The thought of Crystal picking up the phone and calling DYFS in that self-righteous way she had made Jane's face burn with anger.

She had set aside Elaine's contract and started to read a manuscript from a promising new author she was interested in, when Daniel buzzed her.

"Goddess on line one."

Jane couldn't help smiling. She always got a kick out of the eccentric Goddess, the worldwide pop star sensation—and her biggest client. The previous year, Jane had sold Goddess's autobiography, *My Life on Top.* It had now been out for four months and was still selling phenomenally. The previous month, Jane had made a new book deal for the young star—a novelty book called *Can You Stand It?* For this work, a compilation of everything in the world that Goddess hated, she would receive a royalty advance of seven and a half million dollars. Jane's commission would be 15 percent of that.

She pressed line one.

"How's it treatin' ya, Janey?" Goddess said in her trademark blasé tone, chomping hard on gum.

"Can't complain. Are you in New York?"

Among Goddess's numerous homes was a townhouse on the Upper East Side in New York City. That was where she had been spending most of her time lately, while starring in a one-woman Broadway show, *Goddess of Love,* which had been one of the hottest tickets in town for nearly two years. Only two weeks earlier the show had closed. Goddess had grown tired of it.

"Yep, me and the Apple," Goddess replied. "Gettin' bored."

"Bored! What about your new book? And that new movie you're going to be doing?" Goddess had mentioned that this fall she would start filming a movie called *Taking It,* costarring Denzel Washington and Ben Stiller. The film was to be a follow-up to *Doing It,* the movie that had first put Goddess on the map.

"The movie hasn't started yet. Which leaves the book."

"And how is that going?" Jane knew there wasn't really much for Goddess to do on it, since it was being ghost-written, as the first book had been.

"It's wipin' me out, babe. I am, like, pan-fried. I mean, sittin' with that buttoned-up little notebook girl"—she meant her ghostwriter, Adriana Fink—"spillin' my guts. Comin' up with more things I hate. Truth is, I've realized I don't hate that much."

"That's good to hear, but the book was your idea, so I hope you can come up with enough—"

"Yeah, yeah. Don't worry about it. But you see what I mean, right? This writing business is a killer."

"Yes, I do understand," Jane said indulgently, smirking. "And filming your new movie will start soon, won't it? That will be very exciting."

"Jane, you sound like my second-grade teacher. Drop the Julie Andrews bit, okay? Yeah, I'm psyched about the movie. It'll be pretty sweet. That's what I'm calling you about."

"Oh?"

"Mm. Lunch tomorrow."

"What?"

"You're having lunch with me tomorrow."

"I am? Why?"

"Because I'm going shopping today, that's why!" Shopping was one of Goddess's greatest weaknesses.

"Goddess," Jane said patiently, as if talking to a child, "how do you know I'm free for lunch tomorrow?"

"Well, are you?"

"Let me check," Jane said, though she knew she was, and paused as if checking her calendar. "You're in luck. I'm free."

"Yeah, I'm in luck," Goddess said, clearly on to Jane, and snapped her gum with a sharp crack that hurt Jane's ear. "See you then."

"Wait! Where? What time?"

"Unnnh!" Goddess said with a groan. "I don't know! Call the house tomorrow. Seeya."

As time went on, Goddess handled fewer and fewer of the mundane details of everyday life. Jane would call her townhouse in the morning, and one of Goddess's maids would tell her where and when to meet the star. Jane had to laugh. With Goddess, life was always interesting.

Chapter 2

Goddess didn't distract Jane from her thoughts of Crystal for long. By lunchtime she thought she would burst. She decided to have lunch at Whipped Cream, a café straight across the green from her office. Her friend Ginny was the waitress there.

"Want to come along?" Jane asked Daniel as she crossed the reception room to get her coat from the closet.

"Thanks, Jane," he said, slipping on his tweed sport jacket, "but I promised Ginny I'd run a few errands at lunchtime. Give her my love."

"Will do."

She emerged from the office into a blaze of autumn sunshine. Across Center Street, huge old oaks rose from the village green and spread their sharp reds and golds against a cloudless sky of an intense cerulean blue. She crossed the street and took one of the paths that transected the green, passing the big white Victorian bandstand on the right. Now directly ahead she saw the window of Whipped Cream, one of many intricately mullioned windows in the line of shops that curved around the green on three sides. Mock Tudor, half-timbered, with their dark, steeply pitched roofs and multitude of gables, they reminded Jane of something out of a Renaissance fair. As she reached the far end of the green, a brisk wind seemed to come up from nowhere, playing with her hair and finding its way under her jacket, which she pulled tighter around her.

Entering Whipped Cream, she was surprised to find the café nearly empty. In the back right corner of the storefront shop sat an elderly woman with a fluff of blue-white hair whom Jane had seen before. She was crocheting what appeared to be a baby blanket, stopping occasionally to nibble on an immense muffin.

Jane grabbed her favorite table—in the left rear, only a few feet from a fireplace that crackled cozily in the wall of used brick. Sitting down, she scanned the café for Ginny, who appeared from behind the high counter with a coffee-pot and refreshed the elderly lady's cup. Looking up, she saw Jane, and her pretty, pixyish face lit up.

"Hey," she said, coming over.

"Where is everybody?" Jane asked.

Ginny laughed. "It's barely twelve. You obviously had to get out of the office."

"And how."

Ginny plunked down opposite Jane, setting down the coffeepot. She threw a surreptitious glance toward the back of the shop. "Can't talk long. George and Charlie are in a bad mood today because they just found out the rent's going up. Did yours?"

Jane nodded. "But it's not that big an increase."

"Any increase is too big an increase for George and Charlie." Ginny leaned forward on her elbows. "So why the getaway?"

"Crystal," Jane said on a groan.

"Ah," Ginny replied, as if that said it all. "What's she done now?"

Jane took a deep breath and told her about Myrtle

Lovesey and her daughter, Vivian. As Ginny listened, her eyes bugged out.

"You've got to be kidding me."

"Nope. Can you believe that?"

"Jane, this woman's got to be stopped—she's out of control. But why did Myrtle come to you?"

"She felt it would do more good than talking to Crystal directly."

Ginny looked dubious. "Are you going to talk to her?"

"Ginny!" came Charlie's gravelly voice from behind the counter. Jane looked up and saw the top of his head above a carrot cake.

"I'd better go," Ginny whispered, popping out of her chair and grabbing the coffeepot. "Right here!" she called out. "Listen," she said to Jane, "if you do talk to Crystal, *good luck.*" And she hurried away.

Luck indeed. It had never occurred to Jane not to speak to Crystal, but she realized now that doing so would probably do no good. Myrtle had been right: A person who would do such a thing in the first place would be highly difficult if not impossible to persuade to back down.

Ginny reappeared with a mug of coffee for Jane. "What about lunch?" she asked. "What'll ya have?"

"I don't know," Jane said, her voice troubled. "A sandwich, I guess. Tuna?"

"You got it." Ginny hurried over to a table at which two men had just sat down. Jane recognized them as Jonah Kramer and Peter Chu from Up, Up and Away, the travel agency next door to her office.

Jane took a copy of *Publishers Weekly* from her bag and leafed through it while she waited for her lunch. An elderly red-haired woman whom Jane saw here frequently came in and joined the crocheting white-haired woman.

A few moments later the café door opened again, and

Jane looked up to see Eloise Houghton come in. Jane's Nick and Eloise's son Aaron were close friends. Eloise saw Jane, smiled, and waved. She approached the counter as if to place a takeout order, then seemed to think of something and came over to Jane's table.

"How are you, Jane?" Eloise's smile seemed stretched to its limit. Jane often wondered how much of this bouncy little woman's sweetness was put on, but others who knew Eloise said she was a genuinely warm, kind person. Perhaps, but she was also one of the most gossipy people Jane knew, so she was always careful about what she told Eloise. On the heels of this thought came an image of poor Myrtle Lovesey confiding in haughty, holier-than-thou Crystal, and inwardly Jane winced.

All of these thoughts had passed through Jane's head in a fleeting moment. She forced her mind clear and smiled up at Eloise. "I'm well, thanks. And you?"

"Couldn't be better," Eloise chirped. "Jeremy's just been promoted, so needless to say, we're thrilled. How is Nick doing?"

"Oh, he's fine."

Eloise's expression grew thoughtful. "Good . . . good." She frowned. "Jane, has Nick told you what's been happening at school?"

Here she goes. "No, I don't think so." *Please don't go on forever.*

"Well . . ." Eloise dropped into the chair facing Jane's. "It's actually quite awful. Some things have been"—she looked from side to side as if to make sure no one was listening, and lowered her voice to a stage whisper—*"stolen."*

"Really?" Jane frowned, sitting up a little. This was actually interesting. "What things?"

"Computers. A number of them." Eloise wiggled her carefully tweezed brows. "What do you think of that?"

It was, it occurred to Jane, as if the other woman were trying for a good grade in gossip.

"I'd say that's an A-plus—I mean I think that *is* awful. Have they got any idea who did it?"

"Nah. But from what I hear, it's an inside job."

Jane waited for more.

"No break-ins. Several times now the computers have simply been—gone!"

"I see. Surely the police are keeping an eye on things," Jane said, thinking of her boyfriend, Detective Stanley Greenberg of the Shady Hills Police Department.

Eloise gave her a playful wink. "You'd know that better than I would. Anywho-how, I wondered if you knew about that." She rose. "Better run. Got a zillion errands. Thought I'd stop in and pick up a sandwich." She raised her eyes to the ceiling. "So busy I have to eat it in the car!"

Eloise was always extremely busy. That was fine by Jane.

"You have a fabulous day now, Jane," Eloise said, twiddling her fingers, and hurried back to the counter. "I'd like the turkey salad with walnuts on the dark rye," Jane heard her tell George.

Jane returned to her magazine. A moment later Ginny appeared with her tuna sandwich. As she set it down, Jane looked up and saw Ginny watching Eloise. Looking back at Jane, Ginny whispered, "I can't stand that woman." Then she stepped over to Jonah and Peter and asked if they had everything they needed.

Still thinking about the stolen computers, Jane took a bite of her sandwich.

When she returned to her office, there was a pink message slip on her chair. Daniel, who hadn't returned yet from his errands, had written: *Please call Salomé Sutton— important.*

Jane felt a flutter of anxiety in the pit of her stomach. Salomé Sutton, the legendary romance writer, had become Jane's client three months earlier. Sal, as Jane called her, had been unhappy at her longtime publisher, Corsair Publishing, and Jane had pried her loose. Now Jane was trying to find Sal a new home—so far, without success.

She dropped into her chair and dialed Sal's number in California. A maid answered and called Sal to the phone.

"How's it going, Jane?" came the older woman's booming voice. "Any news for me?"

"No, not at the—"

"Never mind, I know you don't. That's not why I'm calling. I want to see you next week."

Jane frowned, puzzled. "See me. In California?"

"No! I'm coming to New York. Staying with my sister Bernice for a month, do it every year. Anyway, I'll be there on Sunday. You free any day next week?"

Jane had no desire to have lunch with Sal but realized there was no way out of it. The sooner she got it over with, the better. She had some things to tell Sal.

She checked her calendar. "How about Monday?"

"Sure, great. Let's do it. I'll call you that morning and we'll figure it out."

"Good," Jane said with manufactured enthusiasm. "Looking forward to it."

"Me, too. Bring me some good news." And Sal hung up.

Jane drove up Lilac Way, crunching leaves under the Jaguar's wheels. It was only a little past five but already dark. She turned into her driveway, through the space in the tall holly hedge, and pulled into the garage of her chocolate brown chalet-style house. As soon as she cut the engine, the garage light overhead was switched on and the door into the kitchen was thrown open.

"Hi, Mom!" Nick—she couldn't get used to how tall he'd grown—stood smiling at the top of the three stairs. At his feet, rubbing up against his leg, was Winky, their small tortoiseshell cat, and in Nick's arms was Twinky, Winky's identical ten-month-old female kitten.

"Hello, missus!" Florence appeared behind Nick. She saw Jane pull her briefcase from the backseat of the car. "Nick," she said softly, "go help your mother."

Nick handed the kitten to Florence, came down the steps, and retrieved Jane's heavy case. She planted a kiss on the soft brown hair atop his head. "Thank you, young man."

He winked at her, and in that moment he looked exactly like his father. "My pleasure, madam!"

Laughing, she followed him into the house. Florence was at the stove, stirring a large pot. The kitchen was filled with the aroma of savory beef and spices.

"Florence, that smells delicious."

"Thank you. It's my best pelau."

At that moment Crystal's immense figure filled the doorway from the family room, and both Jane's and Florence's smiles vanished. Jane had to work hard to put hers back on again.

"Hello, Crystal."

"Good evening, Jane," Crystal said with a grin, and hurrying over, grabbed Jane in a tight embrace. Jane was overcome by a warm wave of Cinnabar perfume. "I can't thank you enough for helping to move me into my apartment this morning." She patted Jane's back soundly. "You are truly a good friend."

"It was my pleasure," Jane said awkwardly, gently extricating herself from Crystal's grip. She marched through the family room toward the foyer closet and hung up her coat, thankful for a reason to get away.

As she slid the closet door shut, there was a frantic scampering from the dining room. An instant later Twinky leaped through the foyer and up the stairs, followed by Winky. Taking up the rear was Alphonse, the latest addition to the Stuart household.

Early in the year, Jane had rescued the collie from an abusive owner and placed him with her friend Penny Powell, a member of Jane's knitting group. Penny and her husband had had Alphonse for eight months when their daughter, Rebecca, developed an allergy to the animal. Jane had agreed to take him back until she could find him a new home.

Watching the beautiful collie bound up the stairs after the two cats, Jane smiled. The poor creature had been so sad and ill when Jane had found him. Now his light gold and white fur was abundant and smooth, his eyes were happy and bright, and it seemed he was always on the run. He let out a loud bark when he reached the upper landing, then trotted warily down the hallway, playing hide-and-seek with his two feline friends.

Crystal appeared at the door to the living room. "Jane, dinner's ready."

Better get it over with. "Crystal, could I talk with you for a minute?"

Crystal gave a little smile and furrowed her brows. "Of course. Is something wrong?"

"Let's sit in the living room," Jane said, and led the way to the sofa, where they sat. "Crystal," she began quietly, "Myrtle Lovesey came to see me today."

Her smile vanishing, Crystal became wary, watching Jane. "Oh?"

Jane nodded. "She's very upset, as I'm sure you can imagine."

Crystal drew herself up, nostrils flaring. "Yes, I'm sure she is."

"Crystal, you had no right calling DYFS like that. What on earth were you thinking?"

Crystal studied Jane for a moment. Then her shoulders

rose and fell in a pitying little laugh. "What was I think-ing? That if more people made telephone calls like the one I made, fewer children would be victims of negligence, abuse—"

"Whoa, whoa!" Jane shook her head in amazement, anger rising. "You've never even *met* Myrtle's daughter. Who are you to take it upon yourself to report her?"

"Who am I? Someone who cares. Someone who isn't afraid to stick my neck out."

"But you don't have the facts. All you know is what Myrtle confided to you."

"And that's a lot."

"All right," Jane conceded, "it is a lot. Yes, Vivian has problems. But she's dealing with them. You have no idea what kind of mother she is. Now, because of what you've done, Vivian's baby may be taken away."

Crystal placed a hand on Jane's and gave her a tiny pa-tient smile, as if speaking to a child. "Jane, dear, no one has said the baby will be taken away. That's the whole point of DYFS sending out a social worker to investigate. If there's no problem, Vivian will keep the baby. End of story."

"It's not as simple as that. I've heard of cases in which DYFS takes a child when there *may* be a problem. Just to be on the safe side."

"Isn't that what they *should* do? Be on the safe side?" Crystal gave Jane a sidelong frown. "Sometimes I wonder about you, Jane."

Once again Jane felt anger boiling up inside her toward this insufferable, meddlesome busybody. "Crystal—"

"And why didn't Myrtle—or for that matter, Vivian—come speak to me directly? How dare you stick your nose in this?"

Jane's mouth fell. "Myrtle asked me to speak to you be-cause she knew you wouldn't listen to her. I want you to call the Department of Youth and Social Services and take back what you said."

Crystal's nostrils flared again and she rose grandly. "Myrtle was right. I wouldn't have listened to her. And I'm not listening to you, either. I know I did the right thing. I'm sorry you can't see that. I will *not* take back what I said. Not a single word of it." She turned and headed for the dining room, where Jane could see Florence serving Nick and casting puzzled glances toward the living room.

Following Crystal into the dining room, Jane realized her hands were shaking. Crystal had taken the seat next to Nick and was playing a teasing game with him, gently pinching his arm. They burst out laughing.

"Missus," Florence said brightly, a plate in her hand. "May I serve you some pelau?"

"Yes, thank you," Jane said absently, sitting at the head of the table.

"Here you are." As Florence handed Jane the plate, she gave Jane a frown of puzzled inquiry. Jane shook her head as if to say, "Not now."

"Well!" Florence said brightly when everyone had been served. "I hope you all like my special dinner."

"Why'd you make a special dinner, Flo?"

Jane said, "Nicholas, I've told you not to call her Flo. She doesn't like it. Her name is Florence."

"Thank you, missus," Florence said.

"Don't call me Nicholas," Nick said.

"See!" Jane replied. "You don't like being called Nicholas—and that's your name!"

"All right, all right," Nick said, rolling his eyes wearily, and turned to Florence. Punctiliously he said, "Why the special dinner, *Florence*?"

"Why, to celebrate my sister's moving into her new apartment. An exciting new beginning in Shady Hills."

Florence frowned. Crystal was digging around in her pelau with her fork.

"What the devil . . . ?" Crystal murmured, then looked up. "Florence, what kind of peas are these?"

Florence hesitated, as if afraid to give the wrong answer. "They're black-eyed peas."

Crystal looked at her as if she were insane. "Black-eyed peas? You're supposed to use pigeon peas. You know that."

"Yes, but I couldn't find pigeon peas." Florence's tone was patient and controlled. "My recipe said it was all right to substitute black-eyed peas."

"Your recipe!" Crystal dug around some more and let out a scornful chuckle. "What Mama would say about this, I can't imagine." Shaking her head, she began to eat, carefully avoiding the peas.

Jane threw Florence a look. Florence shrugged.

Nick was glancing around the table uncomfortably. Suddenly his face lit up. "Something interesting happened today."

Poor Nick, Jane thought, trying to restore peace. "Yes, darling? What happened?"

He put down his fork dramatically. "We had gym class outside today—you know, running on the track? Aaron and me, we were kind of fooling around, so when it was time to go back into the building, we were the last ones."

"Yes?" Crystal said impatiently.

Nick twisted in his chair and looked at her in surprise. "Well, as we were walking through the parking lot, we saw Mr. Stanton—he's the assistant media specialist at our school—putting something in the back of his station wagon."

"Really?" Jane said, though she wondered where this story was going.

He nodded. "It was the weirdest thing. When he saw us, he grabbed a blanket and threw it over the thing he had just put in, but Aaron and I saw it anyway. It was a computer."

Jane frowned, remembering what Eloise had told her at Whipped Cream about the thefts at the middle school.

As if reading her mind, Nick went on, "Did you know a lot of computer equipment has been stolen at our school?"

"How do you know that, dear?" Jane asked pleasantly.

"Aaron told me. I think he found out from his mom."

Jane shook her head. "Now, Nicholas—"

"It's *Nick*!" he cried.

"Nick. You mustn't jump to conclusions without having all the facts." Slowly Jane turned her head and gave Crystal a meaningful look. Crystal looked away.

Nick gave a great shrug. "I'm not jumping to conclusions. I'm just telling you what Aaron and I saw."

"Yes," Florence piped up, "but by telling us both of these things together, you're implying that it's this Mr. Stanton who's stealing the computers."

Nick took a forkful of pelau. "Maybe he is!"

"Nick," Crystal said in a casual tone, "what's the name of your media specialist at school?"

"He's just told you," Jane said. "It's Mr. Stanton."

"No, Jane," Crystal said with forced patience, "he's the *assistant* media specialist. I'm talking about his boss."

"That's Ms. Bryant," Nick said.

Jane eyed Crystal suspiciously. "Why do you want to know that?"

Crystal shrugged. "I'm a librarian, she's a librarian . . . I'm trying to build up my contacts here in town, that's all. You never know."

Florence knit her brows. "You never know what?"

"You never know what the future holds. If things don't

work out for me at the library, I may need to speak to people like this Ms. Bryant."

Watching Crystal, Jane felt distinctly uncomfortable. "How did work go today, Crystal?" she asked, steering the conversation onto more comfortable ground.

"Well, as I've told you," Crystal said with a deep sigh, "Mindy Carter is going to be a problem. I'll admit it was kind of her to give me the morning off so I could move into my apartment. But she's very set in her ways and won't listen to good ideas."

"You mean *your* ideas," Jane said with an icy smile.

"That's right, Jane, my ideas. Some of them are quite good."

Florence looked back and forth between Jane and Crystal, an expression of mild alarm on her face.

"But we shall see," Crystal went on cryptically. "I'm going to give her time." She smiled fondly. "Thank goodness for Ashley."

"Who's Ashley?" Nick asked.

"Ashley Surow, a lovely high school girl who works at the library part-time. She is not only beautiful, she is also very sensible, very levelheaded. A good girl. I enjoy my little chats with her."

"Because she listens to your ideas?" Jane asked.

Crystal's nostrils flared.

Florence jumped up. "Are we ready for dessert?"

"Sure, Flo—I mean Florence."

Florence began clearing the table. Jane rose to help. Crystal turned to Jane. "It was my idea, for instance, to start the reading group at the library. Did you know that?"

"No, I didn't," Jane said pleasantly. "Good for you." *Somebody please get this woman out of my house.* "When is the first meeting, by the way?"

"Next Tuesday, ten A.M. You've read the book, I hope?"

"Sure have," said Jane, who had to admit the reading group had been a good idea. She had recruited her fellow knitting club members, and had heard that several other women in town planned to attend as well.

Florence bustled in with a chocolate bundt cake glistening with white icing.

"Yum," Nick said, and Florence served him the first piece.

"Delicious, sister dear," Crystal pronounced, chomping on a huge piece of cake, and the table was quiet as everyone enjoyed dessert.

When Jane looked up, Crystal, chewing slowly, was watching her with narrowed eyes.

Jane had never been so grateful to finish a meal. Florence and Nick cleared the table and loaded the dishwasher. Crystal, to Jane's delight, said she should be going, and Jane offered to drive her home. They went to get their coats.

On the way through the living room to the foyer, Crystal stopped suddenly and pointed to the end of the sofa. Jane looked and her eyes grew wide. The dark wood was crisscrossed with deep scratches. "Oh, no!" She loved this sofa. It was the first piece of furniture she and Kenneth had bought when they moved to Shady Hills.

Crystal was shaking her head. "Cats do so much damage."

"They've never done this before."

Florence, having heard Jane's exclamation, appeared behind them. "Oh, missus," she said sadly, and made a tsk-ing sound. "Now why would they do this when they have a perfectly good scratching post in the laundry room? I even keep their nails clipped."

"Rip out their claws," Crystal said breezily on her way

to the foyer closet. She took her coat from a hanger and slipped it on.

"It's cruel to declaw cats," Jane said. "They—"

"Blah blah blah," Crystal said with a bored wave of her hand. "I've heard it all, Jane. Don't you think all of you cat lovers go too far with that nonsense? After all, who is the pet and who is the master? Bottom line: If you want to save your furniture, tear out those claws."

Jane could see she would get nowhere on this issue.

Florence came up behind her. "I have an idea about this, missus," she said softly, and Jane turned and gave her a nod and a wink.

Florence and Nick bade Crystal good night, and Jane followed her to the garage, dreading the ride to her apartment.

Chapter 3

As it turned out, except for "Thank you" and "Good night," neither Jane nor Crystal spoke during the ride to Crystal's apartment, which was fine by Jane. When she got home, Florence showed her a magazine she'd found that contained an ad for a scratching post.

"How is this different from what we've got?" Jane asked.

Florence read, " 'This carpeted pole will give your cat a purr-fect place to work out her frustrations and sharpen her claws.' "

Frowning, Jane led the way to the laundry room, where she and Florence regarded Winky and Twinky's present scratching post. It was squat, like a tree stump, and covered with rough fabric.

"Well, no wonder." Florence touched the pole. "This is only burlap. *This* pole," she said, holding up the magazine, "is *luxury carpeted.*"

"Mmm," Jane said, doubtful. Then she shrugged. "All right, I'm willing to try it. Where can I get this luxury model?"

"Let's see . . . It's called the Scratchaway, and it's 'available at all fine pet shops.' "

Jane nodded. "That means it's expensive. I'll pick one up in New York tomorrow."

As if on cue, tiny Twinky walked into the laundry room and let out a sweet little mew.

"See, missus, she's thanking you already."

Jane bent down, picked up the kitten, and held its small furry face close to hers. "I'll make a deal with you. You stop scratching my sofa and I won't use your scratching post."

In answer, Twinky put a tiny paw against Jane's cheek and let out another mew. Jane laughed, cuddling her cheek against the kitten's amazingly soft fur.

In the morning, driving to the bus that would take her to New York City, Jane turned up the windshield wipers against a persistent drizzle that had begun during the night. At the bottom of Lilac Way she turned left onto Grange Road. Ahead on the left stood the elegant stone gates of Shady Hills's new luxury development, Maple Estates. A dump truck was just turning in, engine rumbling.

Approaching the gates, Jane noticed that a small, discreet sign had gone up: MAPLE ESTATES, EXECUTIVE HOMES. She laughed to herself. Executive homes indeed. In Jane's experience, that simply meant expensive. Passing the entrance to the development, she glanced up the new street, which she noticed had also been given a sign: MONTGOMERY PLACE. The street curved gracefully to the left, flanked by large maple trees—new additions as well. Spaced generously along the road were the homes themselves, great sprawling structures of pale stone that looked half-Gothic, half–French châteaux. They were magnificent, she had to admit. Word was they started at a million dollars and went upward from there—considerably upward.

With a little shake of her head, she turned from Grange

onto Packer, which would take her to the bus stop on Route 46.

That morning, Jane had called Goddess's townhouse and been informed by a maid that she was to meet Goddess at one o'clock at Alain Ducasse, the restaurant in the Essex House Hotel on Central Park South.

When Jane's bus reached the Port Authority Bus Terminal on Eighth Avenue, the rain had stopped and the sun had come out, so she decided to walk to lunch, going east to Seventh Avenue and north to the park. As she approached the hotel's black-and-gold art deco entrance, a silver stretch limousine pulled up to the curb and the chauffeur got out. Before he could reach the other side of the car, the door flew open and two tiny legs appeared— legs in leopard-print tights. Jane grinned. Those legs could belong only to Goddess.

The diminutive star hopped out of the limo, ignoring the driver. Seeing Jane, she winked and ran over. Over her tights she wore a crisp pink tutu. An older couple on the sidewalk stopped short, gawking.

Like many stars, Goddess was much smaller than she appeared in her movies. In fact, she was tiny—no taller than four foot ten, with the figure of a little girl. In startling contrast to her size was her famous hair, a thick, lustrous light brown mass that hung to below her narrow waist, silky and straight.

As she reached Jane, her heart-shaped, doll-like face lit up in a beautiful smile. "Hiya."

"Hiya," Jane said, bending down, and they exchanged cheek kisses.

"It's good to see you," Jane said.

"Mm. Come on." Chomping on gum, Goddess led the way into the hotel, through the lobby, and into the high-ceilinged elegance of Alain Ducasse.

Jane had heard this was the most expensive restaurant in New York. She'd also heard it took two months to get a reservation. "How did you ever get us in here?"

Goddess turned to her. "Are you kidding?"

"Of course," Jane said. What was she thinking? Goddess was one of the biggest stars on the planet, a singer, actress, and all-around pop star beloved the world over.

The maître d' had come up to the restaurant's entrance and was beaming at Goddess. "It's good to see you, miss." He turned to Jane. "Good day, madam. This way, please."

They followed him to a small round table. A waiter appeared as if from nowhere and held Jane's chair while the maître d' held Goddess's. She plopped down into the chair as a child would, folding her right leg under her. As she did, the net and tulle of her tutu made a faint swooshing sound.

"Can't stand all this fuss," she said once they were alone. Shaking her head, she removed her gum from her mouth and stuck it on her napkin. Then she gazed blankly at Jane.

No one knew exactly how old Goddess was, but looking at her now, Jane figured she couldn't be much more than twenty-five or -six.

"So," Goddess said at last, her face blank, "what's with the hair?"

Jane frowned. "My hair?" She touched it absently. "What about it?"

"Exactly. It's always that boring red color."

"Auburn. My hair is auburn."

"Whatever. Why don't you do something with it? Make it blond, black . . . *green*. And the way you wear it . . ." Goddess grimaced. "It needs a"—she gave her head a helpless shake—"cut or something."

Jane knew better than to comment on the length of Goddess's own hair. This was Goddess's shtick, changing her appearance daily, coming up with one outlandish costume after another. At last Jane smiled and said easily, "I like myself the way I am, thanks."

Goddess shrugged. "Suit yourself." Their waiter appeared and handed Goddess a menu. "So," she said, putting it down, "what's up?"

Accepting her menu from the waiter, Jane lowered her brows in bewilderment. "You wanted to have lunch. There was something you wanted to talk to me about?" *Please,* she prayed, *don't let it be a problem with this new book.*

"Oh, yeah." Goddess smiled a tiny smile. "I need you to help me with something."

"Of course."

"You know this movie I'm supposed to be doing? *Taking It?*"

"Yes."

"Filming's been put off for a few months, like I told you. Denzel's ready, but Ben's still doing some picture that's gone long. Which is all a good thing, really."

Jane waited, giving little nods of understanding.

Goddess went on, "Anyway, in this movie, I'm playing a secretary."

Jane let out a laugh.

"You think that's funny?"

"Sorry, but yes, I do. Not exactly your kind of role, is it?" Jane thought back to Goddess's other films. In her very first movie, *Doing It,* the movie that had made her a star, she had had wild sex with a man inside a giant running shoe. In *Slick Monkey,* a quirky comedy about an eccentric city girl who offers to take care of her stodgy brother's baby and loses it on the subway, she had basically played herself. In *Adam and Eve,* in which she'd starred with Ben Affleck and Darlene Hunt, she had played a drug addict who makes peace with her dying mother.

But a secretary? "I just can't see it."

Goddess rolled her eyes. "Did I ask you? The point is, I need to do some research. You know, for the role."

An odd feeling of trepidation came over Jane. She narrowed her eyes. "Yes . . ."

Playing with the top layer of her skirt, Goddess leaned forward. "I want to work at your office."

Jane's jaw dropped. "You want to *what?*"

"Mm-hm. I'll be your secretary."

The waiter appeared. "Have you ladies decided? We have some lovely specials today."

"Skip it," Goddess snipped. "Bring me a bowl of croutons and more water. My friend'll have the seared halibut. Salad to start. Glass of white wine."

The waiter gave Jane a perplexed look, opened his mouth to speak, then abruptly nodded and went away.

"That is what you wanted, isn't it?" Goddess asked.

Jane was staring. "Yes," she faltered, "but how did you know?"

"Because that's what you always have. Anyway, like I was saying . . ."

"I already have a secretary," Jane said kindly. "An assistant, really. Daniel. You know Daniel."

" 'Course I know that cutie pie." Goddess rolled her tongue and made a loud purring noise. "I'll be his secretary, too! Don't you see? It'll be perfect research for me." She held out her hands and gave her head a helpless shake. "What do I know about being a secretary? I don't even know what *mine* does."

"But why me?"

"Who else am I gonna ask?"

"How about Yves, your manager?"

Goddess waved the idea away. "Yves doesn't work in an office. He does all his work in his limo or his pool. I need someplace average and everyday like your office. All nice and cozy in that little village of yours, Shadyville or whatever you call it. All-American. Boring."

"Thanks. And how would this work, exactly?"

"Duh! I sit at a desk, answer the phone, do work for you, et cetera. What else does a secretary do?"

Jane shook her head. "I'm sorry, truly I am, but I don't think so. It— You— It would be too . . . disruptive."

Goddess's sweet face softened. She put her thumb under her little pointy chin and pushed out her lips in a pout. "Please, Jane? Pretty please? Pretty please with a big fat cherry on top? I promise I won't be disruptive. I'll be as quiet and boring as you want. I need to do this for my movie. *Please* . . ."

"Oh, all right," Jane couldn't believe she heard herself saying. "But for how long?"

"Not long. How about a month?"

Jane's eyes bulged. "A month? We'll have to see how it goes. I have a feeling you won't last a month."

"Why not?"

"Too boring, as you say."

"We'll see." Goddess bounced up and down in her chair, her skirt puffing. "Thanks, Janey. I'll see that your name gets into the credits. Now, when do I start?"

"When would you like to start?"

"Mm . . . Monday?"

"All right. We start at nine o'clock."

"In the *morning*?"

"That's right. If you think you can't do it . . ."

"Nope, nope, I can do it. Nine o'clock. I'll be there, Janey—oops, I mean Mrs. Stuart," Goddess said, sitting up straight and making a grown-up face.

"That's all right," Jane said uneasily. "Just Jane will be fine."

At that moment her salad arrived. She was grateful for the distraction.

For the remainder of the meal, conversation centered on Goddess's favorite subject: Goddess. Jane learned which shops on Fifth and Madison avenues were the star's new favorites, what kind of miniature dogs (Goddess liked only miniature animals) had been added to her menagerie, and what kind of villa she was considering buying in Cap-Ferrat.

By the time they left the hotel, Jane had a throbbing headache and her stomach ached. After seeing Goddess into her limo—with calls back and forth of "See you Monday!"—Jane walked back along Central Park South and down Seventh Avenue. Gazing through the window of an electronics store, she shook her head, wondering what had possessed her to agree to Goddess's outlandish request.

She had walked eight blocks south before she remembered her plan to stop at Pet Mart on East Fifty-seventh Street and pick up a luxury scratching post. Still shaking her head, she headed north again.

Chapter 4

Jane felt wiped out by the time she got back to the office. She must have looked it, too, because Daniel gave her a funny look and asked if she was feeling all right.

"Fine, just tired. Any calls?"

He spun from his computer to his desk and lifted a pile of pink slips that made her heart sink. "Carol Freund wants to know if you've read her new synopsis yet."

She shook her head.

"Bill Haddad called to thank you for the great work you did on his contracts."

She smiled weakly and nodded.

"Elaine Lawler wants to know if you've received her Kensington contracts yet."

She nodded. "Vetted them yesterday."

"I know," he said. "I told her." He frowned. "Now this one," he said, holding up a slip, "I don't understand at all. Goddess called. She said to tell you: 'Thank you, thank you, thank you. Your girl Friday will see you on Monday.' She hung up before I could ask her what she meant. Do you have any idea?"

With a queasy smile, she sat down in his visitor's chair. "Yes, I do."

He waited, watching her expectantly. When she didn't speak, he frowned, thoroughly bewildered.

"Oh, the heck with it," she said, and blurted out, "She's coming to work here."

For a moment he looked at her as if she had spoken in an unknown language. "Excuse me?"

She nodded simply. "It's true. Goddess is going to work here as a secretary. *Your* secretary, and mine too. Think of it—you can tell Goddess what to do."

"All right," he said, "joke's over. What are you talking about?"

"I swear it's true. She's going to play a secretary in her next movie and needs to do some research. Poor thing, she begged so hard I couldn't say no. She's starting this Monday."

He put down the papers in his hands and sat up straight. "Have you lost your mind? Goddess is one of the biggest stars in the world. How is she going to work here as a—secretary? I'm supposed to give her work to do?"

"Yes, absolutely." She nodded, eyes wide. "In fact, I expect you to. It's the only way she'll learn the job. I thought you liked her."

"Of course I like her. The whole *world* likes her. Ginny and I have all her albums, several of her movies on DVD . . . and she's going to be my secretary." He shook his head as if to clear it.

She rose. "That's right. Speaking of Ginny, you can tell her about this, of course, but tell her to keep it tightly under her hat. The last thing I need is a media frenzy outside the office. Okay?"

"Sure." He shrugged, swiveling back to his computer monitor, and mumbled, "Starting Monday."

"She'll only be here a month," she called back to him from her office doorway. Then with a little giggle—it really was quite outlandish—she sat back in her desk chair and eyed the heap. It appeared to lean slightly to the right today. She'd better watch that.

Suddenly Daniel was in her doorway. "Where will she sit?"

"Sit? Who?"

"Goddess."

Jane nibbled the inside of her cheek. "You're right. I didn't think of that." She got up, went past him into the reception area, and surveyed the small room.

"In the storage room?" he suggested.

"No! It's full of junk. It would take ages to clean it out. No, the only possible place is there where the credenza is. We can move it over, closer to the closet, and put a desk there. We have Kenneth's desk in the storage room. You and I can carry it out here."

He nodded tiredly. "And her equipment?"

"Equipment?"

"You know—telephone, computer . . ."

"No computer. Just a phone. She can take calls, file, call authors."

"You want Goddess to call our authors?"

"Under a different name, of course. I think that'll be all right."

"Okay," he said, studying the area where they would set Goddess up, and shrugged. "Leave it to me."

By the time Jane got home that evening, she had decided not to tell Florence and Nick that Goddess would be coming to work for her. They were both Goddess fans—who wasn't?—and would love the idea, but Jane couldn't risk the news getting out.

She found Florence helping Nick with his math homework at the dining room table.

"Evening, missus. More algebra." Florence smiled. "Dinner in about twenty minutes."

At that moment Alphonse galloped into the kitchen with a loud bark of greeting and pressed himself hard against Jane. "Hmm," she said, "I know what this means."

"Oh, dear," Florence said, "I completely forgot to walk him. Could you possibly?"

"Sure," Jane said. "Just let me change my shoes."

As she passed the kitchen phone, it rang. It was Crystal. All at once Jane realized she wasn't here.

"Well, Jane, have you decided to have the cats declawed?"

"No, I haven't. In fact, I bought them a new scratching post today." She would bring it in from the car after she walked Alphonse.

"I thought they already had a scratching post."

"They do, but apparently it wasn't the right kind."

"Apparently not." Crystal sounded bored. "At any rate, I'm calling to say I'm terribly sorry but I can't make dinner tonight."

"Oh?" *Yes!*

"Something's come up."

"I hope everything's all right."

There was a brief silence. "I hope so, too." Crystal sounded worried about something. "We shall see."

"Anything we can help you with?"

"No, but thank you. So, how are things with you, Jane? What's new?"

If Crystal found out about Goddess, it would be all over town by morning. "Not much. You?"

"I went to see Nina Bryant today. The media specialist at Nick's school."

"Oh?" Jane said warily. "Why?"

"I told you, just to make the contact. She was quite lovely and we got on very well."

"I hope you didn't say anything about Mr. Stanton."

"Mr. Stanton?"

"Yes, you remember. With the computer in his car?"

"Oh, him! No, of course not."

"Good. Better run. Alphonse needs to go out."

Hanging up, Jane told Florence that Crystal couldn't come for dinner. Then she put Alphonse on his leash and let him drag her out the front door.

Cars lined both sides of narrow Lilac Way, which made walking Alphonse difficult, since the street had no sidewalks. Across the street, Audrey and Elliott Fairchild's fifteen-room Tudor looked enchanted—light in every window, people holding drinks as they talked and laughed. Elliott was the medical director of the New Jersey Rehabilitation Institute. It seemed he and Audrey were always entertaining. Idly Jane wondered what the occasion was this time, if there was an occasion at all.

Returning to the house after Alphonse's walk, she entered through the garage and got the new scratching post from her car.

"Winky! Twinky!" she called as she entered the kitchen. They were nowhere in sight. She went down the hall to the laundry room, picked up the old post, and put the new one in its place.

Nick appeared with Winky and Twinky in his arms. "Hey, Mom, that's a nice one." He placed the two cats gently on the floor and gave them a nudge toward the corner of the room where the post stood. They stopped, eyeing it suspiciously. Then they walked up to it. Winky gave it a timid swipe with her right paw, turned, and walked out of the room. Twinky gave the post one last look and followed her mother.

Florence, standing beside Jane, frowned, her chin between her thumb and forefinger. "They probably need to get used to it."

"Right," Jane said doubtfully, and put the old scratching post in the garage to go out with the trash the following day.

But in the morning the number of scratches on the end of the sofa had about doubled. "Oh, dear," Jane said sadly. "What am I going to do?"

"We're going to cover this, for one thing," Florence said, and resolutely set about finding a large piece of thick cardboard and taping it over the end of the sofa.

"I'll call Dr. Singh when I get to the office," Jane said, referring to her veterinarian.

"Good idea."

"Oh, no, Mrs. Stuart," Dr. Singh said after Jane had described the new scratching post. "The carpeted ones are no good. They are not rough enough. Sisal is best. You know, that very hard, rough rope. The post must be tall—tall enough for Winky and Twinky to stretch out all the way. And sturdy, so it doesn't topple over."

Jane nodded tiredly. From the reception room came the sound of the outside door opening and closing, then Daniel's voice and another voice Jane couldn't identify. Focusing again on her conversation, she cradled the phone between her chin and her left shoulder, taking notes with her right hand. She blew out a sigh. "Any idea where I can get this wonderful creation?"

"I believe they carry them at a store in New York City called PetPleasers. You have heard of it?"

"No. Do you have the address."

"It is on Madison Avenue. At Sixtieth Street, I believe."

"Figures."

"Beg pardon?"

"Nothing. Thanks very much for your help."

"It is nothing. Good luck with it, Mrs. Stuart."

Jane hung up and placed her scratching-post notes in

her purse. She'd pick up one of these wonders when she was in New York on Monday for her lunch with Salomé Sutton. From the outer office came voices again. Then her intercom buzzed.

"Jane, Mrs. Lovesey is here to see you."

Jane's stomach did a sickening flip-flop. "I'll be right out."

Myrtle stood waiting for her in the reception area. She stared at Jane, her face completely neutral, her bright blue eyes wide with expectation.

Jane gave her a little smile. When she didn't speak, Myrtle said, "Well? Did you talk to her?"

"Yes."

"And?"

Jane grimaced. "She refuses to take it back. I'm terribly sorry."

Myrtle's eyes narrowed and she slowly shook her head. "I can't believe this." She turned pleadingly to Daniel. "Can you believe this?" He looked at her helplessly.

"Do you know what your Mrs. Ryerson has done?" Myrtle said to Jane. "She's taken my granddaughter from us."

"Not necessarily," Jane said with forced brightness. "I'm sure Vivian is as good a mother as you say, in which case the social worker will file a good report and everything will be fine."

Myrtle regarded her contemptuously. "You've got to be kidding. You know as well as I do that's not going to happen." She took two menacing steps toward Jane, who backed up. "She can't destroy lives like this," she said in a low voice, then slowly shook her head. "She just can't." She turned to leave.

"Myrtle, wait."

The older woman turned.

"I'll speak with her again."

"It won't do any good."

"It can't hurt to try."

Myrtle's thin shoulders rose and fell. "Suit yourself." And she walked out the door.

For several moments Jane remained where she stood, her gaze on the door. Daniel, at his desk, was watching her. "Will you really speak with Crystal again?"

"Yes . . . but Myrtle is probably right. It won't do any good."

Suddenly terribly depressed, she trudged back to her office.

Today she had brought a bag lunch consisting of a sandwich and fruit, having planned to eat at her desk while reading book proposals, but when noon arrived, she knew she had to get out. She wasn't hungry anyway.

"Need any errands done?" she asked Daniel, who looked confused. "I've got to get out of here."

He opened his top drawer and brought out a stack of checks from publishers. "These need to go to the bank," he offered.

"Perfect. I'll walk."

The day was overcast but mild, not unpleasant. She followed Center Street out of the green, then strolled along Packer Road, over the railroad tracks. She passed the police station and considered popping in to see Stanley but thought better of it. He was always so busy, and besides, she'd see him tomorrow for their weekly Saturday night date.

Beyond the police station stood the Shady Hills Municipal Building, and beyond that the Shady Hills branch of Fleet Bank, Jane's bank. Entering the small brick colonial-style building, she waved hello to Betty, Judy, Margaret, and Poonam—her "bank ladies," as she thought of them. They smiled and waved back. She made a mental note to bring them more of her authors' books. They especially enjoyed the mysteries and romances.

As she made her way out of the building, the door into the vestibule opened and Audrey Fairchild came in.

Pretty, blond Audrey was always dressed and made up to the nines, and today was no exception. Tall and busty, she wore a moss green linen pantsuit, complete with matching heels. Her honey blond hair was pulled back in an attractive chignon, and in her ears she wore large diamonds.

Seeing Jane, she broke into a huge bloodred smile and her blue eyes widened. "Well, hello, doll! What brings *you* here, neighbor?" Her tone implied that Jane would have no use for a bank.

"Just depositing some checks," Jane replied, vaguely waving her deposit slip.

"Ah. And how are things at the office?"

Fine. I'm going to have one of the biggest stars in the world answering my phone. "Fine. How are you all doing? How's Cara?"

Cara was Audrey and Elliott's hopelessly spoiled sixteen-year-old daughter.

"She's fine, just fine," Audrey answered cheerily. Then her face grew troubled, her perfectly tweezed blond brows lowering. "She behaved so strangely last night."

"Last night? I noticed you were having a big party."

"Nah, just a little cocktail party to welcome a new doctor at the Institute. Cara was quite rude."

In Jane's experience, rudeness was nothing out of the ordinary for Cara, but she said, "In what way?"

"She wouldn't talk to people . . . kept slipping away. She was definitely somewhere else." Audrey gave a careless shrug, adjusting the shoulder strap of a Louis Vuitton handbag that must have set her back at least six hundred dollars. "Who knows with these kids, right?" she said, stepping over to the ATM and removing a card from her bag. She slid it in and out of the ATM slot, then her fingers went flying across the keypad. "Wha—" she exclaimed, staring at the screen.

Jane turned to her. "Something wrong?"

"What on earth . . . ? It says 'Amount requested exceeds available balance.' That's impossible. Two days ago I had over five hundred dollars in this account. Now let's see here . . ." Audrey pressed some more buttons and a white slip slid from the machine. Reading it, she drew in her breath sharply. "What the devil—? It says I've got only forty-eight dollars!"

"Could someone have withdrawn the money without telling you?"

"No, I'm the only one with access to it. I've got the checkbook in my safe at home, and the only card is right here," Audrey replied, patting her handbag. "How very strange. I'll ask the ladies," she said, tilting her head toward the inside of the bank. "See if they can explain it."

"Well, good luck," Jane said, and went out.

Could Audrey have made a mistake with her account? she wondered. That really wasn't like Audrey, who valued money above all else. Odd. Decidedly odd.

Passing the bank's windows as she headed back to the office, Jane glanced in and saw Audrey seated at Judy's desk, talking animatedly while Judy frowned and slowly nodded her head.

Chapter 5

The following Monday morning, Jane got to work early and pulled into the empty parking lot behind her building. She felt energized after a relatively calm weekend.

Friday evening Crystal and Florence had gone out to dinner, so Jane had been spared Crystal's presence. Jane took Nick out to Giorgio's on the green for pizza, and after that they rented the new Jackie Chan DVD and watched it while eating popcorn and ice cream.

On Saturday, Jane caught up on some work in her study. Then she took Nick bowling and they had lunch out. Saturday night, Stanley took Jane to dinner at a new Indian restaurant in Florham Park. Then they went to his apartment and danced to his Frank Sinatra records.

Sunday, though quiet, had not been as restful, because Crystal had spent the entire day at Jane's house, trying recipes and kibbutzing with Florence in the kitchen. Crystal's presence alone was enough to set Jane's nerves on edge, though she had to admit that Crystal was oddly subdued—less bossy . . . preoccupied. Toward the end of the day she suddenly grew more cheerful—as if, it occurred to Jane, she had made a decision about something troubling her and felt more at ease. If that was true, Crystal shared none of these thoughts with anyone.

After dinner Jane tried to talk to Crystal again about Myrtle Lovesey's daughter, Vivian. But Jane had no sooner spoken the poor young woman's name than Crystal got up and walked out of the room. There would be no more attempts, Jane decided.

She got out of the car and entered her building through the back door. Emerging from the small corridor into the reception room, she smiled. On Friday, she and Daniel had carried Kenneth's old desk from the storage room to the reception area, and Daniel had set it up for Goddess, complete with blotter, pens and pencils, and a telephone. Jane could always count on Daniel.

Hanging up her coat, she shook her head, unable to believe she had agreed to this madness. Goddess—working in her agency—as a secretary! With a laugh she went into her office, set her briefcase on her credenza, and took out a pile of work she'd completed at home. She checked her watch. Still only eight thirty. She'd get even more done before the phone started to ring.

At ten minutes before nine, she heard Daniel come in. A few moments later he appeared in her doorway. "Good morning." He looked uneasy.

"Relax," she told him. "This will be fun—something to tell your grandchildren. Besides, she'll probably be gone by the end of the week. She'll hate this."

"You're right." Looking reassured, he nodded and headed for his desk.

Jane was in the middle of reading a proposal for a science fiction novel when something out her window caught her eye and she looked up. A silver stretch limousine was sliding up to the curb. A uniformed driver got out, came around, and opened the door. Out stepped Goddess. Jane's eyes bulged. The star wore a red leotard to which a profusion of bright orange and yellow feathers had been artfully applied. Her hair was braided and twisted on top of her head, and from it rose a foot-high plume of matching feathers. Jane realized her mouth was hanging open.

She watched Goddess exchange a few words with her driver, who nodded and got back in the car. Then Goddess walked to the front door of the agency, tail feathers bouncing.

"Good morning!" came her voice from the reception area. "Do you remember me?"

Jane had to see this. She hurried out to the front. Goddess stood before Daniel's desk, her left hand on her hip, her right hand playing with her head plume. Daniel was gaping at her. His mouth was open but no words were coming out.

"Hello, hello," Jane said, rushing over. "Welcome."

"Yeah, thanks," Goddess said, and chomped on her gum.

"Rule one," Jane said pleasantly. "No gum in the office."

Goddess looked at her solemnly and nodded. "Right." She removed her gum and looked around for a wastebasket.

Daniel, coming back to life, held his out for her.

"Thanks," Goddess said with a wink, dropped in the gum, and gazed about her, taking everything in. "This is all so . . . cute!" She rubbed her hands together. "So what do I do? Teach me, teach me."

"Here's your desk," Jane said, stepping over to it.

"I'm loving it. It's so . . . battered." Goddess sat down very slowly at the desk, placing her hands flat on the surface in front of her. "And a phone! Do I get to answer it?"

Jane and Daniel exchanged a quick look. "Sure," he said. "Why don't you cover the phone during the morning and we'll see how it goes."

"Okay. What do I do when someone calls?"

He paused a beat, then said, "Just say, 'Jane Stuart Literary Agency,' then ask who's calling and put the call on hold."

"Mmm . . . got it." Goddess turned toward the phone and gazed at it, waiting for it to ring.

"People don't usually start calling till after nine," he told her with a laugh. "So in the meantime I've got some filing for you."

"Filing!" Goddess exclaimed joyously. "Am I going to be convincing in my movie, or what!"

The phone rang. Goddess stared at it, her head feathers quivering like a quail's.

"It's okay," Daniel encouraged her. "You can answer it."

Goddess let out a tiny squeal of glee, then snatched the receiver from its cradle. She held the phone to her ear, waiting.

Jane frowned, then prompted, "Jane Stuart Literary Agency."

"Oh, right! Jane Stuart Literary Agency," Goddess said carefully into the phone, then listened. "*Who?*" Without putting the call on hold, she said loudly to Jane, "Do you know somebody named"—she snorted out a laugh— "Bertha Stumpf?"

Bertha was one of Jane's bigger clients, a bestselling writer of historical romances who published her novels under the pseudonym "Rhonda Redmond." "Put her on hold," Jane whispered.

Goddess hunted down the hold button and carefully pressed it.

"Next time," Jane said gently, "please put the call on hold before you ask us about it."

"Gotcha. Now who is this chick with the bizarro name?"

"She's a client. I'll take it in my office. Please tell her I'll be right with her."

Goddess got back on the line. "Hold on a sec, okay, hon?"

Drawing in her breath, Jane headed for her office to take Bertha's call, exchanging a concerned look with Daniel on the way.

He was right. This was definitely a bad idea.

Salomé Sutton, who liked to eat, had arranged to have lunch with Jane at the Hilton on Avenue of the Americas, because one of its restaurants, New York Marketplace, featured a forty-four-foot international buffet. From their small table in the center of the restaurant, Jane watched Sal's massive back as she moved slowly from one chafing dish to another, loading her plate. Finally she turned and headed back to the table.

"Aren't you eating?" she asked in her deep booming voice.

"In a moment," replied Jane, who dreaded the conversation she and Sal were about to have, and had little appetite.

Sal sat down ponderously in her chair. Gazing across the table at her, Jane realized she'd forgotten just how big Salomé Sutton was: easily six feet tall, and so wide she blocked Jane's view of the restaurant. She wore a vast muumuu in a busy print of ivory, brown, and burnt orange. A Halloween print, Jane realized with a shock, spotting a grinning jack-o'-lantern.

Sal dug into her food, her glossy black bouffant hair catching the light from an overhead fixture. Jane considered opening the conversation now, then decided to get some food first.

She returned from the buffet with a bit of Caesar salad and a small roll.

"That's *it*?" Sal cried. "Why'd I bother comin' all the way up here if that's all you're gonna eat?"

Sal's sister Bernice lived way downtown in Greenwich Village.

"Sorry," Jane said. "I'm not very hungry."

Sal shrugged, savoring a roasted potato. "So," she said, her mouth still full, "let me have it."

"Have what?"

"The scoop. What's going on with my new deal?"

Jane drew a deep breath and leaned forward slightly. "I don't have one yet, as I told you last week. It's . . . a difficult market."

Sal let her fork drop and it landed on her plate with a clatter. Jane jumped.

Sal gulped down some water. "Who do you think you're talking to, some first-timer? For *me*"—she aimed a fat finger back at herself—"it ain't a difficult market. *I* invented historical romance. I am the queen. *Time* magazine called Delilah Dare and Roan Romero from my *Arabian Nights* the quintessential hero and heroine. Kathleen Woodiwiss, Rosemary Rogers, Busbee, Brandewyne—I inspired them all." She cast her glance about wildly. "Where the hell is that waiter with my drink?"

Jane spotted him, got his attention, and pointed to Sal. His expression brightened as he remembered, and a moment later he was setting down Sal's martini.

Meanwhile, Jane had been formulating her response. "That may be true—"

"What do you mean, 'may be'? Of course it's true."

"Right. It's true. But . . . well . . . the publishers . . ."

"Spit it out, wouldja?" Now Sal's mouth was full of roast beef.

"We're asking for a lot of money . . ."

"Damn straight we are! I'm worth it. What, do they think I won't earn out my advance?"

"The editors I've spoken with can't help wondering why we've left Corsair."

"Then tell 'em! Because they were doing squat for me. Because they decided to give all their attention to Stephanie Queen." As Sal said this name, her mouth puckered as if she had eaten something that had gone bad. Abruptly she shook her head. "No. No. You know what it is?" She pointed a dirty butter knife at Jane. "It's you."

"*Me?*" Jane said, fingers to her breast.

"Yup. You ain't got no clout. You're not professional. Who's gonna listen to you?"

Jane gaped at her. She felt her face grow hot. "What are you talking about?" she said, sitting bolt upright. "Why wouldn't anyone listen to me?"

"Look at you. No New York office like the big agents. Where are you? Shady Hole, New Jersey."

"Shady *Hills.*"

"Whatever," Sal said with a flip and a wave of her hand. "Who's gonna take that seriously? Nope"—she shook her head, her lips pressed together—"you're not a New York presence and nobody wants to know from you."

"How dare you speak to me like that?" Jane said, raising her voice. "If that's how you feel, why don't you go back to your old agent, Jory Mankewitz, who had a lot of clout but wouldn't give you the time of day?"

The people at the tables to each side of theirs had turned to stare.

"Hey," Sal said in a conciliatory tone, lowering her voice, "take it easy, Jane. We're just talkin' here."

"No, we're not just talking," Jane said softly. "You're insulting me. I love your work, Sal, and I'm a great admirer of yours, but if you want to work with me, you'd better treat me with respect."

Sal smirked and sat back in her chair, her great body rearranging itself. She ran a finger thoughtfully down a heavily pancaked cheek. "I like that. I do. All right, I apologize."

"Thank you," Jane said, calming herself down with a sip of water. "Why don't you just give me time to do what I need to do, and we'll see what happens."

"Okay, you're on." Sal turned her head to one side and looked at Jane out of the corner of her eye. "*If* I can come out to Shady Hole and see your offices."

Jane gave her head a little shake of confusion. "Why do you want to do that? What will it prove?"

"Humor me."

"No."

"No?"

"No."

"You embarrassed?"

"No, of course not." Jane suddenly remembered that at this moment one of the biggest pop stars on the planet was sitting in her reception room, dressed as a tropical bird. She suppressed a giggle.

"You think I'm funny?"

"No, sorry. But it makes no sense, Sal. You hired me for *me*. You said you'd watched my career, liked how I handled my clients. Give me a chance, all right?"

For a long moment Sal regarded her. Then she burped. "All right," she said at last, "have it your way, Burger King."

"What?"

"I'm agreeing with you, giving you more time. Do your thing."

Jane gave a decisive nod. "Thank you."

"Don't mention it," Sal said, downed the remainder of her martini, and flagged the waiter for another one. As she raised her ham of an arm, her muumuu shifted and a large orange jack-o'-lantern winked playfully at Jane.

Jane couldn't get away from Salomé fast enough. Why, she wondered now, hadn't she just told Sal to find another agent if she thought so little of Jane? Because, Jane answered herself, it was quite possible Jane *would* be able to find Sal a new deal, and if she did, the commission on it would be considerable. *Whore,* she called herself. *Whore with a Jaguar.* And with a little chuckle, she left the Hilton and headed up Avenue of the Americas.

At Fifty-ninth Street she walked along Central Park, ablaze with autumn colors. Then she continued east to Madison Avenue and went one block north to PetPleasers, which looked more like a high-end boutique than a pet shop.

Occupying the entire rear wall of the store was a display of scratching posts, many combined with ramps and cubbies. Jane found a post like the one Dr. Singh had described, and after paying far more than she'd expected to pay, she lugged it out to the street and hailed a cab to the Port Authority Bus Terminal.

When Jane got back to the office at four o'clock, Goddess was nowhere in sight. She gave Daniel an inquiring look. He pointed to the closed door of the storage room. Jane crossed the reception area and opened the door.

Goddess, in her bird costume, sat on a spare desk chair, her legs crossed, engrossed in a paperback book. She looked up brightly. "Oh, hiya."

"Hiya. How's it going?"

"Fab. Have you read this?" Goddess held up the book—*Shady Lady* by Rhonda Redmond.

"Yes, I represented it."

"You did?" Goddess's face grew perplexed. "What do you mean?"

"I represent that author," Jane said patiently, "the way I represent you."

"Ohhhhh."

"In fact, that's Bertha Stumpf, the person who called earlier today. She writes as Rhonda Redmond."

"Well, it's great. I can't put it down."

Jane smiled kindly. "I'm glad you're enjoying it. Please feel free to take it home with you. But in the meantime, how is your work going?"

"Fine, I guess," Goddess said with a shrug. "I was taking a break. Five more minutes, okay? Marguerite is telling Rolando to get lost." She put her delicate nose back into the book.

Jane withdrew quietly. Daniel was watching her.

"How's it going?" she asked him softly.

Looking queasy, he shook his head. "Why are we doing this? It's ludicrous."

"I know, but I told her she could do it and I don't want to go back on my word. What harm does it do?"

He pressed his lips together and lowered his brows, pretending to concentrate. "Let's see. While you were gone, she dropped a nine-hundred-page manuscript on the floor. It took us half an hour to put it back together again."

"Could happen to anyone," Jane said offhandedly.

"She read Bill Haddad's new thriller proposal, found his telephone number on the title page, and called him."

"What!"

"Mm-hm. Told him the story didn't have enough female roles."

Jane winced. "What did he say?"

"He laughed and said he appreciated the input."

"Did he know who was calling?"

"No, he thought it was a new assistant we'd hired."

"Good. Anything else?"

"Yes," he said, shifting uncomfortably in his chair, and looked down in embarrassment. "She said something rather inappropriate to me."

"To you?" She frowned. "What do you mean?"

"Jane, she came on to me."

Her mouth grew huge. She gave a great laugh. "I ... love ... it!"

"You love it? I don't. I ignored it, but next time I won't."

"What did she say?"

"I'd rather not repeat it."

"Oh, come on."

"She said ..." He stared down at his desktop. "She said my pants fit me well and that I have a ..."

"Yes?"

"A nice package."

Jane burst out laughing again, slapping her thigh and nearly falling over. "Oh, dear," she said, recovering herself. "Well," she teased through her tears, "I'd say that's quite a compliment, coming from one of the world's greatest sex symbols."

"Mm," he said, clearly unconvinced, and busied himself at his desk. "What's she up to in there?" he murmured. "I asked her to get a file from the archives."

"Really? When was that?"

"An hour and a half ago."

She smiled and shook her head. "She got distracted. She'll be out in a minute. It's nearly quitting time anyway."

"Thank heaven."

"Come on," she said, sitting in his visitor's chair, "lighten up."

He gave her a grudging smile. "I guess you're right. So, how did lunch with Salomé go?"

Her smile turned into a sneer. "Not good. She said I'm unprofessional and have no clout, that I'm not a 'New York presence.' "

He slammed his hand down on the desk. "What?"

Wonderful, loyal Daniel. "She did," she said.

"And what did you say to that?"

"I reminded her that she came to me because of what I've done for my other clients, and that if she wants to work with me, she's got to treat me with respect."

"Absolutely. Good for you."

"Daniel . . ." Her voice was troubled. "You think I'm professional, don't you? I mean, even though I'm not a 'New York presence'?"

At that moment the door to the storage room opened and Goddess emerged. She looked exhausted. Her head feathers were askew, nearly lying flat, so that she looked for all the world like a bird that had been run over. Tears ran from her eyes.

She held up *Shady Lady*. "Holy smoke, Jane. This really did a number on me."

"I take it that's a good thing."

"Is it ever!" Goddess fell into her chair. "I had no idea there were books like this. You have more?"

"Romances? Lots more."

"Pile 'em up. I am now a *romance reader*." Goddess leaned back in her chair, let out a deep sigh, and gazed off into the middle distance. "Oh, Rolando! Marguerite is one lucky babe."

The street door opened and a young man in a chauffeur's uniform walked in. "Afternoon," he said, looking all around, and then to Goddess, "Your car is ready, miss."

Goddess rolled her eyes. "I told you not to call me miss."

"Sorry, mi— I mean, Goddess. Sorry to bother you, but you said you had to be back in the city by six, and with rush-hour traffic and all . . ."

"*Absolument,*" Goddess said, jumping up from her chair and hurrying to the door in a feathery orange blur. She spun around dramatically. "Till tomorrow, then," she said to Jane and Daniel.

"Yes, till tomorrow," Jane said. Then, walking up to Goddess, she said in a low voice, "Rule number two: No costumes in the office—except for Halloween, of course. Otherwise, office attire. Okay?"

Goddess looked up at her uncertainly. She nibbled on her lower lip. "Office attire." She gave one decisive nod. "Got it."

And she was gone.

"Professional?" Daniel said, and gave a great shrug. "Not sure. Interesting? Definitely."

Together they looked out the front window as Goddess got into her silver limousine, drawing in her small, shapely legs. The driver turned, as if sensing they were watching, and tipped his hat. Then he got into the long, sleek car, and it slithered away from the curb so smoothly that it might have been on ice.

Chapter 6

With a weary grunt, Jane hauled the new scratching post up the three stairs from the garage to the kitchen. Florence, standing at the sink, turned. "Missus, you should have let me help you with that."

"Thanks, but I'm fine." Jane closed the door behind her, and they both regarded the impressive sisal-covered structure.

Nick walked in from the dining room, Twinky curled in one arm, Winky at his left foot, Alphonse at his right. He set Twinky down on the floor, and she and her mother cautiously approached the scratching post. The room was silent.

Winky walked up to the post and stood on its wooden base. Ever so lightly, she rubbed the left side of her face against the rough surface of the sisal rope wound around the tower. She paused momentarily, then suddenly jumped up on her hind legs and, stretching full length, dug her claws into the post and drew them down with a satisfying ripping sound.

"Hey, Wink!" Nick cried. "You like it!"

As if on cue, Twinky prowled around to the tower's opposite side and started to scratch.

"Missus," Florence said with a nod, "it looks like a hit."

"Great." Jane hung up her coat in the foyer, then went into the living room and removed the cardboard Florence had taped over the end of the sofa. "I'll have to have this refinished," she told herself.

She moved the newest scratching post into the laundry room, placed its predecessor in the garage to go out with the trash, and joined Florence in the kitchen to help with dinner.

"I'll set the table," she said.

"Thanks," Florence said. "Only three tonight."

"Oh?" Jane turned to her. "No Crystal?"

"No . . ." Peeling carrots over the sink, Florence looked troubled, her brows lowering over her dark eyes. "She can't make it tonight. She said she has to speak to someone. She's been acting odd, but I don't know why."

Jane was about to say something about not looking a gift horse in the mouth, then thought better of it. "I'm sure she'll confide in you when she's ready." Hands full of napkins and silver, she headed for the kitchen table.

"Oh," Florence said, looking up. "Crystal asked me to remind you that the first book group meeting is tomorrow. Ten o'clock at the library."

Jane had forgotten all about it. She realized now that she had no desire to go. But she'd promised. "Right. Thanks, Florence. I'll be there."

When Jane checked the sofa in the morning, there were no additional scratches. Nick reported that Winky and Twinky had continued to use their new scratching post. With a feeling of deep satisfaction, Jane left for the office.

Most mornings in the fall and winter, Jane stopped at Whipped Cream before work to see Ginny and have breakfast. Today, because of the reading group meeting that would effectively kill most of her morning, she decided to pick up her usual coffee and apple raisin muffin and take them with her.

There was a line at the counter. Ginny busily filled orders and rang them up. When it was Jane's turn to step up, Ginny leaned forward, eyes ablaze.

"Daniel told me," she whispered. "I can't believe it."

Jane frowned. "Can't believe what?"

"That *she* is working at your office. It's . . . unbelievable."

"Mm, that's one word for it." Jane raised one brow. "You must keep it a secret."

"I promise! Can I meet her?"

"I don't see why not. Stop in around a quarter to ten and we'll walk to the library together."

"Oh, right, the reading group." Ginny cast a glance toward the back room. "Charlie and George said they'd cover for me."

"Good. See you then. And remember—mum's the word."

Ginny nodded solemnly and handed Jane the bag containing her muffin and coffee.

Jane had nearly reached her office when Goddess's limo glided around the green and stopped. Jane stopped to watch. Goddess's chauffeur got out and opened the door for Goddess, who stepped out.

Jane blinked in amazement. Goddess had on a beige sweater set and a simple brown wool skirt that came to just below her knees. Her hair was pulled up into a demure bun. She wore black fifties-style "cat-eye" glasses studded with rhinestones. Around her neck was a string of small pearls.

Brimming with amusement, Jane made her way around the car.

Seeing her, Goddess grinned. "Better?" she asked, turning this way and that.

"Much," Jane replied. "I take it this is your secretary look?"

"Yup." Goddess turned and waved her driver away. Then she and Jane headed into the office.

"Jane . . ." Goddess turned to her, eyes narrowed. "Have you got more romance books for me?"

"Lots more. I'll give them to you if you promise to save them for lunchtime and after work."

"I promise!"

Jane laughed. "Deal."

To Jane's surprise, Daniel hadn't come in yet, so she gave Goddess some filing to do. The young woman seemed thrilled at this assignment, immediately yanking open a file drawer.

In her office, Jane called Harriet Green, an editor at Bantam Dell who had expressed interest in Salomé Sutton. They agreed that Jane would send her copies of some of Sal's most recent books, along with information on how these books had sold, and that Harriet and Jane would speak again within the next two weeks.

On her desk Jane had a folder containing royalty statements Sal had received from Corsair Publishing on her previous books. As Jane pulled the statements she wanted photocopied for Harriet, there came from the reception area the sound of Daniel raising his voice—an unusual occurrence.

Curious, Jane went to her office door and listened.

"Why?" she heard Goddess ask in a pouty voice.

"Because it's unprofessional," Daniel replied.

Jane opened her door a crack and peeked out. Daniel sat at his desk, speaking to Goddess across the room. Sitting on Goddess's desk was a tiny portable television.

"All right," she said, "just let me watch the rest of this

story." She gazed down at the small TV screen, brows lowered. Suddenly she threw back her head and shivered sensuously. "Ooh, I *love* it when we topple regimes. It makes me so . . . frisky."

Abruptly she switched off the TV, stood up, and made her way slowly across the room to Daniel's desk. In one fluid movement she was perched at its edge. She leaned down close to his face. "You feelin' frisky?" she asked in a husky voice.

Daniel stared into her face, terror in his wide eyes. He opened his mouth to speak but no sound came out. Goddess leaned closer to him, bringing her beautiful face within inches of his. Ever so softly she placed her hand on his smooth cheek, and in a low, breathy voice she said:

> As I went by a dyer's door,
> I met a lusty tawnymoor;
> Tawny hands, and tawny face,
> Tawny petticoats,
> Silver lace.

She looked into his eyes. "Do you like that?"

He wet his lips nervously, gave a quick nod. "It's from your Broadway show, *Goddess of Love.*"

"I know the name of the show, silly," she replied, pursing her full lips and bringing them toward his.

At that moment the door from the street opened and Ginny walked in. Goddess slid instantly off Daniel's desk and stood facing her like a soldier. "Hello," Goddess said.

Ginny gave a shy nod. Had she seen? Jane wondered.

"Hi, I'm Ginny." She put out her hand and Goddess shook it. "I'm Daniel's girlfriend." She turned to him. "Isn't that right, Daniel?"

He nodded.

"I'm a huge fan of yours," Ginny said, turning back to

Goddess. Then she took two steps forward, bent down—
she was half a foot taller than the star—and whispered
something in Goddess's ear. Goddess straightened, gaze
lowered, and strolled back to her desk.

Jane chose that moment to bustle in. "Ginny! Have you
met—"

"Yes," Ginny said pleasantly. "I was just telling her
what a huge fan I am."

"How nice," Jane said, and looked from Ginny to Daniel
to Goddess. No one spoke. "Well then, I guess we'll be going.
We'll be at the library for a couple of hours." Jane fetched
her reading group book, and she and Ginny left the office.

Out on the sidewalk in the bright sunshine, Jane turned
to Ginny. "What did you whisper to her?"

Ginny scowled. "How did you see that?"

"Easy. I was spying from behind my office door."

Ginny laughed, then leaned toward Jane and whispered
in her ear.

"Ginny!"

Ginny shrugged. "I don't care who she is. She'd better
keep her mitts off my man. This isn't Hollywood."

Jane stole another look at her friend and smiled. "Good
for you."

The Shady Hills Public Library, located across the railroad tracks and around the corner on Packer Road, was an
old, one-story, Georgian-style brick building. Six tall mullioned windows looked out onto a lawn that sloped gracefully down to the road. From the sidewalk a concrete path
led to six wide stone steps beneath the building's double-
doored entrance.

"Good morning, good morning," came Crystal's voice
when Jane and Ginny entered the library's cavernous front
room. Jane looked around and spotted Crystal behind the

massive checkout desk of dark old wood, checking out books for an elderly woman. "I'll just be a moment."

On the checkout desk, to Crystal's left, sat an immense, bright orange jack-o'-lantern made of nylon filled with pillow stuffing. It bore a wicked grin, and seemed to be leering directly at the woman checking out her books, who took no notice of it.

Crystal had mentioned that she and Ashley, the girl who worked here after school, had decorated the library for Halloween. Jane gazed about and noticed that a small jack-o'-lantern sat in the center of each of the tables in the front room. Hanging from the light fixture directly above Jane's head was a cardboard skeleton with articulated bones. It danced and twirled in the breeze caused by a ceiling fan several yards to its right.

"Good morning, ladies." Jane and Ginny turned. Mindy Carter, the library's director, had appeared as if from nowhere and was walking toward them, smiling brightly. She was a small woman—barely five feet tall—and though she wasn't fat, everything about her was round: her face with its pert nose and wide mouth, her reddish brown hair cut in a rounded style, her little figure in a moss green blouse and tweed skirt. "I'm so excited about this reading group." Her face grew concerned. "Do you know who else is coming?"

"Should be a good turnout," answered Jane, who hoped the members of her knitting club would make good on their promises to attend.

"I do hope so," Mindy said. She checked her watch. "Still a little early yet. I'll join you in a few minutes."

As Mindy hurried away toward the checkout desk, Crystal came toward them. "How are you, Jane . . . Ginny?" Before they could reply, she swept on, "I think this is going to work out beautifully, don't you? Have you got your copies of today's book?"

Jane and Ginny nodded dutifully. "Didn't like it much," Jane said.

"That's a shame," Crystal said. "But that's why we're here, right? To talk about what we liked and didn't like."

Ginny said, "Speaking of which, Crystal, I loved that novel you recommended to me last week. Practically inhaled it. Got any more recommendations?"

Crystal beamed, clearly flattered. "Of course. I have just the thing." She led the two women into the library's back room, which ran the width of the building and was filled with closely spaced bookcases. She went to the bookcase on the extreme right. Against it stood a tall ladder with rollers that ran along a track at the top. Crystal rolled it all the way to the end of the bookcase, into the corner, and then climbed it. Watching her, Jane winced, marveling that it could hold her weight.

When Crystal had reached the third rung from the top, she held on to the ladder with her left hand and reached way out with her right to grab a book on the perpendicular wall. "Here we go," she said with a grunt, sliding it out, and climbed slowly down. She handed the book to Ginny. "I loved this one."

"Thanks," Ginny said, leafing through it, and the three women headed back into the library's front room.

"Jane," Mindy called from behind the checkout desk. Jane stopped and turned. "There's a book I've been meaning to recommend to you, but I can't for the life of me remember the title. Ask me again at the end of the meeting and maybe I'll have it."

Jane smiled and nodded. Crystal led them to a long table at the right front corner of the building. "This is the best place for the meeting, I think. It's quietest here."

As if on cue, two members of Jane's knitting group came through the front doors, talking animatedly.

Tiny Louise Zabriskie, with her cropped brown hair

and fine, birdlike features, looked like a child compared to Rhoda Kagan, who was tall, slender, and stylish, with her gently waving variegated blond hair and startling blue eyes.

They approached Jane and Ginny.

"I hope this turns out all right," said Louise, who was nearly always fretting about something. "I hate leaving Ernie on his own like this." Louise and her husband, Ernie, owned Hydrangea House, the only inn in Shady Hills and the venue for the biweekly knitting club meetings.

Rhoda shook her head impatiently. "He's a big boy, Louise. Aren't you allowed a little fun once in a while?"

"I suppose," Louise replied. "Where are we meeting?"

"There," Jane said, indicating the table in the corner.

Louise marched over to it and sat down. From her handbag she took her copy of the novel the group would be discussing, placed it on the table in front of her, and folded her hands primly, waiting.

"Here's Penny," Rhoda said, turning.

Penny Powell, the youngest member of the knitting group, was of medium height, slim, with straight brown haircut in an attractive chin-length pageboy. It was Penny who had taken in Alphonse, only to discover that her daughter, Rebecca, had an allergy to him.

"Good morning," Penny greeted Jane and Rhoda in her breathy voice. She looked excited, her brown eyes gleaming, and cast her gaze about the brightly decorated room, finally looking up. "Isn't this fun?"

Jane often wondered about Penny. When she had first joined the knitting group, she had been painfully shy, dominated by her chauvinistic husband, Alan. Since then she had taken amazing strides, standing up to Alan and asserting herself as his equal. Yet Jane sensed that Penny was still troubled by issues of low self-esteem and unworthiness. Except for the knitting group meetings, she never seemed to have any fun. She spent all her time on Rebecca and Alan, leaving no time for herself. Perhaps it was a hopeful sign that she viewed the reading group as fun.

"Meeting start yet?" came a low, brisk voice at Jane's elbow. It was Doris Conway, thin and stooped, the oldest member of the knitting group. Her dark eyes snapped from Jane to Rhoda to Ginny to Penny. "Penny, what are you so excited about?" Doris didn't miss a trick.

"Why, this reading group," Penny replied. "I think it's going to be really interesting!"

Doris rolled her eyes. "Whoop-de-do," she said in a monotone, boredly twirling her right index finger. Not much excited Doris, a former Shady Hills schoolteacher who had seen it all. She turned to Jane. "If this is dull, I won't be back. In fact, I'll probably leave in the middle."

Jane laughed. "Why are you telling *me* this?"

"Because you hornswoggled me into it. I could be home watching *ER* reruns." Doris looked around. "Oh, there's Louise." She made her way over to the table in the corner and sat down at one end. She and Louise began to chat.

"Guess I'll go sit," Penny said, and Jane, Ginny, and Rhoda followed her to the table. Penny sat down beside Louise, and Jane, Ginny, and Rhoda took seats facing them.

"Not much of a turnout," Doris observed, staring straight ahead as if in a trance.

Jane, who sat to Doris's right, said softly, "Now, Doris, try to be positive. The library needs more events like this."

Doris gave her a pitying look but made no reply.

"Anyway," Jane said, "we're expecting at least two more people."

As she spoke these words, a feeling of dread came over her, for one of these additional people was Myrtle Lovesey. Perhaps, under the circumstances, Myrtle had opted not to attend. That would be fine with Jane.

"Oh, there's Myrtle Lovesey," Penny said cheerfully,

and Jane turned to see the older woman entering the library, her enormous handbag under her arm. She looked around, spotted the other women, and came over to the table.

"Morning, ladies," she said with a little smile. Had Jane imagined it, or did Myrtle's gaze linger on her a bit longer than on the others?

Myrtle took a seat all alone at the empty end of the table. Ginny, noticing this, frowned. Jane avoided meeting Myrtle's gaze.

Mindy Carter marched up to the table and stood at its head, next to Myrtle. "Are we all here?"

Jane looked up. With a start, she realized Myrtle was staring at her, her face expressionless. Quickly Jane looked away. *Please, let this be over quickly.*

Ginny said, "There's one more coming, isn't there, Jane? That woman from the cat shelter?"

"Right. Gabrielle Schraft."

"All right," Mindy said, "we'll wait another minute or two."

"Oh, for Pete's sake," Doris said. Everyone looked at her. Then all heads turned when the library door opened and a woman entered.

"Here's Gabrielle," Jane said.

Gabrielle Schraft would have fit right into the hippie scene of the sixties and seventies. She wore a long-sleeve dress made of panels of variously colored print fabrics sewn together, and over it a pale blue crocheted poncho with a wide, deep blue stripe running through it.

Even her brown hair threaded with gray evoked the styles of the seventies, cut close to her head with a long fringe at the back of her neck.

She looked around and spotted Mindy, who had risen to greet her. "Sorry I'm late," she said. Jane, who had met Gabrielle only once, had forgotten how deep her voice was, almost like a man's. Her face was quite plain, also quite masculine, but when she reached the table and greeted everyone, she broke into the prettiest of smiles. Then she reached into her handbag, brought out a sheaf of brochures, and proceeded to move around the table, depositing one in front of each person.

"What the blazes is this?" Doris asked, holding her brochure between her thumb and index finger as if it were something dead.

"Just some information about my shelter," Gabrielle chirped, sitting in the chair between Myrtle and Penny.

"Your what?"

Jane said pleasantly, "She runs a cat shelter."

Doris fixed her with a look. "I think the woman can speak for herself, Jane."

Jane shrugged.

"Yes, I can," Gabrielle said with a smile. "I run Paws for Love. It's a nonprofit, no-kill, all-volunteer organization. We recycle homeless cats into lifetime pets. The cats are grateful for any and all contributions."

Doris chuckled. "Got your elevator speech down pat, haven't you? Well," she said, flinging the brochure onto the center of the table, where it hit the jack-o'-lantern centerpiece, "it won't work on me. Don't like animals."

Gabrielle looked shocked. "But surely you don't want these poor animals—"

"Can it," Doris said. "Don't care."

Gabrielle's jaw fell.

Jane laughed in embarrassment. "Doris tends to be somewhat . . . blunt."

Doris turned on her. "Don't you make excuses for me."

"Ladies, ladies," Louise said, "please."

"Yes." Mindy, who had resumed her seat, looked horrified. "*Please.*"

The table was silent. Doris glared at Jane for another

moment, then shook her head and looked away. Gabrielle, with an expression of forced indifference, tossed off her poncho, threw it on the floor behind her, and got out her copy of the book to be discussed. Then she took a deep breath and sat calmly, waiting.

"Now then," Mindy said, propping her copy of the book on the table before her. "Let's begin, shall we?"

At that moment there was the sound of heels clicking loudly on the library's ancient wooden floor, and Crystal swept past the table, her gaze on the bookcase along the room's side wall.

Jane glanced at Myrtle, who was following Crystal with her eyes.

Mindy continued, "This week's book is a novel, *River to Yesterday* by Elisabeth Fleischmann. Myrtle, would you like to . . ."

Mindy trailed off, because Myrtle clearly wasn't listening. She had risen from her chair and was gathering up her giant handbag from the floor, her gaze fixed on Crystal ten feet away.

Oh, no. Like someone who can't wrest her gaze from an impending disaster, Jane watched.

Chapter 7

Everyone watched Myrtle step out from behind the table and march up behind Crystal, who seemed unaware of the other woman's presence.

"I want to talk to you," Myrtle said in a loud, menacing voice.

Crystal started and spun around. "What—?"

Myrtle stepped closer to Crystal so that there was barely a foot between their faces.

"I want you to take back what you said to DYFS," Myrtle demanded in a loud voice. "Call them. Say it was a mistake."

Crystal's eyes widened for the briefest moment, then narrowed to slits. Her nostrils flared. "No." She drew out the word, as if savoring it.

Myrtle's mouth opened slightly, but nothing came out. Then, slowly, her lips drew together. "You horrible, horrible woman," she said in a low voice. "Sticking your nose into other people's business . . . thinking you know everything . . . ruining people's lives . . ."

Then she clamped her mouth shut. Suddenly she spun around, her bag swinging wide, and marched into the library's rear room.

Jane looked around the table. All eyes were still on Crystal, who had already turned back to what she'd been doing and looked as if nothing untoward had taken place.

"Now then," Mindy said in a high squeaky voice, and cleared her throat.

Jane realized Ginny was looking at her. Jane gave her a little shrug and returned her attention to Mindy, who was looking across Myrtle's now-empty place at Gabrielle in the next chair, asking her a question. ". . . if Uncle Ned had been in the barn?"

Gabrielle stared at her. "Huh?"

The meeting continued pretty much that way—Mindy cheerfully asking questions about *River to Yesterday,* no one really listening except Penny, who sat attentively, offering answers when no one else would.

Suddenly Gabrielle stood up. "Excuse me," she said in her deep voice. "Need some water." With a little smile, she left the table and went into the library's rear room, presumably to get a drink from the water fountain outside the restrooms.

While she was gone, Jane managed to answer a question about the novel under discussion, since she had, after all, read it. As she finished her remarks, Gabrielle returned from the back room, with Myrtle close behind her. Gabrielle returned to her seat at the table, while Myrtle marched past them all and out the building's front doors.

Ginny leaned close to Jane. "Things ought to be a bit calmer now," she whispered, when at that moment one of the library's front doors opened again and a man walked in. He was young—in his twenties—and quite handsome, with regular features and neatly trimmed brown hair. On his back was a worn green backpack.

He stopped in front of the doors and slowly scanned the library. Simultaneously, Crystal returned to the central area where he was standing. She gave him a polite smile and swept past him.

"You—" he said, and she stopped and stared at him. "Are you Crystal Ryerson?"

She frowned. "Yes . . ."

"You monster!" he cried into her face.

"I beg your pardon?" she said, placing her hands on her ample hips. She tossed her head and glared down her nose at him. "Who *are* you?"

"How dare you go to my boss and tell her I'm a thief! You didn't even see me with that computer. Who told you about it?"

Crystal made no reply, only gazed impassively into his reddening face.

"I don't believe this," Doris said.

So this, Jane gathered, was Mr. Stanton from Nick's school. She remembered her telephone conversation with Crystal the previous Thursday night.

"I hope you didn't say anything about Mr. Stanton."

"Mr. Stanton?"

"Yes, you remember. With the computer in his car?"

"Oh, him! No, of course not."

Jane should have known.

Ginny nudged her with her elbow. "Who *is* he?" she whispered.

Jane gave a quick shake of her head to indicate she didn't want to talk now.

"If you must know—not that it's any of your damn business . . ." Stanton railed, "I was taking that computer home to fix it."

"Were you?" Crystal asked skeptically.

He shook his head as if he couldn't believe someone like Crystal could exist. "You have no idea what you've done to me. It took me nearly a year to find this job. I can't af-

ford to lose it. I've got a wife and a baby at home. Please—
tell Nina you made a mistake."

Crystal took a deep breath through her nose and tossed
her head. "No."

"Unbelievable," he said, shaking his head again.
"You're despicable, do you know that? You've ruined my
life."

He turned and stomped past her, into the library's rear
room.

Jane looked around the table. All eyes were wide and
fixed on Crystal, who remained in the middle of the floor.
Gabrielle's eyes were slits, and she slowly turned her head
from side to side.

After a moment, Crystal gathered herself together and
resumed her walk across the room, positioning herself at
the checkout desk and calmly checking in books from the
return slot.

Mindy cleared her throat. "Well," she began uncertainly, "I suppose we should—"

"We should give it up," Doris intoned from the other
end of the table.

"Doris!" Rhoda said in surprise.

Doris threw out her hands. "The book stinks, everybody seems to have something else to talk about—what's
the point?"

Mindy looked down, deeply disappointed.

"*I* would like to continue the meeting," Jane said, feeling sorry for Mindy.

"Me, too," Ginny said.

"All right, then." Mindy gave a wan smile, looking
vaguely encouraged. "Why don't we—"

At that moment Stanton reappeared from the back
room. His gaze fixed in front of him, he stomped back
across the floor to the front entrance and went out. Jane

glanced across the room. Behind the checkout desk, Crystal appeared to have taken no notice.

"Now then," Mindy tried yet again, "where were we?"

Doris said, "We were talking about what would have happened if Uncle Ned had been in the barn." She sounded unutterably bored.

"Right," Mindy said cheerfully. "Thank you. Any ideas?"

Penny raised her hand. "Then Agnes would have been able to tell him what had happened to her, and he might have helped her."

"Interesting," Mindy said, slowly nodding. "Good, Penny." She frowned, concentrating, then looked up at Jane and laughed. "Talking about the barn reminded me of the book I wanted to recommend to you. It's *Down on the Farm*, by . . . Oh, dear, I can't seem to recall the author's name."

From across the room, Crystal piped up, "Hodges. Lauren Hodges."

Mindy tossed her an uneasy look. "Right," she called. "Thank you. Jane, remind me to get it for you before you leave."

"I'll get it," Crystal said pleasantly. She came out from behind the checkout desk and walked into the rear room.

"Any other ideas?" Mindy asked the group.

"I'm cold," Doris said.

"Yes, it is chilly in here," Louise agreed.

Mindy nodded. "We've been having trouble with the heat. I've asked Rich to fix it, or to call in whoever needs to fix it, but I don't know where he is with that. For that matter, I don't know where he is!"

"Who's Rich?" Jane asked.

"Rich Weldon," Mindy replied, surprised. "He's the custodian. You know Rich."

"Yes," Jane said, vaguely remembering him.

"He never showed up for work today," Mindy continued.

"Here, Doris," Louise said, removing her cardigan. "Put this on."

"Thanks," Doris said, taking it.

At that moment a woman's high-pitched scream pierced the air, followed by a terrible crash. Everyone froze.

Chapter 8

The sounds had come from the back room of the library.

"Dear Lord," Mindy said in a whisper, jumped up, and ran toward the back, the other women close behind her. Together they scrambled into the back room . . . and gasped at what they saw.

An entire wooden floor-to-ceiling bookcase had collapsed. It lay twisted atop a mountain of books—and atop Crystal, whose head lay directly under the bookcase's topmost shelf. Blood ran from a gash at the side of her head.

Jane hurried forward, heart pounding, and picked her way through the books. She bent down and tried to lift the bookcase, but it was no use. The old wood was so heavy she couldn't move it an inch.

"Crystal," she said softly, leaning close, and now she could see her face—its expression frozen, the brown eyes wide with fear.

Mindy took a step toward Jane and said in a low voice, "Is she—"

"Yes," Jane said, "I'm afraid so."

Rhoda came forward. "But how—?" she said to Jane.

Jane looked up at the wall against which the bookcase

had stood. About eight feet up were two heavy metal L-brackets, about a foot apart. The vertical segments of these brackets appeared bolted firmly to the wall. The horizontal segments stuck straight out into the air.

Mindy was studying them. "They were bolted to the bookcase. It's as if they just . . . let go."

"What are you doing?" came Doris's brisk voice, and Mindy and Jane turned to her. "Get ahold of yourselves. A woman has been killed. Call the police."

"Yes," Mindy said with a haunted look. "We should, Jane." Her eyes widened slightly. "Call your boyfriend, Stanley."

"Yes," Jane said. Stanley would know what to do. She ran to the front room and went behind the checkout desk to make the call. As she dialed, she had a horrible thought. She put her hand to her mouth, suddenly feeling so hot she thought she might faint.

How would she tell Florence?

Jane stood on the path that led up to the library's entrance and watched Stanley emerge from the building. Mindy, who had been waiting at the foot of the steps, hurried up to him. As she spoke to him, she had to put her head way back, for although he was of medium height, he was easily a head taller than she. He wore a blue blazer over gray flannel slacks—he'd come out without his coat again, Jane noted. He had such a sweet, concerned look in his dark brown eyes as he listened to Mindy. A wind had come up. It played with his straight sandy hair, which usually remained neatly in place on his forehead.

Abruptly he gave Mindy a vigorous nod, pressed her upper arm reassuringly, then descended the stairs and walked down the path to where Jane waited.

She'd have kissed him hello if there weren't so many

people around—police officers standing at the edge of the library lawn, several of them watching Stanley.

"Are you all right?" he asked her.

She nodded. Suddenly she felt her face contort, and tears sprang to her eyes. "It's so awful, Stanley. I know I said mean things about her, but I—I never—"

"I know." Nodding, he put his arm around her and pulled him to her, clearly unconcerned about who might be watching. "You mustn't feel guilty."

She sniffed hard. "It was so horrible. The whole bookcase— How could such a thing happen?"

Stanley's expression underwent an odd transformation. He was watching her, as if trying to read her the right way. At last he said, "Come to my car."

She frowned. "What?"

He motioned with his hand for her to walk with him. They got into his squad car parked at the far left edge of the library lawn, near the town hall.

"What's going on?" she asked him.

"Jane, I'm going to tell you this because you'll hear it anyway, and I want it to come from me."

She lowered her brows in confusion. "Hear what from you? What is it?"

"Jane, it looks as if Crystal . . . Well, it seems pretty clear that what happened in there wasn't an accident."

"What?" She gave her head a few quick shakes. "Stanley, what are you talking about? The bolts came loose. The bookcase fell on her."

"Yes, the bookcase fell on her, but the bolts didn't *come loose*. They were *removed*."

For a moment she just stared at him, the meaning of what he'd said sinking in. "Removed?" she whispered. "Someone took them out?"

"Yes."

"But why?"

He took a deep breath, considering. "Someone wanted the bookcase to fall."

"On Crystal?"

"It appears so."

"How can you be so sure?"

He looked at her. "Because they're gone."

A movement caught her eye and she looked up. Two men carrying a stretcher had emerged from the library's front doors. A sheet covered Crystal's large body. Carefully the two men descended the wide stairs and moved toward an ambulance Jane now noticed parked a few cars ahead of Stanley's car.

Suddenly she turned to him. "I've got to get home. I've got to tell Florence before someone else does."

"Oh, missus!" Florence wailed, embracing Jane fiercely.

Jane patted her back. She began to cry. "I know. I know. It's horrible. I'm so sorry."

Suddenly Florence drew back and looked Jane in the eye. "Yes, it's horrible, and it's my fault."

"What!"

"Yes. I was the one who told my sister she should come up here and interview for that job at the library. If I had only minded my own business, she would be alive now." Shaking her head miserably, Florence dropped into a kitchen chair. She looked up at Jane imploringly. "But who would have wanted to kill her?"

Was she serious? "Well . . ."

"Oh, I know what you're going to say. She was meddlesome and bossy and some people didn't get along with her. But she had a good heart, missus, she really did. You have no idea how good she was to me when we were growing up in Trinidad. With so many children, my mother was always busy. It was Crystal who raised me, really." She paused, a thought occurring to her. "Thank God our mother isn't alive to know about this."

"Why are you guys crying?"

Nick had appeared in the doorway, Twinky in his arms. Alphonse appeared behind him, padded into the kitchen, and began walking around Jane, pressing himself against her legs. He would have to be walked.

Jane went up to Nick and put her hand on his upper arm. "Honey, something very sad has happened. Florence's sister Crystal . . . well, she died."

Nick's eyes grew wide. "She died?"

Florence nodded. "Yes, Nicholas." She lowered her head and started to cry again.

Nick walked slowly over to her and gave her a hug. Florence hugged him back tightly. "Thank you," she said through her tears. Then she released him, sniffed hard, and stood. "I'd better start getting dinner ready. And Stanley—he'll want to speak to me, won't he, missus?"

"Yes," Jane replied. "You're her next of kin."

"I am," Florence said, turning to the counter, where she had set out carrots and onions for chopping. "I am."

A whistling wind rattled the windows of Jane's study. Gazing out into the darkness, Florence hugged herself for warmth. Then she turned to face Jane, who sat a few feet away. "It makes no sense, missus."

Jane smiled gently. "But I've told you exactly what happened."

"No, I know that. I understand everything that happened up until my sister died. What I don't understand is *why*? Why would anyone want to kill poor Crystal?"

Was it possible, Jane wondered, that Florence really couldn't see what kind of person her sister had been? Florence had apologized numerous times for Crystal's behavior, which meant she must have been aware of how people perceived her. But Jane would not remind Florence of any of this.

Jane frowned, gathering her thoughts. Finally she said slowly, "Who's to say how people will react to another person . . . to something another person has done? Maybe someone was angry at your sister—"

"And *killed* her?" Florence's dark eyes were immense. "Out of anger?"

"It's been known to happen."

Florence cast her gaze down at the floor, pondering this concept. Then sharply she looked up, her face full of resolve. "You have to help me."

"Help you?"

"Yes. You have to help me find out who did this to my poor sister."

"Oh, Florence . . ." Jane began, shaking her head.

"You know how to do it, missus. You've done it before. Please." Florence's eyes searched Jane's. "I'm not stupid. I know what Crystal was. She was bossy and self-righteous, a know-it-all, and she could be a terrible schemer. I know all that. But she didn't deserve to die. I loved her. Please. Help me find out who did this."

"But the police—"

"Pfoosh!" Florence made a sound of disgust and turned her head away. "No offense to your Stanley, missus—you know I love him dearly—but the police here, they are a bunch of bungling idiots! What have they done in the past when someone has been killed? No help at all! It was *you* who figured out what happened to poor Marlene. *You* who found out who that poor girl behind Hydrangea House was. *You* who caught the person who killed Mr. Kenneth's cousin Stephanie. Then there was your poor friend Ivy, and only three months ago, Tina Vale—"

"Okay, okay. Maybe I've been lucky."

"Lucky! Don't sell yourself short, missus. Luck had

nothing to do with it. You have a way of putting the pieces together. And I need you to help me put *these* pieces together for Crystal." Florence leaned toward Jane, wringing her hands. "Will you do that?"

"I . . ." Jane hesitated. Then she let her shoulders drop. "Yes, of course I will."

"Thank you, missus. Thank you." Florence gazed out again into the darkness. A branch whipped by the wind tapped the window glass. Tears came to her eyes. "She's out there, lying in a cold room, all alone. My sister who ran on the beach with me at Chacacabana, who taught me how to cook . . ." She laughed through the tears. "Who poured a bucket of water on my head when I wouldn't eat my vegetables . . . No, missus," she said, turning back to Jane, "my sister did not deserve to die."

Chapter 9

J ane was in no mood for Goddess this morning. Goddess, as if sensing this, had kept a low profile, finishing some filing Daniel had given her, then concentrating intently on a manuscript Jane had asked her to read. Once again Goddess had worn her version of office attire—her secretary costume, this time consisting of a black wool skirt, a gray silk blouse, stockings, and sensible low-heeled black shoes. As if unable to play anything totally straight, she had worn the cat-eye glasses again. These, she had informed Jane, contained lenses of plain glass.

A few minutes after Jane had arrived at the office, Goddess, who had heard about Crystal's death from Daniel, came in and offered her condolences. Now Jane sat very still at her desk, gazing at her papers but seeing the fallen bookcase . . . Crystal's eyes wide with fear . . . two metal brackets extending straight out from the wall into midair.

Distractedly she opened her bag from Whipped Cream, broke off a piece of apple raisin muffin, and slowly chewed it. Who had removed the bolts securing the bookcase to the brackets? Who *could* have removed them? Jane recalled the chaotic book group meeting, the comings and goings.

Shortly before the meeting, Crystal had climbed that ladder to get a novel for Ginny. The bookcase had held fast. Between that time and Crystal's death, Myrtle Lovesey had gone back there. So had Mr. Stanton. Jane decided to speak to each of them. But first she wanted to know more about the bookcase and the ladder themselves. Leaving her office, she grabbed her coat from the closet and hurried out, telling Daniel and Goddess she'd be back soon.

The library was bustling, as if nothing had occurred. A group of six men in their sixties and seventies appeared to be conducting a meeting of some sort at the table where the reading group had sat the previous day. One of them suddenly stood up, raising his voice, only to be ordered to sit down by the others.

To Jane's left, Mindy was helping a college-age young woman find a book. Spotting it, a beaming Mindy plucked it from the shelf and handed it to the woman, who thanked her.

Starting back toward the checkout desk, Mindy saw Jane and her smile vanished. She changed course and hurried over. "Jane," she said solicitously, "how are you doing? How is Florence?"

"We're doing all right, thanks, Mindy. It's just such a terrible shock."

Mindy nodded quickly, her eyes huge, as if to say, *Not just for you!*

Jane's gaze traveled to the doorway into the back room.

"It's all cleaned up," Mindy said softly, following her gaze. "When the police were finished and gave the okay, I had Rich put the bookcase back up. Then he and I put the books back." She moved a bit closer to Jane. "Do you know," she said in an even softer voice, "the bolts were nowhere to be found."

"Really?" Jane said, deciding to play dumb. "What do you mean?"

"Come," Mindy said, and motioned for Jane to follow her to the quiet front corner of the library, where two tall windows bathed the dark wooden floor in warm sunlight. "We can talk here. Anyway, the bolts were gone. Don't you see what that means?"

Jane shook her head, pretending to be at a loss.

"It means," Mindy said impatiently, "that *someone took them.*"

"Really? But who?"

"Oh, Jane," Mindy said, exasperated, "I wonder about you. They were taken by *whoever removed them.*"

Jane dropped her jaw and gaped. "But—but—are you saying—"

"Yes! Someone removed those bolts. Someone wanted that bookcase to fall."

"And kill poor Crystal?" Jane said. "But who? Why?"

Mindy gave her head a helpless shake. "Who knows?" Her reddish brows rose. "No offense, Jane, but she was hardly the easiest person to get along with. For instance, she and I were having a lot of problems."

"Really?"

"Oh, yes. She was so . . . opinionated. She hated doing anything anybody else's way. That's not good when you're reporting to someone."

"No, it's not," Jane agreed. "But since we know *you* didn't remove the bolts, who do you think did?"

"I haven't the faintest idea."

Jane wasn't about to share any of her own theories with Mindy. She began to drift toward the back room. "I'm curious about that ladder."

"The ladder? What about it?"

"Was it sturdy?"

"Of course it was sturdy." Mindy looked up. "There's Rich. He can tell you about it. Rich!"

A man who appeared to be in his late twenties had emerged from the men's restroom at the rear of the building. Hearing his name, he ambled slowly over to where Jane and Mindy stood.

He was of medium height and of average build, neither fat nor thin. He wore putty-colored overalls, open at the neck. His features were plain and unremarkable—perhaps even homely, it occurred to Jane. He had lank collar-length brown hair that badly needed cutting, for it kept falling in front of his eyes, only to be flipped back by a sharp jerk of his head.

As he neared Jane and Mindy, he removed his hands from the pockets of his overalls and put them on his hips. Jane noticed that his nails were raw and red, most of them bitten down to the quick.

Saying nothing, he stood expectantly.

"Rich," Mindy said, "this is Jane Stuart."

His hands remained on his hips. He gave an almost imperceptible nod, his blank expression unchanging.

Mindy went on, "Crystal was the sister of Jane's housekeeper, Florence. Jane's curious about the ladder."

He frowned mildly. "The ladder?" His voice was like the rest of him—average, unaccented, bland.

"Yes, can you tell her about it?" Mindy turned to Jane. "What was it exactly that you wanted to know, Jane?"

Jane led the way into the back room and over to the corner where the bookcase had fallen. There was no ladder on the track near the ceiling. She turned to Rich and Mindy in puzzlement.

"It's over here," Rich said, as if reading her mind, and flipped back his hair. He led the way to the back of the room, where the ladder lay in two pieces against the wall beneath a window. One end of each piece was jagged and sharp.

"It snapped, you see," Mindy said.

"Snapped?" Jane echoed. "How?"

"Well— Rich, you explain it."

Nibbling on the nail of his right index finger, Rich walked back to where Crystal had died. "She reached way out," he said, roughly assuming the position of Crystal's body on the ladder and extending his right arm. "The bookcase wasn't attached to the wall, so when she shifted her weight, it started to fall. All that weight on the ladder snapped it, and the bookcase fell on her." He might have been describing any everyday mishap.

"The weight of the bookcase could have done that?" Jane asked.

Rich looked at her as if she were an idiot. "It did, didn't it?"

"Rich," Mindy reprimanded, "let's not be rude. I think what Jane is asking is whether the ladder was sturdy. Am I right, Jane?"

Jane nodded.

" 'Course it was sturdy," Rich said. "It was a Putnam Rolling Ladder."

"Putnam?" Jane said.

Mindy said, "Putnam makes the best library ladders. We've ordered a new one from them in New York."

Rich indicated the massive bookcase that had fallen. "But these old things weigh a lot, heavy old wood and all."

Jane nodded thoughtfully. "Tell me," she said, turning to Rich, "have you noticed anyone looking at the ladder lately?"

"Nope."

At that moment the men having their meeting in the

front room all raised their voices simultaneously, one of them pounding the table.

"This won't do," Mindy said. "Excuse me." She hurried away.

Rich turned and started to walk away, too.

"Oh, Rich . . ." Jane said, and he turned, his face blank. "I was just wondering . . . This is all probably difficult for you."

"Difficult? For me? Why?"

"Well, with Crystal gone, more work for everyone else."

"I don't do any of her work. My job's the same as ever."

"Do you have *any* feelings about Crystal being gone?"

"Feelings? Like what?"

Jane was beginning to believe Rich Weldon didn't have feelings. "You know, sad that she's gone? After all, you worked with her."

"Only a couple of weeks. Besides, I didn't like her much."

"Oh?"

He simply looked at her.

"She didn't treat you well?"

"No, that wasn't it. She treated me like—like I wasn't there. Like I didn't matter. That was most of the time. When she noticed me, she'd order me around, tell me how to do something."

Jane had no trouble imagining Crystal doing that. "I see. So you resented her."

"Not really. Didn't care much one way or the other. You asked me if I was sad that she's gone. I'm not. That's it." His hands were back on his hips. He turned to leave.

"Wait. I understand you weren't here yesterday morning."

He scowled mildly. "Yeah, that's right. Why?"

"Where were you?"

He let out a bitter little laugh. "What's that to you?"

"Can you just tell me?" she said, figuring blunt would probably work best on this odd young man.

He paused for a moment, thinking. Then he gave a small shrug, as if to himself. "I guess it doesn't matter. I had a doctor appointment."

"Yes?"

"Yes," he said, irritated. "Lady, what are you, a cop?"

"No, but I'm looking into what happened to Crystal in my own way, since you ask."

"Why? What's it to you?"

"She was the sister of my housekeeper, as Mindy told you. I'm doing this for her."

"Which means I'm supposed to tell you my private business?" He flipped his hair.

"No, of course not. But if you have nothing to hide, why won't you tell me?"

He shook his head in wonder. "Lady, you are incredible. Okay, I'll go along with you on this. I had a rash, all right? So I went to see my doctor. It's Lanny Katz, in that office building right down the street."

Jane knew Dr. Katz. His building was on Packer Road, not far from the village green. She forced a smile, intensely disliking this young man. "Thanks," she said.

Without a word, he turned and strolled away, biting on a thumbnail.

As Jane headed for the library's front door, she glanced over at the checkout desk just as Mindy was looking over at her. For an instant their gazes locked and Mindy opened her mouth as if to speak. Jane stopped, waiting, but Mindy appeared to think better of whatever she'd been about to say, and returned to the stack of books she was checking in.

Chapter 10

Jane intended to check out Rich Weldon's doctor, but though she passed his building on her way back to the office, she didn't stop in. She wasn't ready yet, hadn't devised a plan.

To reach her office, Jane had to pass Up, Up and Away, the travel agency next door. She had no sooner passed its poster-festooned entrance than out walked Jonah Kramer, whom she'd seen at Whipped Cream the previous Wednesday. When he saw her, his face lit up.

"Jane!"

She smiled. She liked Jonah, a mild-mannered man in his forties who lived in the neighboring town of Lincoln Park with his wife and many children.

"Jane, can I ask you something?"

"Sure, Jonah. Shoot."

"You've got a new girl—I mean woman—working at your office, haven't you?"

Oh, no. She kept the smile pasted on. "Yes, I have. Why?"

He frowned and shook his head. "She looks so familiar somehow. Do I know her?"

"Do *you* know her? How would you know her?"

"I don't know . . . maybe she's worked somewhere else here on the green?" His face lit up. "Did she ever waitress at Giorgio's?"

"Uh . . . I don't think so."

He scratched a graying temple. "Then how the heck do I know her?"

Jane drew down the corners of her mouth as she made an exaggerated shrug. "Beats me. You know how we sometimes see people we're sure we know from somewhere but we really don't?"

"Yeah . . ." he replied doubtfully.

"Well," she said brightly, "this is one of those times! Seeya!"

"Yeah, seeya, Jane," he said thoughtfully and, nibbling on the inside of his lower lip, turned and went back inside his office.

That was close, Jane told herself as she entered the agency. She frowned. The offices appeared deserted, something she didn't like to happen. When either she or Daniel went to lunch, each always made sure the other would be in, or else they locked up. Where was Goddess?

"Hello!" she called.

Silence. She looked in her office—empty—then had a thought and returned to the reception area, where she opened the door to the storage room. Goddess lay atop an old desk, her chin propped up on her elbow, her nose pressed deep into a copy of *Arabian Nights* by Salomé Sutton. So engrossed was she in her reading that she was unaware of Jane's presence.

"Yoo-hoo!" Jane said softly. "Hello! Goddess!"

Goddess chomped once on her gum but didn't look up. "Mmm, yeah. Hey, babe."

"Goddess," Jane said, slightly louder, "I need to speak to you."

"Hm?" Goddess looked up and frowned, looking around as if awakening from a dream. "What's that?"

"Goddess, I'm sure Daniel explained to you that we never leave the offices unattended. Someone could walk in and steal us blind."

Goddess laughed, looking at Jane as if she were mentally lacking. "Jane, the offices are not unattended. *I'm* here. See?" She curled an index finger back at herself. "Me?"

"You're in the storage room," Jane said, irritation building in her voice, "lost in that book, with the door closed."

"Well, can you blame me?" Goddess asked, sitting up. "It's unbelievable! Roan Romero . . ." She craned her neck and ran her hand down her throat and across her breasts in a very Goddesslike movement. "They just don't make 'em like that anymore."

"They never did," Jane said dryly.

"What's that?"

"It's romance! It's make-believe. Anyway, I'm delighted that you've discovered pleasure reading, but you really need to be out front when Daniel and I are gone. Got that?"

Goddess hopped onto the floor and saluted. "Roger!"

Jane decided not to react to that. Goddess followed her out to the front room.

The door from the street burst open and Jonah from next door stood there, staring at Goddess. She stared back at him.

"Are you . . ." he said.

"Excuse me?" Goddess replied in her best Brooklyn accent. "Do I know you?"

Jonah seemed to deflate. He grimaced, wrinkling his nose, as if asking himself how in heaven's name he could ever have imagined she was who he'd thought she was.

"I—I'm sorry," he said. "Excuse me." And he backed out the door, softly closing it.

Goddess snickered. "Not bad, huh?"

"Very good," Jane said, hanging up her coat. "A close call. Quick thinking."

"Thanks," Goddess said nonchalantly, falling into her desk chair. Looking down, she noticed a pink message slip in the center of her blotter. "Oh, I forgot. Someone called for you."

"Yes? Who was it?"

"Stanley. You represent a writer named Stanley? Funny name."

"He happens to be my boyfriend," Jane informed her.

"You got a boyfriend? You never told me that!"

"What did he say?"

"Mmm, let's see. Oh, yeah. That it's urgent."

"Really?" What could it be? Jane hurried into her office and dialed Stanley's cell phone. She got his voice mail. "Stanley, it's me. Godd— I have a message that you called and that it's urgent. Call me back as soon as you get this."

Then she called the police station. Buzzi at the front desk said Stanley was out but that he'd leave him a message. She knew better than to ask Buzzi what was going on.

Jane sat at her desk but couldn't work, didn't even try. She glanced at a few papers at the top of her work mountain, gazed restlessly out her window, then jumped up and returned to the reception room, where Goddess was filing.

"Back soon," she told her, putting her coat back on, and left the office. She'd visit Dr. Katz, check on Rich Weldon's alibi, while she was waiting to find out what Stanley wanted to tell her.

Following Packer Road across the railroad tracks, Jane recalled the one time she had met Dr. Lanny Katz. It had been three years earlier, at one of Audrey and Elliott Fairchild's dinner parties. Dr. Katz, a tall, handsome man in his fifties with strong features and a full head of crisp salt-and-pepper hair, had told Jane that he was a gourmet cook, then shared with her his recipe for chocolate mousse. Jane had tried it, and it really had been exceptional.

Dr. Katz had a lively, vibrant personality. Jane wondered how he interacted with the bland, uncommunicative Rich Weldon.

Approaching the doctor's building, a modest two-story brick structure on the left, Jane realized how silly it was for her to think Dr. Katz would confide in her about one of his patients. On the other hand, someone on his staff might be willing to at least confirm that Weldon had been there on Tuesday morning.

Katz's office was on the second floor, its waiting room cheerfully decorated in primary colors, presumably to appeal to young patients for whom a large wooden box held a selection of trucks and dolls. Chairs lined the perimeter of the waiting room. At the far end of the room, next to a window looking out on woods, a middle-aged woman sat beside a teenage boy with glassy eyes.

"May I help you?"

Jane turned. To her left, behind a reception window, sat an exceptionally thin woman in her thirties. She had large, doleful eyes that showed a lot of white under their brown irises; a thin, pointed nose; and straight, shoulder-length brown hair threaded with gray and parted exactly in the middle. She smiled at Jane—a lovely smile, her teeth perfect and white. "Do you have an appointment with Dr. Katz?"

Jane approached the window and smiled. "Um, no, I haven't, but I wonder if I could speak to you about something."

The woman gave a mild frown and waited. Jane noticed a book lying facedown on her desk and made out the title: *A Dream of Passion.* Another romance reader. Inwardly Jane smiled.

She had a brainstorm. How fortunate that this woman didn't know her.

"Ordinarily I would call," Jane said, "but I was in the area and thought I'd drop by. I hope you don't mind."

"What is it you want?" the woman asked.

"Well, you see, Ms.—"

"Cohen. Celeste Cohen."

"Ms. Cohen. I work for a manufacturing company in Wayne. I head up human resources. We've had an application from a patient of yours. A Richard Weldon."

Ms. Cohen nodded, her brows knit. "Yes?"

"And he's put down Dr. Katz as a character reference."

"He has?"

"Mm," Jane said, nodding easily. "Many of our applicants use their doctors as references."

"They do?"

"Yes. At any rate, I'm here to see if you—I mean if Dr. Katz—would recommend this young man to us."

Ms. Cohen shifted around in her seat, leaning forward on the counter. "What kind of job has he applied for? I'm just curious."

"We manufacture . . . ladders. Library ladders."

"Library ladders?"

"Yes. You know, the kind you climb to reach those high shelves."

"Ah."

"And Mr. Weldon would work in our plant."

Ms. Cohen looked surprised. "That's the job he applied for? *Rich?*"

"Mm-hm. So . . . would you recommend him?"

"Sure, I guess so."

"You've seen him recently?"

"Yeah. Yesterday, in fact."

"Really? He was here?"

"Mm-hm, all morning."

Jane noticed an ornate silver ring on Celeste Cohen's hand. "That's very beautiful," she said.

Ms. Cohen smiled her lovely smile. "Thanks." She pursed her lips and gazed skyward. "That's my good luck ring."

"Really!" Jane leaned closer. "And what is it you need good luck for? If you don't mind my asking."

Ms. Cohen pursed her lips and her brows shot high, as if to say, "That's my big secret."

"If I tell you," she said in a singsong voice, like a little girl, "then that would ruin my good luck, now wouldn't it?"

This chick's got a few screws loose, Jane thought. "Yes, I suppose it would." She winked at her. "Now, you were saying Mr. Weldon was here yesterday. All morning, you said."

"Yeah. Hated to keep him waiting like that, but it can happen when we squeeze somebody in."

Jane was aware of someone at her right side and turned. The young man with the glassy eyes who'd been sitting near the window was waiting to speak to Ms. Cohen. She saw him and, before he could speak, said, "Soon, very soon, Bradley. Dr. Katz knows you're here."

Bradley nodded glumly and returned to his seat beside the woman who was presumably his mother.

"See what I mean," Ms. Cohen said in a low voice to Jane. "I squeezed him in. I can't help it if he has to wait."

"I suppose Mr. Weldon had an emergency."

Ms. Cohen shrugged. "A rash. Anyway . . ." She looked down and flipped through some papers on her desk, picking one out and placing it in front of Jane. It was a lined sheet with *10/22—AM* jotted at the top. Yesterday morning, Jane thought. Below the heading was a long list of signatures. "See?" Ms. Cohen said, pointing to a signature scrawled at the end of the list: *Rich Weldon.* "He signed in at nine, but Dr. Katz wasn't able to see him until almost noon."

Jane gave a serious nod, marveling at this woman's lack of professionalism—which was proving quite helpful. "Thank you so much for your help, Ms. Cohen."

"No problem. Glad to help. You think he'll get the job?"

"I think he's got a very good chance." Jane winked again. "Good luck with . . . whatever it is you need good luck for!"

Celeste Cohen pursed her lips and looked up again, enjoying her secret.

Definitely off.

Jane had reached the end of the second-floor corridor and opened the door to the stairs when her cell phone rang. It was Stanley.

"Are you all right?" she asked, starting down the stairs.

"I'm fine, Jane. Something has happened. I need to see you."

"Don't be so mysterious. What's happened? Tell me."

"There's a girl who works afternoons at the library. Ashley Surow. Do you know her?"

"Only by name. Crystal mentioned her a few times. Why?"

"Her body has just been found in the woods near the railroad tracks. She's been strangled."

Chapter 11

Stanley's office in the Shady Hills Police Station was a tiny, drab cubicle of cinder blocks painted a pale mocha. A narrow window near the ceiling admitted a thin shaft of light.

Jane sipped the coffee Stanley had brought her and watched him refer to a sheet of notes on his desk.

"Ashley Surow, sixteen years old. Lived on Oakmont Avenue. Attended Shady Hills High School, worked at the library after school." He looked up, regarding Jane with narrowed eyes.

"What?" she said.

He made no response, continuing to gaze at her. Finally he said, "Jane, what are you doing?"

She frowned. "What? What are you talking about?"

"You're playing cop again."

So that was it. She calmly met his gaze, jutting her chin out slightly. "Excuse me?"

"Richard Weldon, works at the library. He called us this morning, said you were harassing him."

"Harassing him! All I did was ask him some questions."

"About Crystal."

"Yes, about Crystal. Harassing him! Why, that little rodent."

"Jane, why are you doing this?"

She drew in an angry breath, then let it out and folded her arms. "Look. Crystal was Florence's sister. Florence asked me to try to find out who would do such a horrible thing to Crystal. I didn't feel I could say no, especially since you and your colleagues don't seem to be doing anything."

He gave an amazed chuckle. "We don't? How would you know that?"

"Well, are you?"

"Of course we are. Do you think you're the only person with a brain in this town? We've already interviewed a number of people about what happened."

"Oh, yeah? Like who?"

"That's really none of your business, but I'll tell you anyway. Myrtle Lovesey, Dick Stanton . . ."

"How did you know to interview them?"

"You mean how did we know they were in the library's back room between the first time Crystal climbed the ladder and the second time when it collapsed?"

She nodded.

"From speaking with Mindy Carter."

"Oh."

"So you see, we're a step ahead of you. You're not doing anything we're not. No, I take that back. You're harassing people."

She decided not to respond to that. Nibbling thoughtfully on the inside of her lower lip, she watched him.

"Besides," he went on, took a sip of his coffee, and set it down, "you're not even speaking to the right people. What's the point of talking to Rich Weldon? He wasn't even at the library yesterday morning."

"I know that. *Now.*"

"Then why did you bother talking to him?"

He had things switched around, but she didn't point that out. "I don't trust him . . . don't like him. I had to make sure."

"Sure of what?"

"That he really was where he said he was."

He turned his head and regarded her obliquely. "He was at his doctor's office."

"I know."

"How do you know?"

"I . . . checked it out."

"There, you see!" He slammed the palms of his hands on his desk. Its rickety steel legs rattled. "Playing cop again. Jane, we don't need you to check things out for us. Besides which," he said, his voice growing gentler, his eyes softening as he looked at her, "there's clearly even more here than we originally thought. This Surow girl worked with Crystal. There's got to be a connection." He shook his head. "Keep out of it, Jane. Please. For your own safety."

She sat quietly for a moment, her gaze cast downward. "She was near the railroad tracks?" she asked quietly.

"That's right," he answered, a little grudgingly. "Apparently her body had been there for about a week, maybe a bit less."

"A week!"

He nodded. "Poor kid."

"What did her parents say?"

He looked up with an expression of disgust. "That she was a 'bad seed.' That she'd been heading down a 'dangerous road,' and this is where it led."

Jane had never met Ashley Surow, but her eyes welled with tears for this poor girl. Picking up her handbag from the floor beside her chair, she rose. Stanley came around his desk, took her in his arms, and held her tight. "I mean it, Jane. There's a crazy person out there, a killer. Keep out of this. Let us handle it."

She gazed up into his warm brown eyes and smiled. He lowered his lips to hers and they kissed deeply. Afterward, she said, "Thank you for caring so much."

He frowned, as if to say she was crazy to think he wouldn't.

He walked her to her car, waving as she pulled onto the street and headed back to the office.

He really was the dearest man. But of course, she had no intention of stopping—especially in light of the news about Ashley Surow. Jane had given Florence her word.

And a promise was a promise.

"Everything all right?" Daniel asked Jane when she entered the office.

"Fine, why?"

"You were gone awhile."

At the back of the room, Goddess looked up from a manuscript, her eyes wide open with curiosity. "Some girl got offed, did you hear?"

Jane gave her a disapproving look. "Yes. How did you know?"

Daniel said, "It's all over town. Poor kid. Did you know her?"

"No, did you?"

"Yes. I saw her at the library a number of times. Sweet kid. Beautiful, too."

Goddess let out a low whistle. "What is it with this town? It's just like New York!"

"People are people," Jane said simply. "Doesn't matter where they are."

Shaking her head sadly, she walked into her office and sat at her desk, her mind conjuring a picture of a teenage girl lying dead in a cold, lonely wood.

*   *   *

That afternoon, a little after four, Daniel buzzed Jane to say that Audrey Fairchild was on the line.

"Janey, honey, I hate to bother you," Audrey said in one breath, "but there's something really important I need to talk to you about. Actually, it's something Cara and I need to talk to you about."

"Cara and you?" Jane frowned. "What is it?"

"Can we come see you?"

"Sure, if you like. Come on down." Then Jane remembered Goddess and quickly said, "On second thought, Audrey, I'll come there. Is everything all right?"

"We'll tell you when you get here. I'll put on coffee. See you soon."

Jane couldn't imagine what Audrey and Cara wanted to talk to her about. She was frowning as she pulled into her driveway, got out, and crossed Lilac Way to the Fairchilds' majestic fifteen-room Tudor. She made her way along the artfully curved path banked with pink and yellow chrysanthemums, climbed the wide brick front steps, and rang the bell.

The door was opened almost immediately by Audrey. Her face lit up as it always did, yet there was something different about it now. There was a haggardness, a strained look, detectable even through her heavy makeup. "Come in, doll, it's freezing out there." She took Jane's coat and hung it in the foyer closet. Then she turned toward the staircase that swept elegantly upward to the wide second-floor landing. "Cara! Come down, dear." She turned to Jane. "I've got coffee for us in the living room. Come."

Jane followed her into the cavernous living room—a room so vast that it was divided into three discrete seating areas that were like individual rooms. Audrey led the way to the one nearest the fireplace, whose mantle displayed part of Audrey's large Lladró collection. Jane loathed Lladró, all those fussy, precious little porcelain figurines in their pale creams and grays.

As if reading Jane's mind, Audrey walked up to the fireplace and touched the largest piece, centered on the mantel—a two-foot-high replica of the Statue of Liberty, all in creamy white except for two doves holding up a colored flower garland.

"My word, that's hideous," Jane said before she could stop herself.

Audrey spun around, aghast. "Jane! This is a very expensive piece. And how can you say that about the Statue of Liberty?"

"I'm not talking about the Statue of Liberty. I'm talking about *that.*" Jane gave Audrey a sorry smile. "You know I don't like that stuff."

Audrey gave her a small frozen smile, clearly irritated. "Well, that's *not* very patriotic," she said in a low voice, then turned toward the foyer. "Cara!" she shrieked. "Get down here!"

There was stomping on the stairs, followed by a petulant "I'm coming!" Then Cara appeared at the entrance to the living room.

Tall and slim, she wore jeans so full of holes that there seemed to be more holes than denim, and an immense royal blue fleece sweatshirt with the words GAP ATHLETIC in white letters on the front. She was a pretty girl, with Audrey's high cheekbones and bright blue eyes, and Elliott's glossy black hair. She had it pulled up into a messy ponytail.

"Hi, Jane," she said shyly, gazing down at the Oriental rug at her feet.

"Hello, Cara," Jane said pleasantly, sinking into a large armchair of mocha leather.

Audrey was settling on the cream-colored L-shaped leather

sofa that faced the fireplace. "Come in here, Cara," she said firmly, pouring coffee into two china cups. Audrey never used mugs.

Cara walked slowly into the room, dragging her feet.

"Stand up straight," Audrey said, and tapped the sofa cushion beside her. "Sit here."

With a roll of her eyes, Cara sat.

"Now," Audrey said, nostrils flaring, and handed Jane her coffee. "Cara has something to tell you, Jane." She turned to her daughter. "Haven't you, Cara?"

Cara nodded, gaze downcast. Then she looked up at Jane and there were tears in her eyes. "I . . . I don't know where to start."

Audrey knew. "Start with meeting that awful man at that awful place."

Cara gave a tiny nod and looked at Jane again. "You know that girl they found dead? Near the railroad tracks?"

"You know about that?" Jane said.

"Of course," Cara replied. "Everyone knows about it."

Of course, Jane thought, and told herself she should have known Shady Hills better than that. "Ashley. Ashley Surow. She worked at the library."

Cara nodded. "She was my friend."

"Your *best* friend," Audrey put in, and sipped her coffee. "Go on."

"She was my best friend. We hung out together a lot. One place we liked to go is Roadside." Cara scrunched up one eye, studying Jane. "Do you know what that is?"

Jane sighed. "I'm not from another planet, Cara. Of course I know it. It used to be called the Roadside Tavern. It's way up on Highland Road. Believe it or not, I've been there." That had been two years earlier, when Jane had been looking for Marlene, her nanny who had vanished. Marlene had hung out there.

"It's not like that anymore," Cara said. "It's a club. It's a cool place."

"I see," Jane said. "Go on."

"Ashley and I were there a couple of weeks ago and we met this guy. His name was Cosmo Blair."

Jane blinked. "Come again?"

Cara gave her head a little shake. "I know it's strange, but that was his name—Cosmo Blair. He was older than us—in his late twenties, I think—and, well, he was really cute. Handsome and sexy, with this great slicked-back hair. I liked him a lot, but he wasn't interested in me. He wanted Ashley."

Cara started to cry again. Audrey, biting her upper lip, patted Cara on the shoulder. "Go on."

"Ashley liked him, too. She gave him her cell number and he said he'd call her."

"Where was he from?" Jane asked.

"From New York City. That's all we knew about him." Cara paused, then continued. "The next day, he called Ashley. They met that night—I don't know where, somewhere here in town. He told her he was a filmmaker. He was looking for fresh talent for a low-budget film he was putting together, and he said he might have a part for her."

At this, Audrey rolled her eyes, then shook her head in sad disgust.

"They agreed they would meet again a week later." Now Cara began to cry in earnest, the tears running down her smooth cheeks. "When they met again, Cosmo said he wanted to drive Ashley to his company's studio. She . . . went with him."

"Oh, no," Jane said softly.

"It was dark—Ashley didn't know where he took her, except that they drove a little while to get there and it was a city. He took her into a big, dirty old building, like an old factory or something, and he started trying to make out with her."

"Go on," Audrey urged.

"At the back of this old building there was a filthy old piece of foam rubber or something lying on the floor, and he tried to have sex with her. He said all his actresses slept with him, that it was the least they could do in exchange for all he did for them. But Ashley had a bad feeling about all this—"

"I should think so," Jane said.

"—and she told him she'd changed her mind about the movie and everything and wanted him to take her back to Shady Hills. But he wouldn't listen. He just kept trying to have sex with her, pulling at her clothes and getting rough. Ashley struggled and tried to fight him, and he hit her. Then he dragged her to a corner of this big room and grabbed some rope to tie her up. He took out a pocket knife to cut the rope, but he couldn't get the knife open and he got so frustrated he hit Ashley again, hard, in the face."

Jane realized she was holding her breath. Shaking her head, she made a soft tsk-ing sound. Audrey met her gaze and shook her head, too, in silent agreement.

"Somehow Ashley got away from him," Cara went on, "but he ran after her and this time when he caught her he beat her up, really bad. She kicked him in the stomach and he fell over. While he was down, she got out of the building and ran across the street and into an alley between two buildings. When she ran out on the other side, a truck was coming down the street. She waved frantically and the driver stopped. She told him she needed to get to Shady Hills. He said he could only take her part of the way. He left the city, drove onto some highway, and after a short while he said he had to get off the highway again. He dropped her off right there."

"Why didn't she call the police?" Jane asked.

"Good question," Audrey said, and Cara gave her a disapproving look.

"Because of her father," Cara told Jane. "He's a terrible tyrant. He was very strict with Ashley, always thought she was doing something she shouldn't. He would have been furious if he'd found out what Ashley had been up to—that she had gone off with this creepy guy. Ashley was terrified. She called me on her cell phone and begged me to come and get her."

"Did she know where she was?" Jane asked.

"Only that she was on Route Eighty."

"So what did you do?"

"Yes," Audrey said, "tell her."

"I took Mom's car and—"

"You *what*?" Jane said. "But you're only sixteen."

Cara shrugged. "I know how to drive. We all know how to drive, Jane. So I found Mom's keys and took the car and found Ashley beside this exit on Route Eighty. It was Route Eighty West, which means Cosmo had taken her someplace farther east."

"Right," Jane said, thinking the same thing. "What did you both do then?"

"Ashley was so afraid. She couldn't go home after what she'd done, so late, looking the way she did. We didn't know *what* to do."

Audrey set down her coffee cup. "Couldn't confide in *me*, of course."

"Oh, Mom!" Cara rolled her eyes and threw herself back on the sofa. "Don't start that again." She turned back to Jane. "We talked and talked and then Ashley had an idea. She wanted to go to Crystal."

"Crystal!" Jane cried.

"Yes. Ashley really liked Crystal. Crystal was the only

person who was nice to her at the library. Crystal listened to her. Ashley admired Crystal."

Unbelievable. "Go on."

"So we called her at her apartment. We said we were in trouble and needed her help."

"And what did she say?"

"She told us to come right over."

Which explained why Crystal hadn't come to dinner the previous Thursday night, Jane thought.

"She was so nice to us," Cara said, holding out her hands. "After she heard the whole story, she said she wanted to talk to Ashley's parents and then to the police. She pointed out that Stanley is your boyfriend. But Ashley refused. She kept saying her father would kill her. Crystal begged her to at least talk to Stanley, but Ashley said no.

"Crystal kept insisting, and Ashley kept saying no. Ashley and I realized that Crystal wouldn't stop until Ashley agreed to talk to *somebody,* so when Crystal suggested this woman at school, the school psychologist—a woman who had helped Ashley with some problems in the past—Ashley said okay. Crystal was happy with this—though, of course, Ashley was lying. She really had no intention of talking to anybody."

"But what would she do?" Jane asked.

"She was going to run away. What else could she do? She couldn't go home. And she was terrified that Cosmo would find her and kill her. So she was going to leave, go away. I pleaded with her not to, but nothing I could say would change her mind."

Audrey said austerely, "Tell Jane what you did next."

"I took Mom's ATM card and got Ashley some cash. Four hundred and sixty dollars. She *had* to have some money! Then I realized I had to hide her, at least for the night. We drove over to that dumpy motel on Route Forty-six, the Rainbow. But they turned us away. They said we were too young. I couldn't hide Ashley here at home, because Mom and Dad were having their stupid cocktail party and there was no way I'd be able to get her in here without people seeing her."

"Which is why," Audrey interjected, "Cara behaved so oddly that night. She had only come in to steal my ATM card."

Cara ignored this. "Then Ashley remembered something. There's this room in the library, kind of a secret room."

"A secret room?" Jane was dubious.

"Well, not really a secret room, a storage room. It's way in the corner of the building, next to the restrooms, and the door is part of the paneling—you know, kind of invisible? Anyway, Ashley said she wanted to sleep in there. She would leave very early in the morning, before anyone got to work. It made sense to me. So I drove her over to the library and watched while she let herself in with the key she had from work. Ashley promised to call me in the morning on her cell phone before she took off."

"Took off?" Jane said. "Where was she going to go?"

"She was going to take a taxi to the Amtrak station in Newark and get on the first train out. But . . ." Cara burst into fresh tears. "The call never came."

"No," Jane said, overcome with a sad shivery feeling. "And she didn't get very far. Do you think maybe she'd decided to take the train from here in Shady Hills?"

Cara chewed her lip, puzzled. "You mean because that's where she—where they found her? I don't think so. She would have been afraid to do that. She was going to call a taxi from inside the library and go to Newark, like I said."

She fingered a stray wisp of hair. "Crystal called me the next morning to find out what happened, to see if Ashley was all right. I lied. I said she was fine but that she wouldn't be at work that afternoon because of her bruises. Crystal accepted that. Monday afternoon Crystal called me again, asking if I knew where Ashley was. I said I wasn't sure but that she was fine." Her eyes grew pleading. "I thought she *was* fine."

"Even though she hadn't called you Friday morning as she said she would?" Jane asked.

Cara shook her head. "I just figured she hadn't had time, that she'd been in a hurry to get away. I didn't think anything of it. Now I know she didn't call, didn't answer her phone when I called her, because she was dead."

She lowered her gaze to her lap and sniffed. "It's my fault she's dead. If I hadn't agreed to let her stay overnight at the library, she'd still be alive."

"Stop it, Cara," Audrey said, and Jane could tell that this wasn't the first time Cara had said this. "You did what you thought was right, to help your friend."

Jane looked at Audrey in surprise. This was uncharacteristically sensitive of Audrey, who must have realized this herself, for as soon as she had spoken, she looked away self-consciously.

Jane wasn't feeling quite so charitable. "You really should have gone to the police," she said, though gently.

"I know." Cara's gaze met Jane's. "You see now why I'm telling you this? Ashley and Crystal's murders must be connected somehow."

Jane blinked. "Who said Crystal was murdered?" she asked carefully.

"I told you, Jane. Everybody knows everything in this town."

Reluctantly Jane nodded. "So you're saying—"

"I'm saying that if Ashley and I hadn't gone to see Crystal, maybe she would be alive, too."

Jane shook her head. "We can't know that yet. Their murders may be unrelated . . . though it seems too much of a coincidence, I agree." Who was this Cosmo Blair? she wondered. Then a picture of handsome Dick Stanton flashed into her mind—Dick Stanton raging at Crystal, then rushing into the library's back room. He was the right age . . .

She drew herself back to the present moment. "Cara, did Ashley describe the building where this Cosmo took her?"

"Sort of. She said it was a long brick building, really big, with three floors. Oh, and she said it had long rows of tall windows."

"You have no idea what city could this have been?"

"Well, it was off the highway, like I told you. Oh . . ." Cara looked up, remembering. "And Ashley said that after they left Shady Hills, Cosmo drove on this highway for about fifteen or twenty minutes."

Audrey frowned in concentration. "Paterson? Passaic? What other city could it be?"

"Sounds like Paterson to me," Jane said, setting down her coffee cup and looking up at Cara. "You realize, I'm sure, that you'll have to tell all of this to the police."

"Yes," Cara muttered.

"Why did you want to talk to me first?"

"Because of you and Stanley," Audrey said before Cara could respond. "We were hoping you could—you know, prepare him."

"So he won't be so hard on Cara?"

Audrey flushed red. "Cara knows she's done wrong, Jane. Taking my car, withdrawing that money from the ATM. But she was just trying to help her friend. I've met Ashley's parents, and I can see why Ashley would have been afraid to go home."

"What are they like?"

Cara looked up angrily. "They're monsters. They treated her like a prisoner, like they have to—had to watch her every second or else she'd do something bad."

"Like what?" Jane asked.

"Like do things with boys. Her father was always calling her a whore."

"Did she have a history of . . . doing things with boys?"

"No! That's just it! She was a good girl. The big thing in her life was her job at the library."

"That may be," Jane pointed out, "but she did go off with this Cosmo without any hesitation."

"I didn't say she was a nun, Jane. But she was a good girl. Please believe me."

"I do," Jane said. "And I will speak to Stanley. I'm sure he'll be in touch right after I do."

"Thank you, Jane," Audrey said.

Jane started to rise.

"Wait," Cara said, "there's more."

"More?" Jane sat back down.

"There's another girl, a girl from school. She's a junior, like me. I don't know her very well. Once in a while I see her at the library. She hasn't been at school for two days now, and some girls who are friends with her say she hasn't been home."

"Who's watching these kids?" Jane asked in disgust.

"Exactly," Audrey agreed.

"Her name is Keiko," Cara said. "Keiko Morikawa. Her friends call her Kiki. She hangs out with kind of a tough crowd."

"Tough?" Jane said.

"Mm. Drugs. Boys."

Audrey said distastefully, "I've seen the mother around

town. She's a real estate agent. So's the husband. They live in Maple Estates, that new development."

Jane remembered driving past its gates Thursday morning.

"They don't care about Keiko," Cara said, "because they're too busy making money."

"Well, we don't know that they haven't called the police," Jane said, though Stanley would probably have mentioned it to her if they had. "All the more reason for you to speak to Stanley. We don't know if this Cosmo has anything to do with her disappearance, but either way, she needs to be found."

The three women rose and walked out to the foyer. Without a word of good-bye to Jane, Cara trudged up the stairs.

Audrey watched her daughter's retreating back for a moment, then turned to Jane and shook her head. "This is a very bad business. What are we going to do with these kids?"

Jane regarded Audrey's helpless expression and was overcome by angry amazement. "What are we going to do with them?" she replied, working to stay calm. "We're going to pay more attention to them. We're going to *be their parents.*"

Audrey gave her a wondering look. "What is that supposed to mean? Are you suggesting that I am not a good parent to Cara?"

"I'm saying that if you watched her more carefully, she would not be going to clubs and meeting men who are rapists and very possibly worse. She would not have been able to take your car keys and drive all over creation without your knowing it. She would not have been able to steal your ATM card and empty your bank account. For pity's sake, Audrey, she's only sixteen."

Audrey's nostrils opened and closed and her mouth

clamped shut. Finally she said, "How dare you? I think you'd better go."

With a shrug that said, "Suit yourself," Jane walked out the front door, down the curving path, and across Lilac Way to her house.

Chapter 12

"Missus, we were getting worried about you. Your car was here, but you weren't."

"I'm sorry, Florence," Jane said, hanging up her coat. "I went to speak with Audrey and Cara. Spent more time there than I expected to. Where's Nick?"

"Upstairs doing his homework. Or else he is talking to all of his friends on AOL Instant Messenger!"

Jane laughed. Lately Nick seemed addicted to this form of instantaneous communication via computer and Internet. At that moment Winky and Twinky appeared at the top of the stairs, meowed in unison, and hurried down to the foyer, where they began rubbing themselves hard against Jane's legs. She smiled absently.

"What's wrong?" Florence asked.

"Hm?"

"Something's wrong, missus, I can always tell. Are you okay?"

Jane gave her a fond smile. "You know me too well. Come into the kitchen. We can have some tea."

They sat at the kitchen table in the pearly gray afternoon light from the big kitchen window, the shadows from the pines at the top of the shallow backyard quickly lengthening, and Jane told Florence everything Cara had said. When she was finished, Florence gazed down thoughtfully at the table. "How horrible. That poor girl." She looked up, meeting Jane's gaze. "There must be a connection."

"Yes, but what?"

"Ashley and Cara went to see my sister on Thursday night. Five days later someone—this Cosmo?—killed my sister. The next day someone—most likely the same person—killed Ashley. Ashley must have known something, something she told Crystal . . . something someone killed Crystal to prevent her from repeating. Then Ashley had to die for the same reason."

"But we know everything Ashley told Crystal," Jane said. "Cara was there. She heard everything that was said. She just told it all to me. Nothing was said that anyone would want to stop Crystal and Ashley from repeating."

Shrewdly Florence narrowed her pretty brown eyes. "Nothing that meant anything to you or me."

"Perhaps," Jane agreed thoughtfully.

"Maybe the police will find something," Florence said. "You did say Cara is going to talk to them?"

"Yes, but I said I would speak to Stanley first. In fact, I'd better do that." Jane drank the last of her tea. "Excuse me."

She went to her study and dialed Stanley. He picked up on the first ring.

"Jane, I don't mean to hurt your feelings, but I'm very busy, so unless you have something important to say—"

"As a matter of fact, I have."

"What?"

"I want to tell you in person. May I come over?"

"I'll come there."

Ten minutes later she was greeting him at the front door.

Outside it had grown quite cold, and Stanley's face was red as he removed his jacket.

"You need some nice hot coffee," Jane said, and turned to find Florence behind her, smiling at Stanley.

"I'll get it, missus."

"Thanks, Florence," Stanley said, and followed Jane to her study. There, sipping the coffee Florence brought him, he listened to Jane's account of what Cara had said. When she was through, he drummed his fingers angrily on the table beside his chair. "These sick animals come out from the city and prey on these innocent small-town girls."

She looked at him. "Are you serious?"

"What do you mean?"

"Stanley, these girls aren't innocent. They're clubbing at places like Roadside and who knows where else. They're seeing boys and taking drugs and running around and most of the time it seems their parents have no idea where they are."

"Yeah, you're right. It's these rich kids. Spoiled rotten and not nearly enough supervision. Be that as it may," he said, blowing out his breath as he got to his feet, "I've got to talk to Cara now. Do me a favor and let her know I'm coming over?"

"Sure." She made the call. "She's ready for you." She walked him to the door. "Be gentle with her, okay?"

"Me? Am I ever anything but gentle?"

She smiled. His face turned serious. "After I speak to Cara, I'm going to pay a call on Mr. and Mrs. Morikawa. I find it extremely odd that they haven't called us."

"Meet them first. Then see if you think it's odd."

He looked at her thoughtfully for a moment, then gave her a kiss and went down the steps and across the street toward the Fairchilds' mansion.

*   *   *

Jane tucked the blankets snugly around Nick and gave him a kiss on the cheek. "Good night." Then she moved to the foot of the bed, where Alphonse lay sprawled on Nick's feet, and gave the dog's luminous coat a long, firm stroke. Alphonse looked up at her with his big moist brown eyes and his tail thumped twice.

"Night, boys," she said, and switched off the light. As she closed the door, leaving a crack so that Alphonse could get in and out, the phone rang. It stopped abruptly, as Florence got it downstairs.

"Missus," she called a moment later. "Stanley on the line."

She took the call in her bedroom. "How did it go?"

"Quite a story," he said, sounding exhausted. "I see what you mean about kids not being supervised. And that Audrey is a piece of work."

Jane smiled. "Isn't she, though? What did she do?"

"Nothing in particular. She kept interrupting, telling the poor kid how to tell her story."

"That's Audrey."

"I called the Morikawas," he said.

"And?"

"They said they got a call from Keiko two nights ago— the first night she was gone. She told them she was with her boyfriend, a kid named Sean Hart, and that she was fine. That's why they didn't call the police."

"I see. And where is this boyfriend, Sean Hart?"

"Darned if they knew! No idea. Didn't even know what town he lives in."

"Why am I not surprised?"

"Well, he doesn't live in Shady Hills," he said, "because I've already checked. I'll see what I can find out in the morning."

"Mm."

"What's that mean?"

"What? What's what mean?"

" 'Mm.' "

"It means I'm thinking. Good night, Stanley."

"Good night, Jane."

In the morning Jane was still thinking, mostly about the rich Shady Hills kids no one seemed to be watching. Over breakfast it occurred to her that the place to find out about teenagers was at the high school. Classes at Shady Hills High School started at seven thirty, which meant staff would most likely be in place around seven. That would give her plenty of time to talk to whomever would talk to her and still get to the office around nine.

The high school was a recently renovated building of pale mauve brick and glass on Highland Road, about half a mile from the center of town. It was a little before seven when Jane parked in front of the building and found her way to the school's main office.

Behind a counter, a sour-looking redhead with a multitude of freckles sat behind a cluttered desk. "May I help you?"

"Yes," Jane said, forcing herself to smile pleasantly at this woman who hadn't even bothered to get up. "I wonder if I might speak to the principal."

"Mr. Kaplan?"

"He's the principal, is he not?"

"Yes," the secretary replied suspiciously. "Do you have an appointment?"

"No, but it's rather urgent and I promise not to take up much of his time. My name is Stuart, Jane Stuart."

"Do you have a child here at the school?"

"No . . ." Jane brightened. "But I will in three years!"

The woman regarded her as if she were insane. "Mrs.

Stuart," she repeated thoughtfully. "What shall I tell Mr. Kaplan this is about?"

This was becoming tiresome. "It's about two of the girls here at—"

"Mrs. Stuart?" came a man's pleasant voice from behind her.

She turned. In the doorway stood a short, chubby man who she guessed was in his late fifties, though it was difficult to tell because of his face, which wore a harried, hanging look. To Jane he resembled an old coonhound. He smiled a tired smile and put out his hand. "I'm Lew Kaplan. Did you say your name is Jane Stuart?"

"Yes," she said, smiling, as she shook his hand.

"I knew your husband. A wonderful man."

"Why, thank you. How did you know him?"

"He was a member of my men's club here in town for a brief time after you and he moved here. Let me say, belatedly, how sorry I am."

Jane vaguely remembered Kenneth joining a men's club, hating it by the second meeting, and dropping out. "Thank you. You're very kind."

"Come in, come in," he said, waving her into his office, which was small and cluttered with books and trophies. He sat behind his desk and motioned for Jane to sit in his visitor's chair. "Now, what can I do for you today?"

She was glad he'd closed the door. "Mr. Kaplan," she began.

"Lew."

"Lew. Thank you. Lew, I wanted to ask you about two girls who attend the high school."

His smile faded a degree or two. "Yes?"

"One of them is poor Ashley Surow, who I'm sure you know about."

He looked down sadly. "Yes. I was just speaking to her parents again. They're taking it very hard. How they'll ever get beyond something like this . . ." He shook his head and his coonhound jowls wobbled. "What exactly did you want to ask me about her?"

She had to proceed carefully. "I don't know how much you know about what happened. I myself don't know much," she lied, "but I do know that she left town before she returned and was—killed."

He winced at the word. "Yes. I did know that." He waited for her to continue.

"There's another girl who has vanished, but this one hasn't come back—at least not that we know about. Keiko Morikawa is her name. I'm sure you know her, too."

He sat up in his chair, working to keep his smile. "Of course I know her. I know all the young men and women in my school. I am aware that she hasn't been at school for a couple of days, but I would hardly say that means she's"—he made quotation marks in the air—"vanished."

"She called her parents three nights ago and told them she was with her boyfriend. The Morikawas don't know where he lives. I'm trying to find him to see if she's really with him."

Lew Kaplan shook his head and blinked a few times. "Wait a minute, you've lost me here. Do you *know* Keiko?"

"No, but I—"

"For that matter, do you know Ashley?"

"Not exactly, but my housekeeper's—"

"Then what business is this of yours?"

Now she sat up straight, making no effort to keep her smile. "If you would let me finish speaking."

"Of course," he said with exaggerated courtliness.

"Thank you. Ashley Surow worked at the public library with my housekeeper's sister, Crystal Ryerson, who you probably know was killed on Tuesday."

"Yes." He shifted uneasily in his chair. "I did hear about that."

"From what I've heard, Ashley told Crystal something before they died."

"And?"

"Something about what happened to Ashley while she was gone. She got herself into an extremely dangerous situation, and it was most likely because of that that she was killed."

"I see."

"And now this Keiko Morikawa disappears, and I find it difficult to believe it's a coincidence. I want to find her, because if I do, I may be able to find out what happened to Ashley, and in turn what happened to Crystal." She leaned forward and, as if speaking to a child, said, "Now do you follow?"

"Yes," he said tightly, "of course I follow, Mrs. Stuart."

"Please, call me Jane."

"Mrs. Stuart. What I want to know, however, is what business any of this is of yours."

"I've just explained that to you."

"Yes, you think you have. What I'm suggesting is that all of this is best left to the police."

"Don't you want Keiko found, Mr. Kaplan?"

"Of course I want Keiko found—if she needs to be found, that is. For all we know, she's with that boyfriend, shacked up in a motel somewhere. Kids do still play hooky, you know."

"Wouldn't it be a simple matter to find the boyfriend and see? I mean, he's a student here at your school."

"No, he's not," Kaplan said, annoyed. "He's a Boonton boy. I've laid eyes on this character, and believe me, he *definitely* does not live in Shady Hills."

Boonton. "Why?" she couldn't help asking. "Doesn't he drive his own Lexus or BMW?"

Kaplan rose. "We're done here, Mrs. Stuart."

Jane rose, too. "Yes, we are done here, Mr. Kaplan. Thank you for your time."

"I won't say it's my pleasure. If I remember correctly, you have a little boy."

"Not so little anymore. He's eleven. As I was telling your charming secretary, in three years he'll be attending this school."

"I look forward to that."

"Oh," she said with an easy laugh, showing herself out, "you won't be here. Not if I have anything to say about it."

His mouth dropped open, jowls wobbling.

Jane turned and walked out, not meeting the gaze of the freckled secretary, who watched with beady eyes from behind her desk.

"That hateful...coondog!" Jane said, banging the steering wheel of her Jaguar. Why had he so resented her interest in those girls? Pompous, self-important bureaucrat.

Shaking her head, she pulled out of the school parking lot. She'd gotten one thing she'd been after: where Sean Hart lived. Pulling onto Highland Road, she headed north toward Route 202, which would take her eventually to Boonton. Presently she passed the club called Roadside on her left. Once, years ago, it had been the Roadside Tavern, little more than a shack with a jukebox. Now it had been remodeled into something sleek and modern, shaped like a long, low, wedge, painted black, with swirls of neon on its side. She imagined its now-empty parking lot at night, packed with expensive cars, expensively dressed young men and women going from these cars to the club and back again, laughing, smoking, making out...

It occurred to her that if Roadside were open now, she

could stop in and probably learn quite quickly where she could find Sean Hart. Instead, when she reached the top of Highland Road, she made a left onto Route 202 and followed it into Boonton, a quaint working-class town with a narrow main street that ran up a steep hill between old tea rooms and antique shops.

There was a surprising amount of traffic on Main Street, people heading to nearby Route 287 to get to work. Jane supposed the most sensible way to go about finding Sean Hart was to approach the principal of Boonton High School—though after her encounter with Lew Kaplan, she was reluctant to try this approach.

Try the easiest way first, she told herself, and pulling into the parking lot of a convenience store, she took out her cell phone and tried Directory Assistance. There were three Harts in Boonton. Jane wrote down all three numbers, then dialed the first one, a Benjamin Hart. An elderly man answered and told Jane there was no one named Sean at that number.

Next she dialed M. Hart. A young man with a deep voice devoid of inflection answered.

"Yes, good morning. I'm looking for Sean Hart, please."

"Speaking."

"Oh, good. Mr. Hart, my name is Jane Stuart. I'm here in Boonton and wonder if I could speak to you for a few moments. It's about Keiko Morikawa."

"Kiki?" he said, his voice rising slightly. "What about her?"

"I'd rather speak to you in person."

"Is she all right?"

"I don't know." Jane rolled her eyes. "That's why I want to see you."

"All right, fine. I'm at 28 Pine Place. Where are you?"

She told him and he gave her directions to his house, only a few blocks away.

Three minutes later, as she pulled into the driveway of a modest white two-story home, one of a tight row of nearly identical houses, the front door opened and a tall young man emerged and came down a short concrete stairway.

"Thanks for seeing me," she said, approaching him.

He was, on close inspection, exceptionally good-looking, with fashionably short dirty blond hair, large pale blue eyes with long dark lashes, and smooth clear skin. Beneath his navy blue sweatshirt and jeans he had an impressive build. "No problem. Come on in."

"I hope I'm not keeping you from your work," she said, following him into the house.

"Nah, not working right now. Looking."

They sat in a tiny front room on either end of a dilapidated sofa covered with white cat hair. A massive white cat wandered into the room from a hallway at the back. Jane smiled. "I have two cats myself."

He ignored this remark. "So what's going on? What did you want to talk about? Is Kiki all right?"

"I'm afraid I don't know. I was hoping you could tell me. You see, she vanished from Shady Hills three nights ago. She hasn't been to school, no one's heard from her. Do you have any idea where she might have gone?"

"Why are you looking for her?"

"I'm . . . with the police." *Forgive me,* she thought.

He looked at her, alarm in his eyes. Then he cast his gaze downward, looking at the cat but not seeing it. Finally he shook his head. "Kiki and I broke up. Did you know that?"

"No, I didn't. When was this, if you don't mind my asking?"

"Let's see . . . five days ago. I haven't heard from her since."

Jane paused. "Had she said anything that might tell us where she's gone?"

He pursed his lips. "Nah, can't think of anything. But with Kiki you never know."

"What do you mean?"

He smiled faintly and looked at her. "Have you ever met her?"

"No, I haven't."

The smile broadened, revealing uneven white teeth. "She does what she wants. She's always hated school, hated living in Shady Hills, hated her parents . . . So maybe she just— took off!"

Jane blinked. "But with whom?"

"No idea. Not with me, unfortunately." Now he leaned down and thoughtfully stroked the fat white cat.

"Do you mind my asking how long you and she were going out?" Was that the current expression? She wasn't sure.

"About six months."

"Please don't be offended, but do you have any idea if she was seeing anyone else while she was seeing you?"

He shrugged, clearly not offended. "Could have been."

Life was so different now, Jane reflected. "Anyone whose name you might know?"

He frowned, remembering something. "When she said she wanted to break up with me, she did mention some guy, but she said he wasn't her boyfriend. I guess he could have been."

"Do you recall his name?"

His eyes wandered as he searched his memory. "It was a weird name." Suddenly he looked at her. "Like a magazine."

"Cosmo?"

"Yeah! That's it, Cosmo. Strange name, isn't it?"

Apprehension overtook Jane. Images from Cara Fairchild's tale flashed into her mind . . . and culminated with

Ashley lying strangled beside the railroad tracks. "What did Keiko say about him?"

He shook his head, as if unable to believe what he was remembering. "She said he was going to take her places."

"Take her places?"

"Yeah, like do things for her career."

Jane knitted her brows. "What career? She's in high school."

"Didn't you know? She's done a lot of modeling. Been doing it all her life. Commercials, too." He gave a derisive snort. "Only thing her parents ever encouraged her to do, because it made so much money."

Interesting. "What did Keiko think Cosmo could do for her career?"

"She said he was a movie director or something. He was going to put her in one of his movies. So," he said, slapping his hands on his knees, "that's where she is, then."

Jane rose, nodding but hoping he was wrong. "That's all she said about him? Did she say where he did his work? What kind of movies he made? Anything?"

He shot her a skeptical look. "Lady, when she told me, *we were breaking up*. The only reason she told me about it was to put me down, show me how much better this guy was than me."

"But I don't understand. You said he wasn't her boyfriend."

He smiled. "If he isn't now, he will be. Have you ever seen Keiko?" When she shook her head, he said, "She's a knockout. Incredible-looking. And I know Keiko. She'll make this guy her boyfriend pretty fast. Especially if he can do something for her."

"Mom . . . Earth to Mom . . ."

Jane shook her head free of thoughts of a handsome

young man luring beautiful girls with promises of movie roles, of these women running from him . . . of these women lying dead where he had left them . . .

Across the dining room table, Nick was staring at her as he cut a sheet of red construction paper for a map of North America he was making for his social studies class. Then Jane became aware that Winky and Twinky were perched on the table to each side of her, and they, too, were glaring at her. In the kitchen doorway stood Florence, one arm curved around a large mixing bowl. She smiled.

"Yes, missus, are you all right?"

Jane laughed, reaching out to stroke the pretty orange-and-brown mottled fur of the cats. "Yes, I'm fine. Thinking, that's all."

"What are you thinking about?" Nick asked, gluing down Canada.

"Um . . . things at work," she replied vaguely.

But Florence gave her a shrewd look from the doorway.

"What about you?" Jane said to Nick, changing the subject. "What's going on with you these days? How's school?"

"Good. Mr. Stanton left."

Both women looked at him.

"What?" Jane said.

Nick gave a simple nod, eyes fixed on his project. "Yup. He's gone."

"Do you know why?" Jane asked matter-of-factly.

Nick looked at her as if she were stupid. "I guess he must have quit!"

But as Jane met Florence's uneasy gaze, she remembered the terrible scene he'd made in the library only minutes before Crystal died. She'd have to find out about his departure from the middle school.

That night, from her study, she called the Morikawas, who, to her surprise, agreed to meet with her the following day.

Chapter 13

After Crystal's funeral service, Jane, Stanley, and Nick waited on the front steps of St. John's Episcopal Church for Florence to come out. An impressive number of her and Jane's friends had turned out on this cold, dreary Thursday, and Florence had stopped in the vestibule to thank as many of them as she could.

Jane turned to see Audrey, Elliott, and Cara Fairchild come out. Elliott, tall and slim, looked handsome in a navy suit. Audrey was dressed predictably in a dramatic black dress and a ridiculous-looking wide-brimmed black fedora, her face its usual rainbow of makeup. On her high heels she walked in mincing steps up to Jane and embraced her briefly. "I'm so sorry, doll. Poor Florence."

Jane nodded and thanked her, then watched the three Fairchilds descend the stairs. In her own way, Audrey was a good egg.

Halfway down the path leading to the road, Ginny stood with Daniel. As if sensing Jane's gaze upon them, they turned and looked up at her, concern in their eyes. She gave them a reassuring smile and nodded. They nodded back and continued along the path toward Renton Avenue.

"I'm here now," came Florence's voice behind Jane and Stanley, and they turned. Florence, in her charcoal gray wool dress coat, smiled at them and then down at Nick, and the four of them started down the stairs.

They worked their way through the crowd to Jane's car, which she had parked a short distance down the street from the church. Presently, as rain began to fall, they pulled out onto the street behind the hearse, following Renton Avenue to Packer Road, making a left onto Highland, then another left onto Cranmore Avenue.

On the right they passed the Shady Hills Senior Center, then came to the black wrought iron fence of Shady Hills Cemetery, and a double sadness washed over Jane, for this was where her Kenneth was buried. In the front passenger seat, Nick, who must have been thinking the same thing, looked quickly at Jane and then sharply away. She gave his arm a gentle squeeze, then put the car in park and switched off the ignition. It was very quiet now, the only sound the tapping of the rain on the windshield.

"Well," Florence said bleakly, and opened her door. She, Jane, Stanley, and Nick, under black umbrellas, joined the other mourners, passing through the cemetery gates and up a paved path, shiny in the rain, that curved gently between expanses of grass dotted with neat rows of gravestones. Soon everyone stood around the grave—a large crowd, Jane thought, and was heartened by this.

Twenty minutes later, after the Reverend Lockridge had finished, they all started back down the path under a sea of umbrellas.

Jane noticed that Nick was watching Florence. Jane turned to her. Florence had cried throughout the service and was crying again, dabbing at her eyes with a white handkerchief. Jane put her arm around her.

Florence gave her a grateful smile. "I still can't believe it. It feels as if it was only yesterday that we were children on the beach . . . my sister chasing me, laughing . . ." She trailed off, her gaze fixed on something ahead on the path. "Missus," she said softly.

Jane looked. Myrtle Lovesey stood on the path, facing them. The others had reached the bottom of the path and were filing through the gate, heading toward their cars. Jane stopped, and Nick, Stanley, and Florence stopped with her. Tall, thin Myrtle wore a black raincoat that hung loosely on her bony shoulders. Over her white hair was an old-fashioned clear plastic rain hat, even though she carried an umbrella. Under her other arm she clutched her large handbag.

Myrtle's piercing blue eyes were wide as she approached. Why was she here? Surely to berate Jane and Florence. Jane couldn't let that happen, not here.

"Myrtle—" she began.

"I'm terribly sorry about your sister," Myrtle said to Florence.

"Thank you," Florence said, clearly surprised.

Myrtle looked from Florence to Jane, ignoring Stanley. "I'm not a monster, you know," she said quietly. "I don't like what Mrs. Ryerson did, but I suppose she meant well, in her way."

Jane studied her closely, eyes narrowed. "Has anything happened?"

Myrtle gave a small shrug. "The social worker from Youth and Family Services is coming out today. Vivian and I hope it won't go any further than that, now that . . . well, under the circumstances." She turned to Florence. "You'll need to take your sister's things out of the apartment, do you realize that?"

"Yes, of course," Florence replied, taken aback.

"I'll be renting it out again. The landlord's told me to get right on it."

"Yes," Florence repeated. "I intend to do it this Saturday."

"Good. Well . . ." Myrtle turned to go.

"Oh, Myrtle—" Jane said, and the older woman turned. "There's something I need to speak with you about."

"Yes?"

"Not here. I'll call you. We can get together when it's convenient for you."

Myrtle paused, clearly irritated that Jane wouldn't tell her what she wanted to talk about. "All right," she said warily, and nodded once. "Any time." She turned again and started down the path.

As Jane turned from Grange Road onto Lilac Way, the rain increased dramatically, beating so hard against the windshield she could barely see the road.

"Missus," Florence said in alarm.

"I know, isn't this rain awful?"

"No, it's not that."

Jane turned to her. Florence's face was frozen in concentration, her brows lowered over glaring eyes. "I just remembered something."

From the backseat Nick said, "What is it, Florence?"

"It was last Friday, when Crystal and I went out to dinner. Something was definitely bothering my sister. All the time we were in the restaurant she was troubled—you know, lost in her thoughts."

"Yes?" Jane said.

"I asked her what was wrong. She said Ashley hadn't come to work at the library that day. Crystal had called Ashley's house, but Ashley's mother said Ashley hadn't come home the night before. She called her"—Florence lowered her voice to a whisper—"a little tramp."

"A what?" Nick said.

"Never mind," Jane said, frowning as she crept up the narrow road against the onslaught of rain.

"Then Crystal became very strange," Florence continued. "She started to ramble—you know, saying odd things."

"Like what?" Jane asked.

"She said . . ." Florence chewed her lip, remembering. "She said, 'You can't really hide who you are, not really.' "

"What's that supposed to mean?" Nick asked.

"Nick, shush," Jane told him.

Florence said, "I thought she was depressed about Dennis, her husband. Then she said, 'There's someone I need to see.' I thought she meant a divorce lawyer. She'd mentioned this to me before. She said she wasn't looking forward to it, which made me sure that was what she was talking about."

Jane turned into the driveway, waited for the garage door to open, and pulled in. She turned to Florence. "But now you don't think that's what she meant?"

"No, I don't. Now I think those things she was saying had something to do with her m— death." Florence began to cry again. She poked her handkerchief at each eye. "Why didn't I press her to tell me more?" she wailed through her tears. "If I had, then—"

"Don't," Jane said kindly, touching Florence's shoulder. "There's no way you could have known. Besides, you can't know for certain that's what she was talking about. Maybe she *was* talking about Dennis."

"No, I'm sure of it now. I know my sister, missus. Knew her," she corrected herself. And with the handkerchief pressed to her nose, she got out of the car.

The Morikawas lived in one of the larger houses in Maple Estates, a true château of cream-colored stone, with an immense turret at each end. A wide circular driveway curved around flat stones and low shrubs artfully arranged to look natural. The house was at the end of Montgomery Place, which was a cul-de-sac.

A housekeeper in a pale blue uniform answered the door. "Yes, they're expecting you," she said when Jane had introduced herself, and led her across a marble-floored foyer larger than Jane's kitchen into the living room, on the right. It was a cavernous room, two stories high. Its entire back wall consisted of the same pale stone that was on the outside of the house. In this wall was the largest fireplace Jane had ever seen, with a deep raised hearth. Above the fireplace hung an abstract painting, a vast canvas covered with lemon yellow paint across which the artist had made several swipes of royal blue that vaguely resembled a tropical bird in flight.

"Mrs. Stuart?" came a man's voice.

Jane turned. She hadn't seen anyone in the room. To her right stood Mr. and Mrs. Morikawa. They were both small in stature—he no more than five and a half feet tall, she several inches shorter than her husband. Mr. Morikawa was a trim, athletic-looking man in his early forties, with handsome Japanese features and neatly combed black hair. He wore expensive-looking black slacks and an olive silk shirt. He smiled a wide, congenial smile and came forward, putting out his hand. "How do you do. Frank Morikawa. This is my wife, Candy."

Candy Morikawa looked younger than her husband, perhaps in her late thirties. Her features were perfect and doll-like, her eyes so dark they looked black, fringed with thick lashes. Her silky hair, a rich brown, hung straight and full to her shoulders, contrasting with the tomato red of her blouse, which she wore tucked into the tiny waist of her charcoal gray slacks. She shook Jane's hand. "A pleasure to meet you," she said, though she barely smiled. There was the faintest hint of an accent in her soft voice. "Please, let's sit down."

Candy and Frank Morikawa sat on a long sofa of creamy

white leather. Jane sat facing them in an ebony leather armchair. "I appreciate your seeing me."

They both gave small gracious smiles. "Our pleasure," Mr. Morikawa said. "You live here in Shady Hills?"

"Yes, on Lilac Way, just around the corner."

"Yes," Mrs. Morikawa said sharply, "I know that street. Are you in the big house at the top of the hill?"

What an odd question, Jane thought, then remembered that these people were in real estate. She laughed. "No, those are my neighbors, the Fairchilds."

Mrs. Morikawa looked disappointed. "Oh." She put her smile back on. "Can we offer you something to drink? Coffee? Tea?"

"No, thank you."

Mrs. Morikawa nodded. "What was it you wanted to see us about, Mrs. Stuart? You said it has something to do with our daughter?"

"Yes." How should she begin? "I . . . This has to do with something that happened here in town earlier this week."

Mr. Morikawa frowned mildly. "Yes?"

She nodded. "I'm sure you've heard about Ashley Surow, the girl who was found murdered."

"Yes." There was impatience in Mrs. Morikawa's voice. "But what has that got to do with us?"

"Ashley had run off with a man named Cosmo Blair who lured her with promises of putting her in a movie. He tried to rape her. He beat her. She got away from him, but it appears he caught up with her."

"Yes?" Mr. Morikawa said, looking uncomfortable.

"Your daughter, Keiko," Jane said, amazed that she had to spell this all out for these people, "has disappeared also, am I correct?"

Mrs. Morikawa drew back her chin and smiled derisively. "Disappeared? No." The silky hair moved with the shaking of her head.

Mr. Morikawa said, "You have to understand our daughter. She is—difficult. Rebellious. She has done this before—skipped school, not come home. But let me ask you, Mrs. Stuart. With all due respect, what has this got to do with you?" He smiled as if to prevent his words from sounding rude.

"Have you heard about Crystal Ryerson, who worked at the public library?"

They both thought for a moment, making small frowns of concentration. "Yes!" Mr. Morikawa said, holding up his index finger. "That poor woman who died when a bookcase fell on her."

"That's right. You see, she was my housekeeper's sister."

"Yes?" Mr. Morikawa said.

"Someone *made* that bookcase fall on Crystal. She was murdered."

They both stared at her.

"Ashley was found the next day. Ashley and Crystal worked together. Before she died, Ashley told Crystal what had happened to her when she ran off with Cosmo Blair. I have reason to believe Crystal was killed because of something she knew. I'm trying to find out who killed Crystal."

"Why?" Mrs. Morikawa asked mildly. "You are not the police."

Jane was grateful that Stanley wasn't here to second this woman's statement. "No, of course I'm not," she replied, smiling politely. "But I promised Florence—she's my housekeeper, and my friend—that I would try to help. I . . . I've done this before—solved murders."

Mr. Morikawa turned his head slightly and glared at her out of one eye. "So what are you saying, Mrs. Stuart? That our Keiko is with this Cosmo?" He laughed easily. "I am pleased to tell you that she is perfectly safe. She called us and said she was fine. She is with her boyfriend, Sean."

"No," Jane said gently, "I'm afraid she's not. In fact, he's not even her boyfriend anymore—they've broken up. He has no idea where she is."

The Morikawas' complacent smiles dissolved.

"What do you mean?" Mrs. Morikawa said.

"How do you know this?" Mr. Morikawa asked.

"I've spoken to him. Just yesterday. He told me that when Keiko broke up with him, she mentioned Cosmo Blair."

Mrs. Morikawa threw her husband a concerned look and wet her lips. "So you came here to warn us?"

"Yes, of course," Jane said. "I'm sure you would do the same thing if the situation were reversed." Though she wasn't so sure of that. "I believe that Ashley's disappearance and Keiko's disappearance are related, in which case your daughter is in serious danger."

"Oh, Frank," Mrs. Morikawa said, putting her hand on his arm.

"Yes," he said, and looked back at Jane, who rose. From somewhere far away came the sound of a telephone ringing.

"I'm sorry to upset you," Jane said.

"No, no," Mrs. Morikawa said, smiling graciously. "You're doing us a favor."

The housekeeper appeared in the foyer doorway. "Mrs. Morikawa, you have a telephone call."

Mrs. Morikawa looked up sharply. "Who is it?"

"A Mrs. Steinberg."

Mrs. Morikawa turned to her husband. "The Victorian six-bedroom at sixty-three Fenwyck Road."

He gave one nod.

"Tell her I'll be right there." Mrs. Morikawa turned to Jane. "Thank you again; you are very kind. My husband will see you out." She hurried off with the housekeeper. Mr. Morikawa walked with Jane to the front door.

"Here," he said, taking a business card from his shirt pocket and handing it to Jane. "If you ever decide to sell your house, call us. We will get you the best price." He opened the door. "Good-bye."

Jane hadn't been to the office all day, what with Crystal's funeral and her visit to the Morikawas. It was past two thirty when she entered to find Goddess, once again in sensible secretary attire, on Daniel's desk, standing on tiptoes while she hung from the ceiling a large pumpkin made of plump stuffed felt.

"Come on," she squealed, "hold me or I'll fall!"

With a laugh, Daniel wrapped his arms around her legs.

"Mm, I like that," Goddess purred, looking down.

He looked up, saw Jane, and removed his arms from around Goddess's legs.

"Hey!" she cried.

"Hello," Jane said pleasantly, looking at Daniel and raising her eyebrows. He looked down, embarrassed. "How is everything going?"

"Fine," Goddess said. "We're doing some Halloween decorating."

Jane frowned. "But Daniel already decorated."

"You call *that* decorating? We're gonna do this holiday up big."

"I see," Jane said. "Are you almost done?"

"Yes," Daniel answered before Goddess could.

Goddess finished hanging the pumpkin and carefully stepped down, taking Daniel's hand as she did. She looked at Jane gravely. "How was the funeral?"

"Like a funeral." Jane shrugged. What kind of question was that?

Goddess had wanted to attend, but Jane had asked her not to. The last thing she needed was a media frenzy at Shady Hills Cemetery.

"Any calls?" she asked, hanging up her coat.

"A few," Daniel said, handing her some pink message slips. Jane flipped through them. One was from Harriet Green at Bantam Dell. Good, Jane thought, she must be calling to talk about Salomé.

Daniel had gone behind his desk and was peering out his window at Center Street.

"Waiting for somebody?" Jane asked him.

"No . . . Did you see anybody outside?"

"What do you mean? Where?"

"Earlier this afternoon there were people on the green. People with cameras."

Understanding dawned. Jane took a deep breath. "Great. So it's leaked out. You see," she said to Goddess, "you can't keep these things a secret. So what happened?"

"Not much," Daniel replied. "We stayed inside. I went out at noon to get sandwiches—"

"And we locked the door," Goddess supplied.

"Good," Jane said. "And they went away?"

"Eventually. I'm surprised they did."

Goddess gave them a queasy smile. "They'll be back. Jane," she said solemnly, "do you want me to leave? The last thing I wanted to do was make trouble for you."

"No, no," Jane said, suddenly feeling very tired. "Just keep a low profile. Maybe they'll give up."

Goddess didn't reply to this, but her expression as she sat down behind her desk and turned the page of a manuscript she'd been reading was skeptical, as if to say, "Suit yourself."

Jane met Daniel's gaze, shook her head wearily, and went into her office, where she called Harriet Green.

"Jane, I was calling you about Salomé Sutton."

"Yes, isn't she fabulous? I think Bantam Dell could do a smashing job for her."

"I'm afraid it's not going to work for us, Jane."

Jane's shoulders slumped. "That's too bad," she said, forcing herself to remain cheerful. "You've got enough romance writers, is that it?"

"Oh, no! We're always looking. It's that—well, her work is really *dated,* Jane. She's still writing the same stuff she was writing back in the seventies."

"Well, I can't say I agree, but—"

"Not only that, but this woman has a reputation of being a *brute* to work with, and that we don't need. Don't you find her difficult?"

Jane nearly choked on that one. "No," she said breezily, "not at all. At any rate, thanks for considering the material, Harriet."

"My pleasure, Jane. We must do lunch again soon."

"Absolutely."

Dejectedly, she hung up the phone and consulted her submission records. Another one down, and not many publishers left. Shaking her head, she drew a line through Harriet's name.

Chapter 14

Jane met Stanley for a late lunch at Whipped Cream. Sitting at her table near the fireplace, she bit into her sandwich.

"How was your visit to the Morikawas?" Stanley asked.

She looked at him sharply. "How did you know I went to see them?"

He rolled his eyes. "You must think we're pretty stupid. They called us right after you left their house."

"Why? To complain about me?"

"No. Actually, they were grateful that you had gone to see them. Once they knew Keiko wasn't with her boyfriend, they wanted to report her missing. Dan Raymond and I went out there. That's some house."

"Amazing, isn't it?"

"Where does so much money come from?"

"Real estate. I think they're more interested in selling houses than in their own daughter. Would you believe he hustled me for business as I was leaving?"

"I believe it. Couple of cold characters, if you ask me."

"What do you mean?"

"Once they realized Keiko wasn't with Sean Hart, that

she may have gone off with Cosmo Blair, they asked us to keep it quiet if we found out she had. Apparently, avoiding embarrassment was more important than finding their daughter."

"See! That's what I've been telling you. The kids in this town have no parents."

"Now, Jane, I don't think I would go that far."

"It's *as if* they don't. Who's watching them?"

Ginny, who had been hovering nearby, came up to their table with the coffeepot and refilled their mugs. "I agree with Jane. It's shameful how these spoiled rich kids run wild. I'll tell you one thing," she said, wiping up some spilled coffee from the table. "If Daniel and I have children, there will be rules." She hurried off to a nearby table, where a man and a woman had just sat down.

Stanley turned back to Jane, placing his hand on hers. "So," he said brightly, "how are things at the office?"

She eyed him suspiciously. "Fine. Why?"

"I understand you've got someone new working there."

She watched him closely. "Yes," she said easily, "a very nice young woman."

"What's her name?"

"Uh . . . Kathy."

"Kathy what?"

She gave him an impatient look. "What is this, the Spanish Inquisition?"

"No, just curious. You know I'm interested in everything you do."

"Kathy . . . Henderson. All right?"

"Touchy, touchy. And how is she working out?"

"Fine."

"She must be working out *really* fine for reporters to want to wait outside your office with cameras, hoping to get a shot of her."

"Who told you?"

He turned on her triumphantly, his mouth open wide. "Then it's true!"

"Yes, it's true," she whispered. "Who told you?"

"I bumped into Jonah Kramer at Home Depot."

"I should have known. Busybody."

He leaned close to her, disbelief in his eyes. "Jane, have you lost what's left of your mind? Goddess—"

"Sh-h-h!"

He lowered his voice. "Goddess is probably the biggest star in the world. If it gets out that she's in your office, you're going to have a riot on your hands."

"But it's not going to get out, is it, Stanley." It was a statement, not a question.

"Not through me! But Jonah seemed pretty eager to talk about it. This is idiotic, Jane. *Why?*"

"Not that it's any of your business," she said coolly, and gave her head a defiant toss. "She's going to be playing a secretary in her next movie and needed to do some field research. She asked me if she could work in my office, and I said yes."

"Unbelievable."

"And, as I said, none of your business."

He moved toward her angrily. "I'm a cop in this town, Jane. It's my business if your little game creates havoc here."

She didn't like the way this conversation was going. She certainly had no intention of sitting there defending herself to Stanley. She rose, pulling on her coat and gathering up her handbag.

He watched her in amazement. "You're leaving? You're mad at me?"

"Well," she said with false cheerfulness, a hot fury rising in her, "I wouldn't want to create any havoc for you. Or subject you to any more of my idiocy."

"What? Jane, I'm sorry."

She turned and looked down on him with a cold little smile. "I don't care if you are a cop, Stanley Greenberg. I don't care if you're the president of the United States."

"Where are you going?" he called after her.

"None of your business," she called back, loudly enough that Ginny and the two women at the nearby table looked up sharply. "You do your job, and I'll do mine."

She walked out of the café and headed across the green. Her words ringing in her ears, she couldn't help laughing at her hypocrisy even through her anger, as she remembered she intended to speak to Myrtle Lovesey today as part of her investigation of Crystal's murder.

She didn't care a fig whether Stanley liked it or not. She'd made Florence a promise.

The rain had stopped and a watery sun had come out. To get to Myrtle's office, Jane cut diagonally across the green instead of walking straight across as she would to reach her own office. She happened to glance at the door of her agency and did a double take. A chubby bald man was banging on the door and hollering something. Close behind him stood three other people, two men and a woman, watching the first man.

She called the office on her cell phone. Goddess answered. "Jane Stuart Literary Agency."

Jane smiled. "Hello, Goddess. That was very nice."

"What was?"

"The way you answered the phone."

"Hey, thanks, Jane. What's up?"

"Who is that man banging on the door?"

"Some reporter," she replied nonchalantly. "Daniel locked the door."

"Did you lock the back door, too?"

"Of course. But sooner or later I'm gonna have to go out there, you know."

Jane gripped the phone tighter in alarm. "Oh, no you're not. I can't have a mob scene." Stanley's words came back to her.

"Okay, but it's only gonna get worse. Jane, you want me to leave?"

"No, of course not. You haven't done anything wrong. Besides, if we ignore these reporters long enough, maybe they'll go away."

Goddess let out a loud laugh. "Are you kidding? That only makes them hungrier."

Jane considered this. "They have no way of knowing it's really you."

"Jane. Sweetie. They know. Trust me. It was all I could do to get into the office this morning."

"Well, if you would arrive with a little less fanfare, maybe you wouldn't draw so much attention to yourself."

"What fanfare?"

"The silver stretch limousine."

"How else am I supposed to get here, by donkey?"

"You could use a plain car—oh, never mind. Anyway, stay put and don't open the door. I'll see you later."

"Roger." And Goddess hung up.

Shaking her head, Jane crossed the street and entered The Home Place. Myrtle was just hanging up the phone. She looked up, her expression blank.

"Hello, Myrtle."

"Jane." Myrtle looked Jane up and down uneasily. "What can I do for you?"

"May I sit down?" Jane asked, her hand on a chair.

Myrtle shrugged. "Suit yourself. What is it you want?"

"I want to talk to you about the morning Crystal died."

Myrtle scowled. "Why?"

"You went into the library's back room for about fifteen minutes not long before Crystal died. What were you doing back there?"

Myrtle leaned back in her chair. "You've got one huge heck of a nerve! Who do you think you are, asking me that? The police have already asked me anyway. Why do *you* want to know?"

"Sometimes the police miss things, Myrtle. Crystal was Florence's sister, and Florence is my dear friend."

"She's your housekeeper!"

"And my friend. So I'm conducting my own investigation, if you want to put it that way. And anything you've already told the police, you can tell me, right?"

Myrtle gave her an unpleasant smirk, followed by an equally unpleasant wink. "Why don't you get it from your friend Detective Greenberg? You know, pillow talk."

Jane gave her a tight smile. "As it happens, I do have some influence with him. Don't you want to tell me what happened so that I can put in a good word for you?"

Myrtle grabbed a ballpoint pen from her desk and began clicking it in and out. "What are you saying—that they think I killed Crystal? In case you didn't notice, *a bookcase fell on her.* Nobody killed her."

"You're going to hear this sooner or later, so I might as well tell you. The bookcase fell on her because someone removed the bolts securing it to the wall."

Myrtle's mouth fell open. "And you're saying I did that?"

"No, I didn't say that at all. But the fact remains that you had an opportunity to remove those bolts while you were in the back room. Just tell me what happened back there."

"Fine, you win. If you really want to know, I was so upset that I ran into the ladies' room to pull myself together. I was embarrassed, too." Myrtle shook her head ruefully. "I don't know what possessed me to make a scene like that."

"Of course you know what possessed you. You were furious at Crystal for reporting Vivian to DYFS. Your granddaughter could have been taken away, put in a foster home." Jane paused. "Do you still think that could happen?"

Click-click, click-click. "I don't know. That was Vivian on the phone just now. The woman from DYFS had just left. Like I told you this morning, with Crystal gone, who knows what will happen?"

"So Crystal's death may help you."

Myrtle looked at Jane incredulously. "You really think I killed her, don't you? Lady, I'm no killer. I'll be the first to admit I hated that fat busybody, but climb up that ladder and unscrew a couple of bolts so that she would get crushed under a bookcase . . . That's not my style."

"Who said you climbed the ladder to do it? Who said there were two bolts?"

"Very clever. *Of course* someone would have to climb the ladder to get to the bolts. And I just guessed there were two."

"If you had climbed the ladder and unscrewed the bolts while you were on it, wouldn't the bookcase have come down?"

Myrtle squinted her eyes. "What is this? Why are you asking me that? This is your theory, not mine. How would I know? Maybe Crystal brought it down because she was so heavy."

"Maybe. Myrtle, why did you attend Crystal's funeral?"

"Why? Why not?"

"You hated her."

Myrtle smiled sadistically. "Yes, I hated her. Guess I wanted to enjoy watching them put her in the ground."

Jane rose. "That's sick."

Myrtle jumped up. "Is it?" she screamed, making Jane jump and draw back. "Honey, you tell me how you're gonna feel when somebody tries to take your grandkid away from you."

Jane looked down, at a loss for words.

"Yeah, see what I mean? So don't you go tellin' me what's sick! Now get outta here. You're as nosy as Crystal was, playing cop like you—you—run this town. Get out!"

Jane walked to the door.

"And tell Florence if Crystal's junk isn't out of the apartment by the end of the day tomorrow, I'm throwing it out!"

"The reporters are gone," Jane said brightly when she got to the office.

"No, they're not. They relocated," Daniel replied, and pointed toward the small corridor leading to the parking lot behind the building.

"Oh, I see."

Goddess was filing. She looked up. "Jane, you *sure* you don't want me to leave?"

Daniel looked up, waiting for Jane's answer.

"I told you, no," Jane said, and out of the corner of her eye she saw Daniel's shoulders slump.

"Okeydokey." Goddess closed the file drawer and sat down behind her desk.

Jane began removing her coat, when the phone rang. Daniel grabbed it, spoke a few words, and put the call on hold. "It's a Dick Stanton for you."

"Oh, good. I'll take it in my office." She hurried to her desk and picked up the phone.

"I got your message, Mrs. Stuart," Dick Stanton said. "I'd be happy to see you."

"I appreciate that. What time would be convenient for you?"

"Now is fine, but would you mind coming to my house? I've got my baby daughter here."

"Not a problem. Just tell me where you live."

He gave her directions and they agreed she would go right over.

"See you later," she told Daniel and Goddess, and started down the back corridor toward the parking lot.

"Jane, they're out there!" Daniel called after her.

She turned and gave him a dismissive scowl. "So's my car!"

Daniel hurried after her. "I'll lock it behind you."

Through the window in the office's back door, Jane could see that there were more reporters in the parking lot than she had expected—easily a dozen. They stood just outside the door, talking among themselves, looking quite jovial. At the back of the parking lot sat three TV news vans.

Holding her breath, Jane opened the door and rushed through. Behind her, Daniel immediately locked it.

"Mrs. Stuart! Mrs. Stuart!" They all charged forward. Suddenly there were several shoulder-mounted cameras in her face.

"Mrs. Stuart, why do you have Goddess in your office?"

"Jane, what is this, some kind of publicity stunt?"

"Are you representing talent as well as writers now, Jane?"

She cast her gaze about, took them all in. "No comment." She loved saying that. She pushed through them. They followed her to her car.

"Nice Jag, Jane! Is it a gift from Goddess?"

"Hey, Jane, who you gonna hire next, Madonna?"

She couldn't help laughing at that one. They ran after her even as she drove slowly out of the parking lot, through the alley beside her building, and out onto Center Street. There she put on some gas and finally left them behind.

Should she tell Goddess to call it a day? Was Stanley right? Was all this publicity a bad thing, or perhaps good for her and the agency? She would certainly become more visible. Maybe Salomé would like that.

But she couldn't think about any of that now. Following the directions Dick Stanton had given her, she drove to the north end of town and found Poplar Place, a narrow dead-end street with four tiny houses on each side. Stanton's house was the last one on the left, one story and covered with old aluminum siding that may once have been white but was now a grimy gray. A battered black Volvo station wagon sat on the gravel driveway.

Jane got out and made her way up a flagstone path overgrown with weeds and tufts of grass. There was no doorbell, only a rusted door knocker, so she tapped it a few times, then waited. Only about a foot to her right was a window, and through it she could see the top of a large-screen TV and behind it a wall hung with family photographs.

Stanton was smiling as he opened the door to her. He wore khakis and a brown V-necked sweater over a T-shirt, a look Jane found very sexy. His hair was tousled, as if he hadn't bothered combing it today, and he was unshaved.

"Come on in," he said, holding the door open. He smelled faintly of some citrusy cologne.

"I appreciate your seeing me."

"Not at all!" In the small living room, he grabbed a blue crocheted afghan from the end of a worn gold-and-white plaid sofa and tossed it on the floor. "Have a seat. Can I get you something to drink? Coffee?"

"No, thanks very much." She glanced around the room. She was facing the huge TV. The entire wall behind it was covered with a mosaic of photographs—men, women, and children of all ages in seemingly every possible combination. Against the wall to Jane's left, a stereo system shared a low table with messy stacks of CDs. To her right sat a chair that matched the sofa. Stanton fell into it, crossing his legs.

"You'll have to excuse me if my daughter wakes up."

"Of course," she said.

"Now, you said you knew Crystal Ryerson?"

"Yes," Jane said, "and I have to tell you I'm surprised that you're being so friendly to me, Mr. Stanton."

He frowned, puzzled. "Why wouldn't I be?"

"Well, in light of the fact that I told you I wanted to speak with you about Crystal . . ."

"You know her, right? You're a friend of hers?"

"Yes."

He shrugged. "I was hoping she wanted you to talk to me about what she did, that she'd decided to take back what she said about me."

Jane stared at him. "Then you don't know."

"Know what?" He smiled pleasantly.

"Crystal is dead."

He drew back a little. "Dead?"

Was he truly surprised, she wondered, or an excellent actor? Either way, she had to play along. "Yes. As a matter of fact, she died only minutes after you confronted her in the library."

He raised one brow. "You know about that?"

"Yes, I was there. My reading group was meeting at a table only a few feet away."

"I see. And you say she died right after that? How?"

"A bookcase fell on her."

He looked horrified, his jaw dropping. "Whoa. How'd that happen?"

"Someone unbolted it from the wall."

"You're kidding, right?"

"No, unfortunately I'm not."

He shook his head slowly. "Dead. Then you're not here to talk about her taking back what she said."

"I'm afraid it's too late for that."

"Then what did you want to talk to me about?"

The faint cry of a baby came from a back room. Stanton took a sharp breath, let it out, slapped his hands on his knees, and rose. "Just give me a minute."

He was gone several minutes, during which Jane pondered what he had said. If he was to be believed, he had thought Jane came on Crystal's behalf, to make things right.

He reappeared, smiling, and sat back down. "All changed and back to sleep—we hope."

"I remember those days," Jane said with a laugh.

"You have children?"

"Just one. A boy, eleven. In fact," she said, remembering, "you may know him." She wasn't about to mention the time Nick and Aaron had seen him hiding a computer in the back of his Volvo. "He goes to the middle school here in Shady Hills. Nicholas Stuart?"

"Yah, sure! Sweet kid. Spends a good bit of time in the school library. Stuart..." He looked thoughtful. "Hey, you're that literary agent!"

"That's right."

"Now I'm putting it all together," he said, nodding. "Anyway, where were we? You were telling me why you wanted to talk to me."

"Yes. I want to ask you about Crystal, what happened between the two of you."

"Why?" he asked, meeting her gaze.

"As I just explained, Crystal was murdered—"

"And you think I murdered her?" His voice rose with disbelief.

"No, of course not—though you did have an opportunity to remove the bolts from that bookcase."

"What are you talking about?"

"After you had your confrontation with Crystal, you went into the back room of the library."

He shrugged, shaking his head, as if to signify he barely remembered. "Does that matter?"

"Certainly. You weren't back there very long, but you were there just long enough to remove the bolts from the bookcase. Then you stomped out."

"Is that why you're here—to find out whether I yanked out my monkey wrench and did a little quick handiwork before I left? You've got to be kidding. Would I admit it if I had? Not only that, but how would I have known she would get onto that ladder?"

"What ladder?"

He closed his mouth, then said cautiously, "The library ladder."

"Who said Crystal was on the ladder? I simply said a bookcase fell on her."

"Okay, okay," he said, holding out his hands, "I confess. I knew about what happened. Heard it all. And I can't say I was sorry to hear it."

"Who told you?"

"Are you serious? It's all over town."

"Why did you pretend not to know?"

"I don't know . . . so you wouldn't think I'd done it. Which I didn't!"

"All right," she said, "let's say I believe you. You have to admit you had a strong motive to kill her."

He drew his brows together. "Wait a minute. Tell me again what business any of this is of yours? You're no cop."

"No, I'm not a cop. But Crystal's sister is a close friend

of mine, and I promised her I'd try to find out who did this horrible thing."

"Oh, right!" he said, nodding. "Now I remember all about you. You had that nanny who disappeared, and you found her. Then *People* magazine did that story about you. 'New Jersey's Miss Marple,' or something like that, because you solved the murder."

"That's right," she said modestly. "And I've solved several others as well."

"Right. So now you're playing Miss Marple again, trying to find out who crushed Crystal. Don't you have any faith in the police?"

She gave no answer, just waited.

For several moments he stared at the floor, as if deciding what more to say. Finally he looked up.

"All right, I admit I hated her. But wouldn't you hate her if she'd done that to you? Somehow she knew I'd taken a computer home, and she decided I was the one who'd been stealing computer equipment from the school. *And* she told this to my boss, Nina Bryant, who'd never liked me much to begin with, and was only too happy to have an excuse to get rid of me."

"Did she give that as the reason she was dismissing you?"

"No, of course not. But she told me she believed I was the thief. As for the official reason she was letting me go, she said my work was substandard, and that she and I had a personality clash. Legitimate reasons. The net effect is that I'm out of a job."

"Yes . . . but Nina Bryant could have fired you for only those reasons—without suspecting anything about the computers."

"Absolutely. Except that my work has been excellent—others will back me up on that—and for the most part,

though I don't like Nina, she and I got along just fine. You
see, the computers were her blackmail material. She told
me that if I challenged the dismissal, she would tell everyone I was the thief. She had me. Because as it happened, I
did have one of the library's computers here at home, to
repair it."

"Was it Crystal who'd told Nina you'd stolen the computers?"

"Yes, you know it was."

"How did you find out?"

"Nina wouldn't tell me at first. When she came into my
office to fire me Tuesday morning, she said 'someone' had
seen me putting a computer in my car and covering it with
a blanket. I told her I was taking it home to fix it—I *enjoy*
fixing computers—I've taken others home, *and* brought
them back—but she wouldn't listen to me. She said that if
I would resign immediately, she would make sure no one
found out what I'd done."

His nostrils flared as he recalled the scene. "I was enraged. I demanded that she tell me who had told her about
the computer in my car. At first she wouldn't tell me. Then
she blurted out that it was Crystal Ryerson.

"I said, '*Who?*' She told me Crystal worked at the public library."

"So you stormed over there to confront her."

"That's right. Wouldn't you have done the same thing if
someone had accused you of something you hadn't done—
and lost you your job?"

"Yes," she replied, "I would."

He looked at her beseechingly. "It's so unfair. I had re-
paired all that equipment for the school—for free, because
I'm good at it and I wanted to help—and now Nina was
using it against me!"

"Why didn't you tell anyone you were fixing equipment? Hadn't it occurred to you that someone might think you were stealing it? I'm sorry," she said, shaking her head, "but it doesn't make sense to me."

"I have no answer to that except that I was incredibly naive. It never occurred to me that anyone would think that. I never made a secret of taking the computers home. But I never broadcast it, either."

"Why did you cover the computer in your car with a blanket?"

He laughed. "To protect it, of course. I've always kept an old blanket in the back of my station wagon. Most people with station wagons do. Whenever I took home a monitor or a CPU, I'd wrap it in a blanket to keep it from getting damaged."

They sat in silence for several moments. Jane sighed. "Which brings us back to Crystal's murder."

"It does?"

She met his gaze. "You still haven't answered my question. What were you doing in the back room after you told Crystal off?"

He laughed in disbelief. "I did *nothing*! I was infuriated beyond words. You saw me. I just stormed off. I wasn't thinking about where I was going. I ended up in the back room and I stood there, trying to cool down, trying to think of something else to say to that monstrous woman. But then I realized it was no use. So I walked out."

At this moment Jane realized that—she wasn't quite sure why—she believed this man. "I'm sorry," she said.

Tears came to his eyes. "You have no idea what she did to me, losing me that job. It took me a year to find it. I wasn't making much money but I enjoyed it, in spite of working with Nina, who was tolerable if you kept your distance. Ellie—that's my wife—she and I have Katherine, and the mortgage on this house. Ellie's a teller at a bank in

Wayne. She doesn't make much money, but it was nice to have along with what I made. Now, with just her salary, I don't know what we're going to do."

"You can collect unemployment."

"Yeah, I can collect unemployment, but what I need is a new job. Trouble is, positions for librarians are few and far between. We may have to move." Suddenly he looked up and smiled archly. "Hey, I know. I'll apply for Crystal's job."

"Not funny."

His face fell. "I know. Sorry." He put his face in his hands and his next words were slightly muffled. "I don't know what we're going to do."

Jane rose. "Thank you for seeing me."

"Wait," he said. "I'd like to show you something."

He led her down the hallway off the living room, past the baby's room, to a room at the end. "Take a look," he said, pushing open the door.

She peered in. It was a long, narrow room, and against one of its walls ran a table constructed of two doors set on top of low file cabinets. Lined up on this table Jane counted seven computers, all on, screens full of moving color.

"This one on the end," he said, pointing. "That one's from the school. But that's the only one. The hard drive was shot, so I put in a new one. I was going to bring it back on Wednesday. I'll do it on Monday. The rest of the computers are mine, put together from used parts I pick up at computer shows, garage sales, that kind of thing. It's a hobby of mine. If I need a computer, I can put one together for practically nothing. I don't need to steal one." He turned and looked at her, his handsome brows drawn slightly together. She could see the individual hairs of his beard. "Do you understand?" he asked.

"Yes. I . . . I'm sorry about what happened."

She turned and walked back down the corridor. He held the front door open for her.

"Good luck," she said, and felt embarrassed as she got into her Jaguar, sleek and silver, beside his shabby Volvo.

Chapter 15

Bright sunlight poured through the living room of the apartment that had been Crystal's, illuminating a small stack of self-help books on the coffee table. Florence briefly examined each book in turn. As she set down the last of them, there were tears in her eyes.

"I know what she was like," she said to Jane, who sat across from her, sorting through the contents of a drawer from the kitchen. "She thought she knew everything. But at least she was always trying to—" Her voice broke and she lowered her head, wiping away her tears.

It was ten thirty Saturday morning and they had been working for about an hour and a half. Disposing of Crystal's belongings wouldn't take much longer. She hadn't had much. Jane and Florence had already gone through Crystal's bedroom. Florence had kept a few things—a scarf, a few pieces of costume jewelry—and the rest they had put in boxes for Goodwill. Florence had nearly finished sorting through the contents of the living room, while Jane dealt with the kitchen, first the countertop and cabinets, then the drawers, one at a time.

"What about this?" Jane asked Florence, pointing to

the stainless steel silverware in a drawer on her lap. "Would you like to keep it?"

"No. What would I do with it?"

With a nod, Jane placed the knives, forks, and spoons into a box on the floor near her feet. The drawer she held was empty now. She set it down on the floor at the end of the sofa, picked up another drawer, this one full of papers, and started through it. There were takeout menus, a small address book, a copy of a letter from an attorney representing Crystal's husband, Dennis. He had begun divorce proceedings. Silently Jane handed this to Florence, who read it and nodded sadly.

Next Jane found a small black appointment book. She riffled its pages. Crystal hadn't written much in it. Jane flipped past October 22, the day Crystal had died.

"This is interesting," she murmured, gazing down at an entry for October 26 at 8:00 P.M. *Dinner with H.,* Crystal had written. "That's tonight." She looked up at Florence. "Who's H.?"

"I have no idea."

With a shrug, Jane set the book aside.

Under the book she found a copy of another letter. Frowning, she examined it. It was a copy of a letter Crystal had written to the head of the Shady Hills Board of Health.

John A. Favorito, Jr.
Health Officer
Shady Hills Municipal Building
68 Packer Road
Shady Hills, NJ 07059

Dear Mr. Favorito:

I am writing to you to make you aware of an alarming situation in our town.

I am a resident of the apartment building at 12 Fremont Lane. Situated behind this building is a cat shelter called Paws for Love, run by a Ms. Gabrielle Schraft. This establishment is the subject of my letter to you.

This so-called "shelter" is the most shocking example of cruel and unsanitary conditions I have ever had the misfortune to find. Hundreds of cats are crowded together in filthy cages that go uncleaned for days on end. As I'm sure you can imagine, the stench from this place is horrendous. It hits me every time I leave and enter my building.

I trust you will promptly investigate this shameful situation and take the appropriate action to protect the health of these poor defenseless cats, not to mention the health of the residents of 12 Fremont Lane; i.e., closing the shelter immediately.

Very truly yours,
Crystal Ryerson

"Have a look at this." Jane handed the letter to Florence, whose eyes grew wide as she read it.

"Crystal never mentioned anything about this to me. And she hated cats. She wouldn't have cared if their cages were cleaned."

"No, she wouldn't," Jane agreed. "Very strange." Thoughtfully she put the letter aside.

Two hours later, around half past twelve, they had finished. On one side of the living room were stacked boxes destined for Goodwill; on the other side, one large box containing the few things Florence wanted to keep.

They had rented a U-Haul Mini Mover truck again.

Jane couldn't quite believe they were carrying down everything they'd lugged up here only ten days ago, but of course she made no comment about this.

Finally they stood breathless and sweating in the apartment doorway.

"I guess that's it, then," Florence said. Jane gave her a sad smile, pulled the door shut, and followed Florence to the elevator. Downstairs, Florence headed for the van.

"Just a minute," Jane said, and as Florence turned, Jane drew from the pocket of her jeans the copy of the letter Crystal had written to the Board of Health. She tapped the sheet of paper. "I'd like to pay this place a visit."

"Really? Why?"

"I know this woman, Gabrielle Schraft," Jane replied, though she realized she wasn't answering Florence's question. "She came to the reading group meeting on Tuesday."

Florence looked at her sharply. "Then she was there when—"

"Yes."

"What is she like?"

"Um, I think *bohemian* is the word. You'll see."

Jane turned around. In her letter Crystal had said Paws for Love was behind the apartment building. To the right lay a parking lot for residents. To the left, a narrow drive led into the woods. "Let's try this way."

They followed the drive between thick trees and bushes. When they had walked about fifty feet, the woods opened up and they found themselves on a scruffy patch of grass before a small, ramshackle two-story house painted a brilliant sky blue. Above the front door hung a wooden sign featuring the face of a cat, with the words PAWS FOR LOVE above it.

Approaching the building, Jane noticed a discreet plaque beside the door that read: ONLY CAT LOVERS NEED

ENTER. She pointed this out to Florence, and smiling, they went inside.

Instantly the two women gasped in wonder.

"Oh, missus, what a wonderful place."

Before them lay a vast room, far larger than one would have expected from the outside. On the walls of this room was painted a mural featuring oversize caricatures of cats of all types—Siamese, Persian, Maine coon, sphinx—all overlapping and in various stances and poses. As for the room itself, there wasn't a cage in sight. Instead, the room had been fitted with a wonderland of stairs, ramps, cubbyholes, and perches in bright orange, turquoise, gold, lime green, magenta, and purple. Throughout this amazing structure cats could be seen—crawling, sleeping, scratching, rolling around. Jane guessed there were about two dozen of them.

"You like it?" came a woman's deep voice.

They turned. Gabrielle Schraft stood smiling in a side doorway. She wore a dress not unlike the one she had worn to the reading group meeting—a wispy long-sleeve garment of a faded mauve print fabric. She was positively beaming.

"It's wonderful," Jane said. "I don't know if you remember me . . ."

"Of course I do. You're Jane."

"Yes," Jane said, smiling, "and this is Florence."

Florence smiled and shook Gabrielle's hand.

"Are you in the market for a cat?" Gabrielle asked, and without waiting for a reply, continued, "Let me show you the rest." She turned and led them into the room from which she had come, a smaller room fitted with cages along the far wall.

"This is the kitten room. We need cages here, of course."

In these cages were three kittens, tiny white balls of fluff moving playfully about.

Gabrielle went on, "We also need them in the intake room—that's at the other end of the house—and in the quarantine area. That's in back. No one there now, I'm pleased to say." She pointed upward. "My son and I live upstairs."

"How long has this been here?" Jane asked, amazed that she hadn't known about it.

Gabrielle led them back into the main room. "The shelter itself—about six years. This amazing creation," she said, indicating the feline playland, "about a year." She smiled proudly. "Designed it myself. Got my boyfriend to build it for me."

Jane said, "It must have—"

"Cost a lot?" Gabrielle said. "It did. But I had some money from when my mom passed away, and we get a lot in donations."

Jane nodded, still taking it all in. How could Crystal have written such a letter?

"So!" Gabrielle said. "You didn't answer my question. Are you in the market for a new friend?"

"No, I'm afraid not," Jane said a little sadly. "We've already got two tortoiseshell cats and, at the moment, one rambunctious collie."

"Then . . ." Gabrielle looked puzzled, clearly wondering what they were doing there.

"We're here," Jane said carefully, "about Crystal Ryerson."

Gabrielle frowned. "Crystal? But she's—"

"Yes," Jane said. "Of course."

"I mean, we were there, right?" Gabrielle said. "It was horrible."

"Yes. Florence is Crystal's sister."

Gabrielle's mouth fell open slightly and she turned her head a little to one side. "I am so sorry."

"Thank you," Florence said.

"But what does that have to do with me?" Gabrielle asked.

Jane brought out the letter and handed it to her. As Gabrielle read, she began to nod. Then she looked up. "I figured as much. She told me she was planning to write a letter, and though I never read it, the Board of Health sent someone out here." She laughed. "As you can imagine, the woman saw immediately that Crystal's allegations had no merit. This shelter is regarded as one of the best in the state."

"I don't understand," Jane said. "Why would Crystal have written those things? Do you have any idea?"

"Sure," Gabrielle said easily.

At that moment the door at the back of the room was thrown open and a small boy with a wondrous mop of golden hair came running in, followed by a very old beagle, panting hard.

"Come here, you," Gabrielle said, grabbing the little boy lovingly around the waist. "Meet our new friends. This is my son, William," she told Jane and Florence. "William, shake hands."

William took two steps forward like a little soldier and put out his hand to the two of them in turn. "And this," he said in a high voice, turning to the beagle who was now beside him, "is *my* friend, Skipper."

"Hello, Skipper!" Florence said, and crouched down to pat the dog's smooth brown-and-white head.

"Hey, sport," Gabrielle said, "do you think you could bring in some of those supplies that came yesterday?"

"Sure!" William cried, and ran toward the rear door, Skipper in slow pursuit.

"Only the small boxes!" Gabrielle called after him, then turned back to Jane and Florence. "I love him to death.

His father walked out on us when William was eleven months old. As for Skipper, he's been through a lot with me, ten years' worth."

"He's only ten?" Jane asked, surprised.

"Yes. He looks a lot older because he's got cancer." Gabrielle's face turned sad and she lowered her gaze. "I'm going to miss that sweetie. Anyway," she said, looking up briskly, "you were asking me why Crystal would write those things. Easy. She hated my guts."

"But why?" Florence asked.

"You sure you want to know?"

"Of course."

"My boyfriend, the one who did all this work for me—his name is Henri, and he's originally from Tobago. One day about two weeks ago, he and I were at the ShopRite in Parsippany, picking up some groceries, and we separated. He was looking at plantains when Crystal spotted him, and *man*, did she start flirting with him." Gabrielle shook her head in wonder. "Henri, he's a bit of a tease, if you know what I mean. He kind of liked your sister, and he played along—you know, just for fun. Then I appeared, and I knew immediately what was going on. Women do."

Jane and Florence nodded.

"I was friendly to her—I liked her, too, *at first*—but she went cold as ice on me. She'd seen Henri put his arm around my waist, you see. She turned on her heel and walked out, hips swaying. She was embarrassed, of course. I gave Henri what for—leading that poor woman on like that. And then we both forgot all about it.

"But Crystal didn't. You see, she'd seen me around here. She knew who I was. The next day she came in here and said she was looking for a cat. She didn't choose one, but the day after, she came back again, this time saying she thought my shelter was filthy and that she intended to write to the Board of Health, demanding that this place be closed down. Can you imagine?"

Florence shook her head in dismay.

"I knew she was jealous of me, but I never thought she'd go to this extreme." Gabrielle handed the letter back to Jane. "*Then*, as if that weren't enough, she somehow found out where Henri lives and called him. Invited him over for some home-cooked Trinidadian cooking."

"Oh, dear," Florence said.

"When your sister wanted something, she didn't give up easily."

"No," Florence agreed, "she didn't." She looked up timidly. "Did he?"

"Did he what?"

"Did Henri accept my sister's invitation?"

Jane looked at Florence in surprise.

Gabrielle's face turned stony. "Yes, I believe he did. Men! Like I told you, he's a terrible tease. I figured he felt sorry for her."

"I see," Florence said, a knowing look in her eyes. "When was this dinner?"

"It never happened. It was supposed to be tonight, I believe."

"And that's why Crystal hated you," Jane said, doubt in her voice, as she slipped the letter into her pocket. "Sounds as if you may have things turned around."

Gabrielle's eyes snapped to Jane and darkened.

"By the way," Jane said, as if on an afterthought, "when you got up during our reading group meeting and went into the library's back room, what did you do back there?"

Gabrielle looked at her in bewilderment. "What the blazes are you talking about?" An orange tabby brushed against her legs and she bent down, scooped it up, and cradled it in her arms.

"It's a simple question," Jane said. "What were you doing?"

"I was getting a drink of water." Gabrielle's voice rose. "I believe I said that's what I was going to do when I left the table. What else could I have been doing?"

Jane didn't answer, instead merely giving a little shrug.

Suddenly Gabrielle's eyes widened. "Hey, wait a minute. You don't think— Oh, you gotta be kidding."

"What?" Jane asked innocently.

"Forgive me," Gabrielle said to Florence, "but I heard how Crystal died—I mean, how that bookcase fell on her. Some sick individual had removed the bolts securing the bookcase to those two L-brackets. You think I did it!"

"I said no such thing," Jane said.

"You don't have to. But what possible reason could I have had to do that? *Crystal* hated *me*, remember?"

"And your Henri was going to have dinner at my sister's apartment," Florence said, her face expressionless.

Slowly, as if in slow motion, Gabrielle put down the cat in her arms, then straightened. "You are two sick ladies. You actually think I would *kill* a woman because I thought she was taking my man away?"

"I didn't say that," Jane said.

"I think you'd both better leave."

Florence met Jane's gaze. Jane gave a tiny nod, and they both turned and walked out.

They were silent until they had reached the street end of the narrow drive. Then Florence looked at Jane, her dark eyes bright. "Missus, that is one strange woman."

"Only toward the end," Jane replied.

"I don't think she killed my sister."

Jane turned to her. "Why not?"

"For what reason? Because her boyfriend accepted a dinner invitation from another woman?"

Jane lifted her brows. "People have killed for far less," she said in a low voice, and led the way across the road to the truck.

Sitting at her vanity, Jane carefully closed her eyelash curler over her lashes, then counted to ten. She repeated this on her other eye, then put down the curler and took up her mascara brush. She was careful to apply more mascara to her outer lashes and less to the lashes beside the bridge of her nose. Ginny had told her that this method would lift her eyes and make them almond-shaped.

She shook out her hair, making sure it curled dramatically at the collar of her jade green cashmere jewel-neck sweater.

When she was satisfied, she got up and went out into the corridor. As she neared the staircase, a yell came from Nick's room. In the next instant Nick was barreling down the corridor, followed by Alphonse, Winky, and Twinky, all in a gallop.

"Make way, Mom!"

Laughing, she pressed herself flat against the wall and watched them rush past her, down the stairs, into the living room, and out of sight.

There was more thumping, the sound of Nick laughing, and then the smashing of glass.

Jane winced. All was suddenly silent. Then into her line of vision slid Nick, head down, eyes upraised. "Sorry, Mom," he called up the stairs.

"What was it?" she asked.

"That jar thing that was Dad's mom's."

She drew in her breath sharply, grimacing and stomping her foot once. Then she hurried down the stairs and moved past Nick into the living room, where Alphonse, Winky, and Twinky stood very still, watching her.

On the floor at the foot of the étagère on which it had

stood for years, Jane's favorite Murano glass vase lay in a thousand peacock blue pieces. "Oh, Nick," she wailed.

"Mom, I said I'm sorry."

She looked over at the two cats and the dog. They all looked down. She couldn't repress a tiny smile.

"First of all," she said, "I want you all to quiet down. Nick, I am leaving you alone again tonight because you are eleven years old and you're mature enough to take care of yourself. Is that true?"

"Yes, Mom."

"All right. You get the dustpan and brush, and I'll get the vacuum cleaner."

He nodded and hurried off to the kitchen. At that moment the doorbell rang. Jane checked her watch. Seven o'clock. It must be Stanley.

She went to the door. He was smiling, handsome in charcoal slacks, a gray silk shirt, and his black leather jacket. In his hands was a bunch of exquisite lavender roses.

"How beautiful," she breathed.

"They mean I'm sorry for those things I said to you at Whipped Cream."

"Me, too," she said, and brought her lips to his. "Mm."

"Mom," Nick said, "I think I got all the big pieces."

"An accident," she told Stanley. "Come in. I'll just be a second. Would you like something? Some wine?"

"No, thanks," he said, and smiled when he saw Nick and the animals. "Hey, fellas!"

"Hi, Stanley," Nick said, heading back to the kitchen with a dustpan full of glass.

The telephone rang.

"Now what?" Jane crossed the living room to get it.

"Where's Florence?" Stanley asked.

"Off," Jane told him, and grabbed the phone.

"Mrs. Stuart?" It was a woman's voice, low and without inflection.

She frowned. "Yes?"

"Mrs. Stuart, my name is Agnes Shaughnessy. I need to talk to you."

Still frowning, Jane glanced up to find a puzzled look on Stanley's face. "About what?" she asked the woman on the phone.

"It's about my daughter, Roxanne. She's disappeared. Can you come see me?"

A shiver ran through Jane. "Let me grab a pen. Hold on." She set down the phone. "Stanley, could you do me a favor and put those beautiful roses in some water? There's a perfect vase in the kitchen. Then could you please start the car?"

"I thought we were taking my car?"

"Don't you want to drive the Jaguar?"

"Not especially."

"Well, I do. All right? Will you start it? I hate getting into a cold car. The keys are on the kitchen counter."

He gave her a suspicious look as he left the room, carrying the roses. Jane yanked open the drawer of the telephone table, grabbed a pen, and picked up the receiver. "Okay, Mrs. Shaughnessy, I can come see you tomorrow if that's all right. Ten o'clock?"

"Yes, that will be fine." Mrs. Shaughnessy gave Jane her address. "You'll really come?"

"Of course I will. I promise."

"I believe you. Oh, and Mrs. Stuart. I know your boyfriend is Detective Greenberg. I guess he's there at your house now—I heard you call him. Please don't say anything about this to him, all right? At least not yet."

"All right," Jane answered, mystified. "I'll see you tomorrow, then."

She had to force a smile back onto her face as she said good-bye to Nick and headed out to Stanley in the car.

Chapter 16

When Agnes Shaughnessy had given Jane her address, she had jotted it down without thinking. Now, as she entered the garage and walked to her car at nine forty-five Sunday morning, she took the scrap of paper from her coat pocket and did a double take at what she'd written there: *12 Montgomery Place.* That was in Maple Estates.

Mrs. Shaughnessy had sounded uneducated. How was this possible?

Jane drove down Lilac Way, made a left onto Grange Road, and another left onto Montgomery. Number 12, almost directly opposite the Morikawas' house, was nearly twice the size, so big that to Jane it looked like a hotel.

Baffled, she parked on a circular driveway of bricks laid in a herringbone pattern and walked up to the front door, deep in the shadows of a high colonnade. As she reached for the doorbell, the mammoth front door slowly opened.

Standing there was a petite woman who looked around sixty. She wore a maid's dress, black with a white eyelet collar and cuffs. Though her face was small, her features were coarse and poorly defined—her mouth large, her nose an odd flattish shape. She had wispy thinning hair of a pale reddish brown, and her eyes were a beautiful bright green.

"Mrs. Stuart?" she asked softly.

"Yes. Is Mrs. Shaughnessy in, please?"

The woman shot a wary glance back into the house. "That's me. Can you do me a favor and come around back?"

Surprised, Jane hesitated for a moment, then recovered. "Yes, of course."

"Follow the path all the way to the end," Mrs. Shaughnessy said, leaning out and pointing toward the left side of the house, "and you'll come to the service entrance. It's a white door with an awning. I'll meet you there and let you in."

"All right." Jane found the path at the side of the house, between banks of shrubbery and tall ornamental grasses. The path was made of brick in the same herringbone pattern as the driveway. She followed it past an immense picture window that gave her a view of a richly decorated living room and beyond it the house's spacious front hall. Turning the corner at the back of the house, she found herself looking down a magnificent terraced yard that culminated in an oversize swimming pool, tightly covered for the winter. Behind it, to the left, stood an elaborate wooden swing set with a hunter green canvas canopy over a vinyl slide in a paler green.

"Over here!" came an urgent whisper.

Jane turned. Mrs. Shaughnessy stood on the path outside the service entrance, under a white awning. She went inside, holding the door for Jane, who followed the older woman down a short corridor, past a large laundry room, into a small room furnished with a beat-up dinette set of brushed steel with bright red vinyl cushions on the chairs. Against the far wall was a tiny kitchen, the kind you'd find in a small apartment, and on the counter was a large Mr. Coffee machine, its carafe full.

Mrs. Shaughnessy pulled out a chair for Jane, then went to the counter. "Would you like some coffee?"

"No, thank you."

Mrs. Shaughnessy nodded once, turned, and poured a mug of coffee, which she carried to the table, sitting down opposite Jane. "Thank you for coming," she said, her voice still lowered, as if she were doing something forbidden and someone might walk in at any moment. "I'm sorry to be so mysterious and all."

"That's all right," Jane said graciously. "What is it I can do for you, Mrs. Shaughnessy?"

"Call me Agnes." The mug in the small woman's hand began to tremble and she set it down. "Like I told you, it's about my daughter, Roxanne. She's . . . gone away. When I heard about what's been going on, I got so scared . . . I wanted to speak to you as soon as possible. That's why I asked you to come see me at work." Suddenly she screwed her eyes shut tight and silently began to cry.

"Please," Jane said gently, "tell me how I can help."

Agnes opened her eyes, sniffed once, and gave a tiny smile. "I knew you'd be nice." She scowled. "Not like these people I work for. The Kellys. Do you know them?"

"I don't think so."

"Beverly and Kevin. He's a stockbroker or some such. She does nothing, doesn't even take care of her own brat. I'd quit this job in a second if something better came along."

"About your daughter . . ."

"Yeah, my Roxanne." Agnes slid a photograph from the pocket of her dress and handed it to Jane. Roxanne Shaughnessy was an exceptionally beautiful girl, with thick red hair that fell like a waterfall to her shoulders, creamy skin, and large almond-shaped eyes the same vivid green as her mother's."

"How old is she?" Jane asked.

"Sixteen and a half. She goes to the high school here in Shady Hills. She's a junior. We live in an apartment at Hillside Gardens, other side of Route Forty-six. My husband and I moved there when Roxie was little so's she could go to the good schools here."

Jane knew Hillside Gardens, a shabby low-rent complex at the southernmost end of town.

"One day about a month ago," Agnes continued, "Roxie didn't come home. The next day she called me and said she was fine, but that she wouldn't be back."

"Did she tell you where she was?"

"No, she wouldn't."

"What did you do?"

"Well, I haven't told you the whole story yet. Y'see, early last month, at the beginning of school, Roxie started stayin' out late. We figured she was seeing a boy, but she wouldn't tell me and Ralph—that's my husband—who it was. My Ralph, he's kind of strict about things, and maybe Roxie was afraid to tell him anything, I don't know. Anyway, she starts stayin' out late and my husband starts givin' her a hard time, sayin' she's no better than a hooker and like that."

Jane frowned. "That's pretty harsh, don't you think?"

"Yeah, but what could I do? He's like that, thinks that way about women. Roxie never answered him when he asked her where she was going or where she'd been. The only thing she ever said, she said to me one day when we were alone. She said, 'You don't have to worry about me, Mom. I can't tell you what I'm doing, but it's not anything bad. If it works out, we won't have to worry about money for college.' "

Jane frowned. "What did you think she meant?"

"I had no idea. It didn't make no sense. She said she wasn't doin' nothin' bad, but on the other hand, she said she was makin' money, which made me think maybe she *was* doin' something bad. I didn't mention nothin' about this to Ralph, that's for sure.

"Anyway, Roxie just went about her business, did what she liked. Ralph would scream at her and she'd walk out, calm as you please. And then, one day, like I told you, she was gone."

"Did you report her missing?"

"Ralph, he didn't want me to. Said it was a shame on our family."

"I don't understand."

"He said the only reason Roxie wouldn't have come home was that she'd got herself knocked up, in which case he didn't want her back and good riddance to the dirty tramp and like that."

"How horrible."

Agnes nodded in agreement. "So I went to the police myself—you know, secretly."

"You did?"

"Yeah. About a week after Roxie left."

"Whom did you speak to?"

"The chief of police himself. Ward, his name is."

Eric Ward, Stanley's boss. "What did he say?"

"That he'd look into it and get back to me, but he never did. I don't understand why." Agnes's hands began to tremble again and she lowered her head, crying. "I'm a terrible mother. I feel so guilty. What with everything Ralph was saying, I was afraid to go back to the police. If Ralph had found out, he would have been furious at me. But I should have stood up to him. She's my daughter, too."

"Yes, she is," Jane said, reproach in her voice. "And now you've called me about her. Why now, and why me?"

"Because I heard about those other girls, y'see. That poor Ashley Surow they found lyin' there at the tracks, strangled. And now there's all this gossip goin' around about this Morikawa girl. The Morikawas live across the street, you know." Agnes curled her lip. "More rich trash, like these people here."

She indicated her surroundings with her eyes. "Mrs. Kelly, I heard her talking to Mr. Kelly yesterday morning about the Morikawa girl, how shocking she thought it was that her parents didn't do a better job of keeping track of her." She let out a laugh which came out too loud and her hand flew to her mouth, her eyes sliding from side to side. In a lower voice she said, "Like Mrs. Kelly gives a flying— like she cares about little Carter . . . such a sweet little boy. It's his nanny and me who take care of him, not her!"

"Why did you want to tell me all this?" Jane asked.

"First of all, because I've heard—well, that you've found some missing people in the past."

Dead missing people, Jane thought, and knew Agnes was thinking the same thing, but said nothing.

"Second, because I knew Detective Greenberg was your boyfriend. I've seen him around town, in stores and like that, and it seems to me he's a kind man."

"Yes," Jane said with a smile, "he is."

"And since I've already been to the police, and that didn't get me nowhere, I thought maybe I could do it this way— you talkin' to Detective Greenberg, and him lookin' into things for me, find out where my Roxie went to."

Those bright green eyes, full of concern, were fixed on Jane, who gave a nod of understanding. "Of course I'll do what I can, Agnes."

"Bless you." Agnes glanced at a black plastic clock on the wall. "I better get back to work. They like brunch on Sunday."

"Of course," Jane said. "I can let myself out." At the

door a thought occurred to her and she turned. "Oh, Agnes. Hasn't the high school been in touch with you about Roxanne's absence?"

"No," Agnes answered, her face blank.

Pensively Jane nodded and went out.

That afternoon, Jane dragged Nick to the Willowbrook Mall in Wayne, where she bought him some warm shirts for the winter and a new winter coat. She rewarded him with lunch in the mall's food court. When they got home, Jane went to her study and called Stanley on his cell phone. He was spending the day with his sister, Linda, and her thirteen-year-old daughter, who lived at the north end of town.

"Can't talk long, Jane. I'm helping my niece with her Halloween costume. She's going to a big party."

"How nice. I won't keep you, just a couple of quick questions."

"Shoot."

"What are Ashley Surow's parents like?"

He was silent for a moment. "What makes you think I know?"

"Stanley, stop playing games. Either you tell me what they're like or I'll meet with them and find out myself."

"All right," he said with a groan. "The father—Dave, his name is—he's just as Cara Fairchild said. A big dumb guy. Domineering, small-minded, always thought the worst of his daughter. Never gave her the benefit of the doubt, if you know what I mean."

"Yes, I do. And the mother?"

"Helena. Meek little mouse. Lets Dave order her around. No mind of her own."

"Interesting. Thanks. One more thing. Have you ever heard of a girl named Roxanne Shaughnessy?"

"Uh . . . no, don't think so."

"I was afraid of that."

"What's that supposed to mean?"

"Thanks, darling. Have fun."

She hung up, then set her mouth tightly and banged her desk with her fist, filled with a sudden fury. Grabbing her Day Runner, she wrote herself a reminder to pay another visit to Lew Kaplan, principal of Shady Hills High School, first thing the following morning.

"Mrs. Stuart, I really am very short on time today." Lew Kaplan kept his eyes focused on some papers on his desk. Finally he looked up, meeting her gaze. "I thought I answered all your questions last Thursday."

"Mr. Kaplan, what can you tell me about Roxanne Shaughnessy?"

His brows lowered slightly. "Roxanne? She's a student here."

"No, she's not. Not for a month."

"Listen," he said, his patience clearly gone, "not only do I not want to discuss my students with you, but I can't. How would you like it if some woman came in asking about your son, and I told her anything she wanted to know?"

"A valid point. And a convenient one." She gave an easy shrug. "We can let the police ask the questions."

"What do you mean by that?"

"Why haven't you been in touch with Roxanne's parents about her absence?"

He kept his gaze steady. "I have nothing to say to you."

She knew she would get nothing more out of this odious little man. Without saying a word, she got up and walked out.

As she passed through the outer office, she noticed that Kaplan's secretary was standing at the counter. "Mrs. Stuart?" she said softly.

Jane stopped and turned. The redhead beckoned Jane over with a curling finger and Jane approached the counter.

"Listen, could I talk to you?" the secretary asked. "Privately, I mean?"

"Why?"

The woman leaned even closer, lowering her voice to a whisper. "I can hear everything that goes on in there." She turned and pointed to a heating vent in the wall between her desk and Kaplan's office. "I heard what went on when you came here last week, and I heard what you just said. I think I can help you."

"All right," Jane said, excitement shooting through her. "Where would you like to meet? At my office?"

"No, someplace less suspicious. How about that little coffee place on the green?"

"Whipped Cream? I know it well."

"Good. My name's Debbie, by the way. Debbie Hagen." As she shook Jane's hand, she smiled and didn't look at all sour anymore. "I can meet you on my lunch hour. Twelve fifteen work for you?"

"Absolutely. See you then."

As Jane moved away from the counter, Kaplan's door opened and he emerged. He cast a suspicious glance from Jane to Debbie Hagen. Jane met his gaze, her face expressionless, and walked out.

Jane introduced Debbie Hagen to Ginny, who brought them coffee and sandwiches and then hurried off to check on other customers.

"I knew Ashley," Debbie said, "and I know Keiko and Roxie. I know all the kids."

"What can you tell me about Roxanne?"

Debbie smiled fondly. "Roxie's a good girl. Smart as a whip, sweet as can be, and beautiful—like a model." She curled her lip. "She's not trash like her parents. Mother's a maid, can you believe that? As for the father, I don't think he's worked in years, useless old parasite."

She took a bite of her sandwich. "Of course, the reason the Shaughnessys are in dumpy old Hillside Gardens is that that's the only place they can afford to live in Shady Hills so that they can use our school system. Don't get me started on people who do that."

Debbie Hagen was apparently an incredible snob. But that didn't mean she wouldn't prove a source of useful information. Jane nodded in understanding.

"But like I said, Roxie's a good girl. She's ambitious, wants to make something good of herself. She told me she wants to go to college, even asked her guidance counselor if he would help her apply for scholarships when the time came." Debbie shook her head. "It never made sense to me that Roxie would leave like that."

"Do you think she might have run off with someone?"

Debbie looked at Jane askance. "You mean a boy? No way."

"Really? A beautiful girl like that?"

"I know, she's exquisite, a knockout. But it's true. She and I, we joked around a lot, and I asked her once, 'How come a stunner like you has no guy?' Know what she said? That she didn't have time for boys. She was going to be either a doctor or a lawyer and her career goals were more important to her than silliness like dating and boys. You wouldn't believe all the clubs she belonged to. Forensics. Marketing. Art Club. She wrote for the school newspaper. On top of which, she studied hard. No time!"

Setting down her sandwich, Debbie looked around warily. "Mr. Kaplan would kill me if he knew I was talking to you like this. I can't stand him, but I need the job."

"I understand, and I appreciate it. Tell me," Jane said, "can you think of any connection among Ashley, Keiko, and Roxanne? Were they friends, do you know?"

"Hmm." Debbie concentrated. "I don't think so."

"Because of their different backgrounds? You know, the Morikawas are wealthy, the Surows middle-class, the Shaughnessys lower-class."

Debbie waved away that idea. "That never matters at school! At least not in Shady Hills." From Debbie's faint scowl, it was clear she didn't approve of this state of affairs. "They're very democratic when it comes to friendship. Of course, that all goes out the window once they grow up and see what's what."

Jane nodded, forcing herself to keep silent.

"The only thing those three girls had in common," Debbie Hagen said, "was that they were all stunningly beautiful."

Jane took a bite of her sandwich and waited, watching Debbie, but it appeared she had said all she had intended to say. Jane managed to make small talk but didn't have to for long, because Debbie had to get back to work. "You know," she said, shrugging into her coat and picking up her purse, "when Roxanne hadn't come to school for a while, I heard our vice principal say to Mr. Kaplan that she had probably run off with some guy. I went to Mr. Kaplan and told him I didn't think that sounded like her."

"And what did he say?"

Debbie flushed dark red behind her freckles. "That it was none of my business—I'll leave out the bad word he used—and that I was not to talk about Roxanne or anyone else anymore."

"Interesting. Tell me," Jane said, "have you ever heard of a man named Cosmo Blair?"

Debbie wrinkled up her nose. "No. Strange name. Who is he?"

"I don't know," Jane replied truthfully.

"I'll tell you who you really ought to talk to," Debbie said, heading for the door. Jane waited. "The mayor."

"Oh? Why is that?"

Debbie looked around furtively. She looked like a hunted rat. "Can't say more than that. As I said, I need my job and shouldn't have said this much. Good luck." And she hurried out the door of the café, leaving Jane with the check.

That was all right. The information Jane had gotten from Debbie Hagen was more than worth the price of lunch.

The reporters and news vans were back today, hollering outlandish questions at Jane. She pushed her way through them and into the corridor at the back of the office, Daniel slamming and locking the door behind her.

"Jane, why are you letting this go on?" he whispered.

"Because I gave her my word," she whispered back. "What's the matter?" she said, giving him a mischievous eyebrow lift. "She getting under your skin?"

His mouth dropped open in horror. "*What?*"

"I saw your arms wrapped around her legs last Friday."

"That was to keep her from falling!"

"Methinks thou dost protest too much."

He shook his head in exasperation and walked away. *Good*, she thought. *Now he'll leave me alone about Goddess, at least for a little while.*

The star in question was reading a manuscript Jane had given her, a literary novel by a new client, Isabel Wayland.

"What do you think of it?" Jane asked her.

Goddess looked at Jane over her cat-eye glasses. "Bor-r-ring!"

"Really? I thought it was absolutely beautiful. So moving."

"Not my cuppa, Janey girl. Give me more *romance*."

"Man cannot live by bread alone," Jane pointed out.

Goddess rolled her eyes. "Whatevah."

With a laugh, Jane went into her office. On her chair was a pink message slip: *Please call Salomé Sutton. Urgent.*

Groaning, Jane dropped into her chair and dialed Salomé's number.

"How are ya, Jane?"

"Sal, are you all right?"

"Yeah, I'm fine, why?"

"Your message said urgent."

Sal let out a bellowing laugh. "I knew that would get you to call me back fast."

"I don't appreciate that, Sal. Please don't do it again."

"Whoo-hoo-hoo, touchy, are we?" Now Sal sounded irritated. "Maybe if you did something for me, I wouldn't have to bother you like this."

"I didn't say you were bothering me." What was the use? Jane let out a long breath. "What can I do for you, Sal?"

"What can you do for me? *Get me a deal, Einstein!*"

That did it. "Sal, do you want me to tell you why I haven't been able to get you a deal?"

"Yeah, enlighten me."

"All right. Editors are telling me your writing is dated and that you have a reputation for being difficult to work with."

"What! Dated? Difficult? Now you listen to me. I am a titan of the romance genre. A titan! My work is not dated. It is classic. And I am not difficult. I'm . . . particular."

"I'm just repeating what's been said to me. I should have told you this a long time ago. I certainly won't spare you from this kind of thing in the future."

But Salomé wasn't listening. "I know what the trouble is. It's you."

"*Me?*"

"Yeah, like I told you when we had lunch. You ain't got no clout. You're unprofessional. No New York office."

Jane sizzled. "I am not going to dignify any of this by arguing with you. I will only say that you are wrong, dead wrong."

"Then let me come out there, see your operation."

"No."

"Why not? Think I won't find it professional?"

"We are as professional as any agency in the country. I am hanging up now, Sal. Good-bye."

Fuming, she put down the phone. At that moment Goddess walked in without so much as a tap on the door.

"Jane," she said, "can you tell me something?"

"Sure," Jane replied with a sigh, "what is it?"

"Why don't you guys use colored filing tabs? They're so much prettier than the plain clear ones."

Chapter 17

"Whoo-oo, Janey!" Across the street, Audrey stood in her driveway beside her smoke-colored Audi, and waved a white handkerchief. On the other side of the car, her hand on the door handle, Cara kept her gaze fixed on the driveway.

Jane crossed the street. "Good morning. Audrey, I want to apologize for those things I said."

Audrey put up her hand. "Thank you, Jane, but you were right. Elliott and I do need to keep a closer eye on Cara. I just didn't want to hear it."

Jane smiled. "Friends?"

"Of course! It would take a lot more than that!"

"Good . . . There's something I want to ask you both."

"Sure. Cara, come over here!"

With a scowl, Cara came around the car to stand beside her mother.

"What's on your mind?" Audrey asked.

"There's a third girl who's disappeared, have you heard?"

They both shook their heads, eyes wide.

"Who is it?" Cara asked.

"Her name is Roxanne Shaughnessy."

Cara nodded. "I know her, but not very well. She used to hang out at the library, too. What happened?"

"One day about a month ago she didn't come home. She called the next day and said she was all right, and that's the last her parents have heard from her."

Cara drew a ragged breath and looked anxiously at Audrey, who pursed her lips. "Jane," she said, "what is going on in this town?"

Jane shook her head. "Cara, if you hear anything about these girls—anything at all—will you let me know?"

"You know she will, Jane." Audrey turned to Cara. "Which reminds me, young lady. No more going out at night."

"*What?*"

"You heard me. From now on, when you're not at school, you will be with us. Understood?"

Whether Cara didn't see the point of arguing or saw the wisdom in this edict, it was impossible to tell, but she made no further argument. "Bye, Jane," she muttered, and got into the car.

As Audrey slipped behind the steering wheel and closed the door, she threw Jane a look of wild alarm.

Robert Bergman, the mayor of Shady Hills, was a lawyer with offices on Packer Road, in the same building as Rich Weldon's physician, Dr. Katz.

Jane, who had met Bergman a number of times at various community functions, had called his office the previous day and asked for an appointment this morning. To her surprise, his secretary said that Mr. Bergman would be delighted to see her.

Jane parked behind the office building and found his office on the ground floor. In a modest reception room, Bergman's secretary, a tall, buxom blonde in a tight tomato red turtleneck, hung up Jane's coat and then showed her into Bergman's dark-paneled office.

When he saw Jane, a smile bloomed on his face and he practically jumped up, thrusting out his hand. "Jane, hello. Such a pleasure to see you."

She was surprised and perplexed by this reception. She barely knew him.

"Sit, sit," he said, indicating a comfortable-looking chair covered in golden leather that faced his desk. When she was seated, he lowered himself into his chair, folded his hands on his desk before him, and beamed at her.

He was a handsome man, around fifty, sleek and fit, with dark brown hair that looked as if it had been trimmed that morning. A receding hairline augmented a broad forehead. Prominent cheekbones, a sharply sculpted nose, and thin, rather red lips combined pleasingly. His eyes, a deep brown, were large with dark, almost feminine lashes. He blinked twice.

"You know, it's uncanny that you called me last night," he said, "because I wanted to talk to you, too."

She smiled. "Really? About what?"

"You go first," he replied playfully.

She gave a little shrug. "I'll get right to it. I'm curious to know whether you know anything about Ashley Surow or the two girls who have disappeared, Keiko Morikawa and Roxanne Shaughnessy."

His smile dimmed, but only slightly. "I know no more than you do. The Surow girl . . . that's a horrible thing, of course. The police are working on that and will, I'm sure, get to the bottom of it."

Jane had no such confidence in the police, despite her affection for Stanley, but she kept this thought to herself.

Bergman went on, "As for these other two girls—yes, I have heard that they are missing." He narrowed his eyes.

"May I ask why you're so interested in them? You have a child of your own to worry about, if I'm not mistaken."

It was her turn to blink. "I beg your pardon?"

He gave a forced little laugh. "These girls aren't your concern. Why are you asking people about them?"

"How do you know I'm asking people about them?"

"You're asking me."

He was smooth. She said, "It appears that no one else is much interested in these girls. *Someone* needs to be, so I felt it might as well be me."

Now his smile fell away altogether, any attempt at cordiality abandoned. He lowered his head and positively sneered at her. "You know, women like you give me a pain in my ass."

She gaped at him. "What did you say?"

"Who the hell do you think you are, minding everybody else's business, bothering people. Lew Kaplan says you've been up to the high school hounding him not once, but twice! Now me. Who's next?"

Now it was her turn to sneer. "Why, you pompous fool! How dare you!"

"Mind your own business, lady!" he suddenly shouted, then slammed down the palm of his hand on his desk. "And another thing—which is very definitely *my* business. I understand you have a pop star, someone named Goddess, working at your office. Don't you care what that does to our town, how it disrupts life here? Do you really need to stage such colossal publicity stunts? Shame on you!"

She stared at him, breathing hard, as if she had just been hit on the head with a brick.

Before she could speak, he rushed on. "A friend of mine used to be the mayor of Mountain Lakes. He said a stunt like this would *never* be tolerated in his town."

"I—"

"We don't need this kind of publicity in Shady Hills, Mrs. Stuart. Million-dollar homes are being built in Maple Estates, which I believe isn't far from where you live. Sixty million dollars' worth of real estate." He pushed his head even farther forward. "Prospective home buyers won't be interested in a town where girls vanish and offices are turning into—rock concerts! You're a businessperson, of sorts! I assume you don't want any trouble, any more than I do. *So what the hell's wrong with you, lady?* Butt out!"

She shot up like a rocket and slapped him hard across the face. He flipped back in his chair, his cheek red, his mouth hanging wide. "Oh, you have made a very big mistake," he said in a low, ominous voice.

"No, you have," she said. "If you ever speak to me like that again, I'll slap you even harder."

The door to the reception room burst open and Bergman's secretary stood there, bosom heaving. "Mr. Bergman, do you want me to call the police?"

Jane swept past her, grabbing her coat from the closet.

"What good would it do!" Bergman screamed out at her. "She's dating one of them!"

Emerging into the corridor, her coat over her arm, Jane had to smirk at that last comment. He was right, though in truth, dating Stanley wouldn't do her much good if Bergman filed assault charges. She wouldn't put it past the weasel. She'd have to watch her temper in the future.

In the meantime, she knew more than she had going in. And slapping him *had* felt awfully good.

Early that evening, Jane and her fellow members of the Defarge Club met in the spacious living room of Hydrangea House. The weather outside had turned unseasonably cold, but it was always warm and cozy here, thanks in large part to the fire that Ernie, Louise's husband, had made in the massive old stone fireplace.

Jane needed this meeting tonight. Here, among her friends, she could relax, be herself. Knitting, though fun (Jane was the fastest knitter in the group), was only an excuse, as far as she was concerned.

"So, Jane," said Ginny, who sat beside her on one of Louise's floral print sofas, "how are things at the office?" Leaning forward, she removed the aluminum foil covering from the plate of assorted cookies she had brought for the group.

Jane looked at Ginny. Her expression was positively wicked. Jane gave her a warning look, and Ginny giggled.

Nestled in her special chair at one end of the coffee table, Doris looked up from the afghan she was knitting, a vast creation in blues and golds that never seemed to end. "You mean that actress you've got working in there? What's up with that, Jane?"

Penny Powell, sitting on the sofa directly across from Jane, was winding wool. She looked up with a puzzled frown. "Goddess isn't an actress, is she, Jane?"

"Yes, she is— Wait a minute. Doris, who told you there was anyone working at my office?"

Doris gave her a pitying look. "You're kidding, right? Jane, this is Shady Hills. So is she an actress or isn't she?"

Jane laughed. "Now *you've* got to be kidding. She's only the biggest star on earth. She's a singer, an actress, an author."

"Whoa, hold it," said Rhoda, seated next to Penny. "This is us you're talking to, Jane. She's no author. You've told us yourself that her books are ghosted."

"Well, yes, but—oh, never mind. To answer your question, *Ginny*"—she threw her another reprimanding look—"everything at the office is fine."

"Not from what I hear," Louise said, and immediately looked around as if punishment would come swiftly, for this was highly unlike Louise.

"What's that supposed to mean?" Jane demanded.

"Well, for one thing," Louise said, "the green is covered with paparazzi. And for another, I don't think our Ginny is too pleased about her significant other being cooped up in that little office with the world's greatest sex symbol."

"Louise!" Ginny cried.

"We're all friends here, Ginny," Louise said sweetly. "Any of us would feel the same way." She returned her attention to the slipper she was knitting.

Jane looked at Ginny, who now had tears in her eyes. "Oh, Ginny, stop worrying. Daniel loves you and only you. You know that." She raised one eyebrow. "You started this."

"I know," Ginny said with a weak smile. "I think we're all kind of on edge, after what happened to poor Crystal."

"And that girl by the train tracks." Rhoda turned to Jane. "How is Florence holding up?"

"Very well, considering. On Saturday she and I went through Crystal's things, cleaned out the apartment."

Doris grabbed an oatmeal raisin cookie and bit into it. "This is dry, Ginny."

"Sorry, Doris," Ginny said with a quick roll of her eyes. "They're from the shop."

Doris spoke with a mouth full of cookie. "You've got to admit, none of this is good publicity for our town. Murders—we've certainly had our fair share of *those,* haven't we, Jane—and now I hear girls are vanishing."

"What?" Rhoda asked sharply, her face blank. "What girls?" She looked at Doris.

"A couple of high school girls," Doris said without looking up. "That's all I know."

Jane looked around the group. She hadn't expected to talk about this—hadn't even thought word had gotten around town—but maybe someone in the group could shed some light on it. "Their names are Keiko Morikawa and Roxanne Shaughnessy," she informed them. "Both disappearances follow the same pattern. They disappear, call home the next day to report that they're all right, and then they're never heard from again. In the case of Keiko, we know that she ran off with a young man named Cosmo Blair—who is also the young man Ashley Surow ran off with before she was murdered."

"By Cosmo Blair," Doris said flatly.

"We don't know that," Jane said.

"Who else could it have been, Jane?" Doris shook her head, her knitting needles flying.

Jane gave in. "Apparently he lures these girls with promises of putting them in movies."

"Oldest trick in the book," Rhoda said, grabbing the largest chocolate chip cookie.

"What is?" came a man's voice from the doorway. They all turned. It was Ernie, looking as fat as Jane had ever seen him look, in jeans and a black sweater. His hair was neatly trimmed, as if it had been cut that day.

"Hello, darling," Louise said. "We were just talking about these poor girls who have gone missing. There's some awful young man who's luring them away by saying he'll put them in a film."

"And killing them," Doris put in matter-of-factly.

"We don't know that," Jane put in. "Not for certain."

"I do," Doris said. "He strangled Ashley by the railroad tracks, and heaven knows what he's done with Keiko and Roxanne."

A violent chill shook Jane. It was, of course, highly likely that Doris was right, but Jane hadn't ever put the thought into words, not even to herself.

Ernie waddled into the room and grabbed two cookies. Jane saw Louise start to speak, then stop herself and shake her head as if to say, "What's the use?"

"What I hear," Ernie said, perching on the arm of Louise's chair, "is that people are keeping their daughters home at night."

"Good!" Jane said, and everyone looked at her. "If they had done that before, these poor girls would still be with us."

"Got a point, Jane," Ernie said, and as he looked at her, a sparkle came into his eyes. "Hey, Jane, I hear you and Rob Bergman are best friends these days."

She glanced up at him sharply. "Come again?"

"You and he have a little . . . tussle today?" He burst out laughing.

"What's he talking about, Jane?" Penny asked.

"Ernie, how do you know about that?"

Ernie guffawed, slapping his knee. "Can't keep secrets in this town, you know that, Jane. Okay, listen to this. This afternoon I went to my barber, Sal, and Sal says to me, 'Hey, Ernie, you know that lady on the green with the movie star workin' for her? And I says, 'Yeah?' And he says, 'She smacked the mayor today!' "

"Jane!" Penny cried in a whisper. "You smacked the mayor?"

"Wait," Ernie said. "So I says, 'Really? How do you know?' And he tells me that his wife, Donatella, goes to the same yoga class as Bergman's secretary—you know, the blonde with the big—"

"Ernie," Louise broke in. "Her name is Letty."

"Right," Ernie said. "So they were at this yoga class today, and Letty told them all!"

"Oh, no," Jane said, putting her face in her hands.

Ginny said, "Why did you hit him, Jane?"

"He said some awful things to me. But it wasn't just that. He was angry at me for not minding my own business. He went on and on about how this town doesn't need this kind of publicity . . . that people don't want to move into a town where girls are disappearing . . . and didn't I know that, being a businessperson."

"Well, of course Rob would feel that way, Jane," Ernie said, looking at her as if she were mentally deficient. "What did you expect?"

"What do you mean?" Jane asked.

"Jane, he's a major investor in Maple Estates."

"What?"

Ernie nodded. "Everyone knows that."

Louise tugged on the sleeve of her husband's sweater. "Obviously not *everyone* knows it, dear. Try not to be so mean."

"No, no, that's okay, Ernie. In fact, thank you."

"What's the matter, Jane?" Doris said, peering over her sea of afghan. "You're acting spooky all of a sudden."

"Am I? It's just that this all makes a lot more sense to me now."

Smiling to herself, she concentrated on her knitting, her hands flying faster than ever.

At eight thirty the following morning, Jane pulled into the parking lot of the Shady Hills Police Station and took a space at the very back, hidden between two immense SUVs. Stanley would find out eventually that she had been there, but she didn't want him to know now—at least, not if she could avoid it.

She watched for him as she entered the station and told Buzzi she had an appointment to see Chief Ward. Fortunately, Stanley's and Ward's offices were at opposite ends of the station's main corridor, so that when Buzzi took her to Ward, she didn't pass Stanley.

Eric Ward was an immense man, tall as well as broad, with a massive head topped by glorious, thick silver curls.

He smiled a huge white smile and rose to take Jane's hand in both his own.

"Good to see you, Jane, good to see you," he said in his deep, gravelly voice. "Sit, sit. You're looking as beautiful as ever, by the way."

She looked down modestly. "Thank you, Eric, you're always so kind." She glanced at his open door. "Would you mind if I closed this?"

He looked surprised but quickly recovered. "Sure, no problem at all!"

She closed the door gently and resumed her seat as he resumed his. "Now what's on your mind, Jane? Don't tell me we've got another visitor on the green?"

He was referring to a homeless man who had lived in Shady Hills the previous year. "No, no, nothing like that."

He smiled another huge smile. "Okay, then I'll let you start. Oh, by the way," he said, gesturing toward the glass wall between his office and the corridor, "you want Stanley in on this?"

"No!" She hadn't meant it to come out like that.

"Fine, fine," he said lightly, and gave her a little wink whose meaning she couldn't begin to imagine. "Shoot!"

At that moment Ward glanced out to the corridor. Jane followed his gaze and found herself looking straight at Stanley, only two feet away. He looked dumbfounded, his mouth hanging open, his brow wrinkled. He glanced from her to Ward, clearly expecting to be invited in, but Jane only gave him a weak little grin, and Ward lifted his big mitt of a hand in a friendly wave. Baffled, Stanley shook his head and moved on.

"Now," Ward said, and waited.

"Eric, I want to talk to you about the girls who have vanished from town."

Very slowly, his face darkened. "I beg your pardon?"

"You know what I'm talking about," she said mildly. "First there was that poor soul Ashley Surow, who ran away and made it home only long enough to get killed. Then there was Roxanne Shaughnessy, who vanished about a month ago. And less than two weeks ago there's Keiko Morikawa."

"Jane," Ward said on a sigh, "what does any of this have to do with you?"

"Before Crystal Ryerson and Ashley Surow were murdered, Ashley told Crystal something. I believe they were killed because of whatever it was they knew."

"Okay," he said, playing along. "Then I'll repeat: What has any of this got to do with you?"

"Crystal was the sister of my housekeeper, Florence. Florence is also my friend. I promised her I would try to find out who killed Crystal."

"Why?"

"I just told you, because she's my friend."

"No, I mean on what authority are you investigating these murders? Or these girls' disappearances, for that matter."

"On—my own authority," she blustered. "I don't have to be a cop to solve a murder. In fact, as I'm sure you're aware, I have already solved five murders in this town. Murders your department failed to solve."

His expression grew stony. "So you're playing detective again." He threw out his hands. "You're right, Jane, I can't stop you from doing that. But I don't need to cooperate with you in your 'investigation,' and I certainly won't let you get in our way."

She drew back. "I'm not getting in your way."

He looked down at his desk in embarrassment. "You're starting to get in the way when you barge into the mayor's office and attack him."

"I did not attack him. We were having a perfectly civilized conversation until he started abusing me. That's when I slapped him—which I admit I shouldn't have done. But I certainly never 'attacked' him."

"Jane, let's not split hairs. You're making a nuisance of yourself. You like this crime stuff—maybe that's why you like Stanley."

She stared at him in amazement.

"But the fact is, it's none of your business."

She was so tired of being told this. "You know what I think?" she said.

"No, what?"

"I think people like you and Rob Bergman don't want this to be any of my business because you want to keep these girls' disappearances quiet. I think you want to keep them quiet because you're both heavily invested in Maple Estates, and it isn't good for sales if it gets out that Shady Hills is a dangerous place for teenage girls."

His nostrils flared. "Who said I'm an investor in Maple Estates?"

"Well, aren't you?"

"Yes," he conceded, "I do happen to be. That's public knowledge. But I hope you realize the seriousness of your allegations."

"Yes," she said, meeting his gaze levelly, "I do." She leaned forward. "Why else would you have blown off Agnes Shaughnessy when she called you a month ago and reported Roxanne missing."

"What do you mean, blown her off?"

"You never got back to her!"

"We're still working on it!"

"Are you?" She laughed. "I don't think so."

He placed his hands flat on his desk. "Believe what you like. And let me tell you something. If you don't think most of the people with money in Shady Hills aren't invested in Maple Estates, you're pathetically naive. In fact,

I'm surprised that with your money, *you* aren't an investor." He cocked his head to one side. "But maybe you're too busy minding other people's business and playing private eye to get involved in smart deals."

She wasn't going to let him get to her the way Bergman had. Besides, she was already going to be in enough trouble with Stanley. She rose. "I appreciate your time."

"Not at all," he said, getting to his feet. "Sorry I couldn't help you more."

No, you're not, you corrupt liar.

"Oh, Jane . . ." he said, and she turned at the door. "I'm a little concerned about whatever you've got going on at your office. All those reporters, news vans. I was going to ask Stanley to speak to you, but I might as well do it. We've had a couple of complaints from other business owners on the green. They feel you're creating a disturbance."

Perhaps she was, but she wasn't about to agree with him. "And?" she asked coolly.

He gave an easy shrug. "And people who create a disturbance get fined." He winked. "Just a word to the wise."

She turned and left his office. As she reached the reception area at the center point of the corridor, she saw Stanley emerge from his office and glare at her. To her relief, he didn't move toward her.

She hurried out to her car.

Chapter 18

In her fury she had no trouble barging through the reporters and getting into the office.

Daniel and Goddess both looked up from their desks. "Jane—" they said in unison.

"Can't talk," she said, rushing past them, and made a beeline for her office.

She stopped short. Stanley was sitting in her chair.

"Close the door," he said.

She looked him in the eye. "You've got to be kidding. First of all, don't you ever talk to me like that, Stanley Greenberg."

"Or what?"

"Or what?" she said, her tone deadly. "Or you'll wonder how you lost your girlfriend so fast. Second, get out of my chair. Now."

Very slowly, his gaze fixed on her, he rose and moved to her visitor's chair. Passing perilously close to him, she moved into her chair, which he'd warmed up considerably. How had he gotten there so fast?

"Okay," he said. "What do you think you're doing? Do you have any idea how much trouble you've gotten me into?"

She'd had enough. "No. Sorry, Stanley. I don't answer to you. You are not my father. You are not my boss."

He ignored this. "Jane, you're making enemies all over town. The chief of police. The mayor. Did you really slap him?"

"Yes," she replied calmly, as if confirming that she'd bought groceries. "He deserved it, believe me."

"Jane," he said, leaning forward at the waist, "why are you doing this?"

"Doing what? Confronting these men who care more about money than human life? That's evil, Stanley. That's corruption. Don't you see? Your boss, the chief of police, is corrupt!"

"Jane, life isn't so black and white."

She squinted at him pityingly. "Not you, too. Oh, Stanley, don't you hear what you're saying? There's no gray area here. It's quite simple. I'll spell it out for you. Your boss, Eric Ward, chief of police in Shady Hills, New Jersey, and Robert Bergman, mayor of Shady Hills, New Jersey, and who knows how many others in this wonderful town, are working together to cover up the fact that innocent teenage girls are vanishing. The reason they're doing this is so as not to discourage people from buying homes in Maple Estates, in which they have invested money. There. Is that simple enough for you? No gray there, Stanley. Black and white, plain and simple."

For several moments he stood looking at her, his face twisted into a frown, as if he were seeing her as he had never seen her before. Then, very slowly, he began to shake his head. "I'm sorry, Jane, but I think you're wrong, dead wrong. I don't know, maybe it's because you're upset about what happened to Crystal—I know you're very fond of Florence and you feel for her—but this kind of conspiracy theory . . . it's just crazy."

It was those words that put her over the edge.

"Get out."

"What?"

"Get out!" she shrieked, coming out from behind her desk, and she pushed at him, moving him toward the door.

"Jane, stop," he said, even as he lost his footing and nearly tripped.

But she kept pushing at him until he threw her hands from him, stared hard at her for a moment, and then left her office and went out the front door.

She watched him go, then slammed her office door so hard the room shook.

Then she collapsed into her visitor's chair and burst into hot, angry tears at the realization of what she'd just done.

At her desk, Goddess sipped her Dr Pepper, then took a big bite of her meatball hero. "Jane?" she said timidly.

Jane, sitting in Daniel's visitor's chair with a slice of pizza in her hand, looked over. "Hm?"

"Is this how all offices are?"

Jane had to laugh. "Fortunately, no."

"You gonna go to him? Say you're sorry?"

"After what you heard him say to me? Would you?"

"No."

"All right, then."

Daniel looked at her and blinked sadly. "I'm sure you two will patch things up."

She shrugged. "I don't know . . ."

He gazed down at his chef's salad. She knew he couldn't believe it. Neither could she. A terrible, empty sadness crept through her. Was that it? Were she and Stanley through?

"It's all so hard to accept," Daniel said. "I mean about Chief Ward and Mayor Bergman and the houses and everything. How can such terrible things happen in such a sleepy little town?"

She looked at him in disbelief. "How can you, of all

people—you, who lost your wife the way you did—ask that?"

He nodded. "You're right."

Hearing the mention of Daniel's wife, Goddess looked over, her eyes wide, but said nothing. She knew all too well what had happened to his wife. She had been closer to his wife than anyone had ever suspected. But that was another, painful story, Jane told herself, and put it from her mind.

"I think," she said thoughtfully, taking a bite of pizza, "that things like this actually happen *more* in places like Shady Hills, *because* no one expects to find them there."

"Jeepers," Goddess said, crumpling her bag into a ball and dropping it into her wastebasket. "And I thought New York was bad!"

Jane and Daniel burst out laughing.

"Boy, Jane, now you've gone and done it." Ginny nibbled distractedly on her thumbnail, gazing at Jane across the table at Whipped Cream. "Are you going to apologize?"

Jane stared into the fireplace. "For what? Confronting people who have done something wrong?"

Ginny shook her head. "No, for screaming at Stanley and kicking him out of your office."

"Oh, that. Yes, I suppose he does deserve an apology for that. But if we're finished anyway, what difference does it make?"

At the thought of this prospect, Ginny's face took on a look of horror. She got up. "I'll get your breakfast."

A moment later she returned, setting down a steaming mug of coffee and a large muffin on a plate.

Jane looked at the muffin and did a double take. Its top was slathered with bright orange frosting, and in the center was a piece of black candy in the shape of a cat.

"Happy Halloween!" Ginny said. "Charlie and George told me to decorate all the muffins today. I *must* stop eating the candy corn."

Jane smiled. She realized she had become so caught up in Crystal's and Ashley's murders and Keiko's and Roxanne's disappearances that she had completely forgotten about Halloween. Nick, who at eleven no longer wanted to go trick-or-treating, would attend the town's Halloween party that evening. In the past she had helped him with his costume, but this year he had informed her that he intended only to apply some face makeup. Daniel and Goddess had decorated the office, so Jane hadn't had to do that. It made Jane a little sad that the fun lead-up to Halloween had passed her by this year.

Suddenly she was aware that Ginny was still standing beside the table.

"Yoo-hoo," Ginny said. "Anybody home?"

Jane gave her head a shake. "Sorry."

Ginny put her hands on her hips and smiled sympathetically. "Don't be so hard on yourself. I know you love Florence—we all do. But it's not your job to find out who did that awful thing to Crystal. You've done your best. Why not leave it to the police now?"

"The police!" Jane gave a mirthless chuckle. "The way I've left it to them in the past? I may *have* to give up, and yet I feel I'm so close."

"You do?"

"Yes. It's like a jigsaw puzzle. There are all these different pieces lying on the table, none of them fitting together. But one piece is missing. If I can find it, I'll know how *all* the pieces combine." Shaking her head, she got up.

"You haven't touched your muffin!"

"Sorry, Ginny, but I don't think I can deal with orange frosting on my apple raisin muffin."

"I can get you a plain one."

"Thanks, but that's all right. I'm not very hungry. I *will* let you put my coffee in a cup to go, if you wouldn't mind."

"Not at all."

It was a magnificent morning. Strolling across the green, Jane gazed up at a cloudless sky. The sun was bright and warm, the air unseasonably balmy. A gentle wind played with the dried leaves on the grass. They skittered onto the path in front of Jane as she walked.

Far to Jane's left, a police car turned from Packer Road onto Center Street and glided slowly around the green. It was Stanley. Jane felt a little leap in her stomach. As he turned onto the section of road that ran in front of Jane's office, he turned his head and saw her. Her heart stopped. Her head told her to smile at him, but she couldn't. And when he saw that she hadn't, he turned his head away, his face expressionless, and drove on.

What was the matter with her? Perhaps she should call him when she got to the office, apologize for the way she'd treated him the day before. She'd humiliated him, taken advantage of the fact that he would never push her back. *Oh, Stanley.* Misery washed over her.

She looked up at her office about fifty yards away and stopped short. Across the street from the agency's front door, the largest crowd of reporters yet had gathered. Now she noticed the two TV news vans parked far to the left, in front of Up, Up and Away. A buzz of talk and laughter rose from the crowd, as if they were having a small party. This really was too much.

At that moment a black Lincoln Town Car pulled off Packer Road and started around the green. *Oh, no.* Goddess must have taken Jane's advice and selected this less conspicuous means of getting to work than her stretch limousine. But why was she so late? Jane's watch said ten o'clock.

The car pulled up in front of the office, obscured by the crowd of reporters. This should be interesting, Jane thought, and moved off the path, craning her neck so that she could see the car again.

The door on the side of the car closest to Jane was thrown open, and after a moment two plump legs appeared, then a bright green muumuu.

Oh, no.

It was Salomé Sutton.

Chapter 19

How dare she come here, after Jane had expressly told her no!

Jane watched. She had no intention of making her presence known. Salomé had taken it upon herself to come out here unannounced and uninvited. She could very well turn around and go right back to New York City.

Sal was looking at the crowd of reporters, a baffled scowl on her large face. She put a hand up to her shiny black bouffant hairdo and scratched her head, throwing a troubled look at her driver. The reporters, for their part, didn't know what to make of Salomé, either. Jane saw them looking at one another as if to ask who this woman was.

Now Sal trotted to the sidewalk and up to the agency's entrance. She peered at the plaque that read JANE STUART LITERARY AGENCY.

At that moment Jane noticed movement in the alley to the left of her building. She frowned, confused. Someone was coming through. Jane saw bright rainbow colors, swirling and shaking, and thought at first that she was looking at someone in an elaborate Halloween costume. Then she gasped when she realized that, in effect, she was.

For the person was Goddess. Transfixed, Jane watched. So did Salomé.

Goddess wore a dress that was all swirls of ruffles in bright tropical colors—hot lime, tangerine, lemon yellow, orange, red, and peacock blue. On her tiny blond head sat a tall headdress made up of artfully stacked fruits—lemons, oranges, bananas, grapes, a pineapple. She was Carmen Miranda. She emerged from the alley, stopped, gave the crowd her trademark Goddess smile, and threw her arms into the air.

The crowd went wild. Salomé, only about twenty feet from Goddess, watched in horror as the star clip-clopped back to the alley on seven-inch heels and retrieved a small boom box, which she set on the sidewalk and switched on. Suddenly its speakers blasted music, loud and lively with a Latin beat.

Goddess began to dance, dipping and twirling in the way she'd made famous, one hand going to the other elbow, then reversing, and when a voice was added to the music, she began to lip-synch.

Jane threw back her head and laughed. It was Carmen Miranda's *"Mama Eu Quero."* Around and around Goddess spun, tossing her fruit-topped head and wiggling her arms, her rainbow ruffles swirling.

Then the song was over and she suddenly stopped, breathing hard, and took a bow. The crowd cheered, several of the reporters crying, "Brava! Brava!" Goddess threw them kisses. Then she grabbed the boom box, minced to the door of the agency, and turned to face everyone again. "Happy Halloween!" she cried. And as the crowd went truly nuts, the door behind her opened and she slid inside.

Still the crowd cheered and applauded, and with a start Jane realized Ginny was standing beside her on the path, laughing uproariously. "Unbelievable," she said, and shaking her head in wonder, turned and headed back to Whipped Cream.

Jane glanced back at the road. Coming toward her, her face dark red, her nostrils flaring like an enraged bull, was Salomé. She stepped onto the green, crossed the grass, and stomped up to Jane. "You've got some explaining to do."

Jane gave her a bright little smile. "I have?"

"What the blazes was that all about? I come all the way out here to check out your operation—which you've insisted is as professional as any agency in New York—and I find a Vegas floor show right outside your door. Well? Start explaining."

At that moment, as she gazed at Sal, Jane felt a great weight lift from her shoulders. She shook her head. "Nope, no explaining."

"What!"

"I'm sorry it's taken me so long to get to this point. Sorry for me, that is. Life is too short for me to spend one more minute of it being abused and insulted. So hit the road, Sal. You're fired."

Sal looked as if her face were about to explode. Her eyes bulged dangerously. "I'm—what?"

"Fired. We're finished. I'm releasing you from our representation agreement." When Sal still looked baffled, Jane added, enunciating carefully, "I don't want to be your agent anymore. Good luck, no hard feelings—I hope—and have a good life."

This Sal understood. With a shake of her head that set her jowls quaking, she turned and stormed back to her hired car. Throwing open the door, she got in, shouting something to the driver. Then she yanked the door shut and the car sped away. Watching it go, Jane had never felt more empowered.

The reporters were banging on the agency door. She

pushed her way through and turned to face them. The crowd grew quiet. "Show's over," she said with a smile. "Happy Halloween!"

The door opened behind her and Daniel yanked her in and slammed it shut, locking it. Goddess sat on her desk, her fruit headdress askew. "What'dja think?" she asked, still breathing hard.

Jane went up to her. It was time to ask Goddess to leave. "I loved it. We all loved it. But—"

"This is really hard for me to say, Jane, because you and Daniel have been so wonderful, letting me work here and teaching me and everything." Goddess smiled sadly. "But it's time for me to go. This . . ." She indicated the office. "It's just not me."

"I understand," Jane said solemnly. "It was fun having you here."

Goddess hopped off the desk. "You're a total friend," she said, and gave Jane a peck on the cheek. Then she ran up to Daniel, still standing at the door, grabbed the back of his neck, and planted a kiss hard on his lips. When she pulled away, he was smiling.

"And you," Goddess said to him ruefully, "are one yummy boy toy. Ginny's a lucky girl." She put her hand on the doorknob, then stopped. "Oh! I almost forgot!" She ran into the storage room and appeared a moment later with a stack of romance novels balanced under her chin. "Can't forget these. Jane, baby, keep sendin' 'em, okay?"

"Okay," Jane promised, and she and Daniel watched through the window as she burst out the door and struggled through the reporters to the curb. At that moment, as if by magic, her silver stretch limousine pulled up. The driver hopped out, held the door, and she dived in. Then the driver ran back around to his door. Before he got in, he looked over at Jane and Daniel in the window and tipped his cap. Then he jumped in and the car glided away.

On the sidewalk, the crowd of reporters slowly began to disperse.

It was hard to get much work done that day. During the first hour after Goddess's departure, the phone rang continuously, as people called to offer their congratulations. One of them was Florence, who had heard all about it from her friend Noni. "Missus, I cannot believe you kept such a secret from me and Nick. Tonight you will have to tell us all about it." Jane wondered how Mayor Bergman, Chief Ward, and Stanley felt about Goddess's media event.

Gradually the exhilaration gave way to sadness, as Jane remembered her argument with Stanley the previous day . . . the way he'd looked at her from his squad car and then looked quickly away . . . the murders of Crystal and Ashley . . . the disappearances of Roxanne and Keiko. Would these mysteries ever be solved?

Her intercom buzzed and she jumped.

"Jane?" came Daniel's voice. "It's three fifty. Don't you have a nail appointment at four?"

At first she had no idea what he was talking about. Then she remembered her biweekly manicure appointment. Originally she had planned to have outrageously long, creepy nails to scare the trick-or-treaters, but now all she wanted to do was honor her appointment and go home.

She bade Daniel good night and crossed the darkening green to Nails by Gail, a tiny shop nestled between a pharmacy and Giorgio's.

Gail Girard, who owned the shop, was a pretty dark-haired woman in her late forties who never stopped talking. After offering Jane her condolences about Crystal and asking Jane to convey them to Florence as well, she moved on to the subject of Goddess.

"An unbelievable treat," she said, adding a pinch of salt

to Jane's soaking water. "So your hands won't get pruney," she explained, as she did every time. Then she added a bit of scented oil. "To make your hands even softer. Now put them in . . ."

Jane obeyed. Gail prattled on.

"What a talent. Truly an original. I wonder what kind of nails she's got. Hey, you had her right there in your office, Jane! What kind of nails has she got?"

Jane shrugged. "They're . . . nails."

Gail rolled her eyes. "You're hopeless. Are they long? Short? What?"

"Um, medium."

"Okay, fair enough. Medium. I would have expected long nails on her." Gail gave a little shrug. "Only because nails are so empowering, and Goddess is the ultimate empowered woman."

"Empowering?" Jane asked skeptically. "Nails?"

Gail looked shocked. "I'm surprised at you, Jane. Smart woman like you. Did you know . . ."

Oh, no.

". . . that in ancient China—three thousand B.C.!—royalty painted their nails black and red? Yes. I've always wondered why black and red," Gail said to herself, then shrugged. "In ancient Egypt, if you were in the highest social class, your nails were red. Cleopatra did her nails deep red, and Queen Nefertiti liked ruby! Isn't that fascinating?"

Jane was anything but fascinated, especially because she got roughly this same manicure history lesson every time. She would change the subject. Nails made her think of the trouble she'd been having with Winky and Twinky's claws. She related to Gail the saga of the scratching posts.

"I had the same problem with my sweet little George and Gracie," Gail said, removing Jane's right hand from the soaking bowl and drying it gently with a soft towel.

She rubbed cuticle oil onto Jane's fingers, then got to work with an orange stick. "I was at my wit's end. Then I got the right kind of scratching post, same as you, and . . . *viola!*"—this was one of Gail's little idiosyncrasies, saying *viola* instead of *voilà*—"the scratching on my dresser stopped!"

Jane nodded. "Amazing, isn't it? That you can get them to stop without having to have them declawed?"

Gail looked up in horror. "Never! I mean, my word, can you imagine how frustrating it must be for a cat to want a nice scratch but have no claws?"

Jane froze. "What did you say?"

"I said . . . can you imagine what a cat must feel like—you know, wanting to scratch but not being able to?"

"No, no. You said 'frustrating.' "

"Yeah, well, it would be!"

Jane jumped up, jerking her left hand from the soaking bowl. "It's my puzzle piece. And that book! It's not a romance!"

"What? Jane! What are you doing?"

Jane grabbed Gail's towel and hurriedly dried off her hands. "I'm sorry, Gail, but I have to go." She fished frantically in her purse and threw down some bills. "You've been great," she said, already at the door. "Happy Halloween!"

She ran across the street and onto the green. She must speak to Stanley. What happened yesterday didn't matter anymore. Well, it did, but they could deal with that later. Hurrying across the grass, she got out her cell phone and called him. She got his voice mail. "Stanley," she said after the beep, "I have to talk to you. It's *urgent.* I know you're mad at me, and I apologize for what I did yesterday, I really do, but please, *please* call me the second you get this message."

She would wait for his call at home. She ran through the

alley to her car in the lot behind her building. Jumping in, she started the engine, drove out to Center Street, and followed Packer across the railroad tracks. On her left was the office building in which Dr. Katz and Mayor Bergman had their offices. She passed the police station on the right, followed by the municipal building, then the library.

With a frown she slowed the car, squinting into the darkness. On the library's wide front steps, someone lay facedown, arms outstretched. Jane pulled up to the curb and peered out the car window. "Oh, no," she whispered. It was Mindy Carter. She must have fallen.

Jane cut the engine, hopped out of the car, and ran up the path to the building. "Mindy!" she called, approaching the steps. "Mindy!" She stepped closer, bending over to get a better look.

"Trick or treat," a man's voice whispered in her ear as two strong arms encircled her waist from behind, pulling her off her feet and dragging her swiftly around the side of the building into the shadows.

Chapter 20

Jane screamed, struggling against the iron grip around her waist, against the man who had dragged her behind a large bush. Someone appeared from the front of the building—to help her?

Jane's scream froze in her throat. It was Mindy, very much alive, and smiling a mild smile. She held something in her hand, which she suddenly raised up and swung at the side of Jane's head. Jane felt a terrible jarring pain—

She came to, a dry rag shoved into her mouth, her hands bound painfully behind her back, her head throbbing unbearably. At first she felt movement. Then, as her awareness returned, she realized she was in a vehicle. She looked to her right. She was in the front passenger seat of a van, driving on a dark road, a highway. She looked to her left and found herself gazing into the eyes of Rich Weldon. In jeans and a sweatshirt, he drove silently, giving her an indifferent look before returning his gaze to the road.

The gag in Jane's mouth tasted like dirt and grease. She fought to keep from gagging. The pain in her head intensified. She groaned.

"Doesn't matter," Rich said casually, nibbling on a fingernail. "It will all be over for you soon."

Suddenly she remembered leaving a message for Stanley. Her cell phone! Then she remembered she'd left it on the seat of her car when she'd jumped out to help Mindy.

He pulled off the highway. The van rolled down an exit ramp, evened off, and entered a tangle of dark streets—squalid city streets, bound by decrepit old buildings of stone or brick . . . vacant lots filled with garbage and weeds . . . rusted chain-link fences topped by razor wire.

Abruptly he slowed the van and turned left into a narrow alley between two dark, looming brick buildings. Glancing up, Jane saw three long rows of tall windows.

He parked in a sort of courtyard behind this building. Turning off the engine, he got out and came around to Jane's side, throwing open her door. Brutally he grabbed her from the seat, his arms around her waist again—he was surprisingly strong—and then he was dragging her again, as if she were a sack of flour. She would have walked if he had let her, but he kept dragging her, through a door in the side of the soot-blackened building and into a cavernous, shadowy room. Here he changed course, now pulling her toward the room's right-hand wall.

Savagely he flung her to the floor. She expected to hit it painfully, but something softened her fall—a cushion of some sort. Then she glanced down and saw that it was a large piece of foam rubber, filthy and darkened with age. She was on her back now. Looking to her right, to the wall at the room's other end, she made out machinery of some kind, long banks of intricate black metal.

All of a sudden he bent over and ripped the gag from Jane's mouth. The rough movement intensified the pain in her head. She spat bits of dirt and cloth.

"So which movie are you going to put me in?" she asked him, her voice low and contemptuous.

He put his hands on his hips and laughed, then tossed his hair. "So you *have* figured it out. What I want to know is—how?"

"It wasn't hard, once I had my missing piece. It was fingernails."

"What?" he said, looking at her as if were insane.

"I suddenly remembered something Ashley Surow had told Cara Fairchild. She said Cosmo got so frustrated when he couldn't open his pocket knife that he slapped her. Why would opening a pocket knife be so difficult? Because your nails are bitten down to the quick." She lowered her gaze to his hands, which he put behind his back self-consciously.

"And that was it?"

"No, not only that. It was also Celeste Cohen."

He frowned, watching her.

"She was the link, you see, between you and Cosmo Blair. To Roxanne Shaughnessy, Ashley Surow, and Keiko Morikawa, you were Cosmo Blair, the handsome young filmmaker looking for new talent. But then you needed an alibi for the time Crystal died. So, *looking* like Cosmo Blair but *calling yourself* Rich Weldon, you asked Celeste, the secretary at Dr. Katz's office, to lie for you, to say you had been there.

"Poor deluded Celeste with her good-luck ring, reading *A Dream of Passion,* which I suddenly remembered isn't a romance at all, but an *acting book.* The subtitle is *The Development of the Method* and it's by Lee Strasberg, the famous acting teacher. Celeste was preparing for the movie role you'd promised her." She looked at him curiously. "I'm surprised you haven't killed her yet."

His eyes narrowed to slits. "Who says I'm not going to?" He wet his lips. "Were those the only giveaways?"

"No, there were other clues, clues I couldn't see at first. Obviously, Ashley never realized you were Cosmo Blair, though she saw you at the library five days a week."

"Exactly," Rich said smugly. "No one pays any attention to the shy custodian. He's invisible."

Jane nodded. "But when Ashley described Cosmo to Crystal, she must have mentioned a gesture or mannerism that was familiar to Crystal. Maybe it's that annoying way you have of tossing your hair to get it out of your eyes. I bet it's become such a habit that you do it even when you're Cosmo with your hair slicked back.

"Crystal said something to her sister Florence about how a person can't really hide who he is. Florence thought Crystal was talking about her husband, but what she actually meant was that disguises don't always work. Then Crystal told Florence she had to speak to someone and wasn't looking forward to it. My guess is that that someone was Mindy Carter, who it appears is in cahoots with you."

"Of course she is," Rich said. "She's my mother."

Jane blinked in surprise. This she hadn't guessed, but it made sense. "A perfect setup . . . High school girls come to the library to study, allowing you and your mother to select the ones you want, the most beautiful girls in town."

"Right, because that's how our clients like 'em." Rich smiled, and suddenly Jane could see that he *was* handsome, that there was an attractive face behind the scraggly hair. "Those are the girls who fetch the most money."

"White slavery," Jane said flatly, and Rich smiled again, proudly now.

"People think it never happens *here,* but it happens everywhere, right under people's noses. My mother and I have done it in the last two towns we lived in, and we're going to continue to do it in Shady Hills."

"You weren't about to let a busybody like Crystal Ryerson get in your way, were you?" Jane said contemptuously. "After Crystal made the fatal mistake of confiding her suspicions about your dual identity to Mindy—unaware that she was your mother and your accomplice—Mindy told you to remove the bolts on the bookcase."

"That's right."

"How clever she was to have you do it at a time when any number of people could have had access. You were right there in the library the whole time, weren't you? In the 'secret' room where poor Ashley had tried to hide."

"Right again. I popped out when I was sure no one was in the back room of the library, removed the two bolts, and ran back to the secret room."

"And to make sure Crystal climbed the ladder, Mindy recommended a novel to me that Crystal would have to climb the ladder to get."

"Climb the ladder *and* reach way out," Rich said with a clever smirk. "We had to make sure she pulled the bookcase over on herself. Crash!" He threw back his head and laughed.

Jane winced. "But one murder wasn't enough. Next was poor Ashley, and only a day later. You had to be sure she would never connect Cosmo Blair with Rich Weldon."

He nodded. "I took great pleasure in killing her. She deserved to die for the way she looked through me at the library, like I was air. Then, when I was good-looking and could do something for her—oh yeah, she was interested then, wasn't she? She was so easy to kill. After she ran out of here and got away from me, I figured she'd get back to Shady Hills somehow. Maybe she hitched a ride—I don't know. Anyway, I drove right back to Shady Hills and set myself up outside her friend Cara's house. Cara was her best friend. They were together a lot at the library, or else I'd hear Ashley talking about her with Crystal. I knew Ashley would go to her."

"What made you think she wouldn't go to the police?"

He shrugged. "I couldn't be sure, but I'd heard her telling Crystal about her father, how strict he was and everything, how he would kill her if he ever thought she'd done anything 'cheap.' " He laughed. "Cheap. I guess running off with a movie producer and almost getting raped is kind of cheap, huh? Turns out I was right. Cara and Ashley pulled up to Cara's house. Ashley waited in the car while Cara ran in for something."

The ATM card, Jane thought.

"When Cara came out again, I followed them. First they went to Crystal's apartment, way up off Fenwyck Road. Then they drove to the library. It was perfect. Ashley went inside—Cara drove away—I went inside." He made a grotesque strangling motion. "I dragged her body out the back and dumped it in the woods. And do you know what?" he said, leaning over and putting his face only inches from Jane's. "You're next. I gotta make a call, then I'll be back for some fun."

"Fun?"

"I can't sell you—you're too old, though you must have been a knockout once. But *I* can still enjoy you . . . before I kill you. It's the least you can do for me, after all the trouble you've put me through."

He turned and walked off into the shadows. Vaguely she could make out his silhouette in the darkness. Then, from far away, she heard him talking on his cell phone.

"Yeah . . . I got her here . . . Yeah, at the mill, where do you think? . . . I'm gonna do it here, then dump her somewhere . . . I don't know yet. Listen, did you think about my suggestion? . . . Well, I think she's just right, the kind they want. Okay, good, I'll look for her at Roadside tomorrow night, then, tell her she oughta be in pictures!" He barked out a laugh.

Frantic, Jane glanced about her. So this cavernous room had once been part of a silk mill. Her and Audrey's guess that Cosmo Blair had taken Ashley to Paterson had been correct, then. Paterson had once been the silk capital of the world.

She turned and looked behind her. Machines similar to the ones on the far left wall ran along this wall as well. These were nearer to Jane—only five or six feet away— and she realized that they were broken-down looms, black with age. She was afraid to stand up because he might see her. She lay back and rolled over so that she could study the machinery more closely. Her gaze raked the floor. There, among the dust and dirt and cobwebs, lay a pile of black metal rods about a foot long. She threw a glance back at Rich's shadow, listened. He was still on the phone, planning future abductions.

Slowly, carefully, she moved so that her back was to the pile of metal rods. Then, bending in the middle and propelling herself with her feet, she moved her bound hands toward the rods . . . inching closer . . . and then she felt them. Cold, covered with filth. But solid metal. It seemed to take forever for her tied hands to gain a firm grip around only one of the rods.

When Rich returned, she was back on the sheet of foam rubber, exactly where he'd left her.

He dropped to his knees before her and with a little smile began unbuttoning his jeans. She lay perfectly still, watching him, as he leaned forward to touch her.

With a sudden movement she drew her legs in sharply and then delivered a powerful kick directly to his crotch. He grimaced, letting out a grunt of pain, and fell forward.

She scrambled to her feet and ran, forcing herself to adjust to the clumsiness of running with her hands tied behind her back, gripping the metal rod. She made for the door they had come through. She could see that it opened outward. She pushed on it. It was locked tight. The pounding pain in her head grew stronger. She glanced over her shoulder and saw Rich get to his feet and start toward her. She ran some more, along the wall, and suddenly spotted another door. She pushed on it. Locked.

She ran again. Now there was a seemingly endless expanse of solid wall. She heard him getting closer, heard him panting, heard her own ragged breath, felt her head about to explode.

At the end of the wall was another door, her last chance. She threw her shoulder against it and it opened easily. Bursting through, she found a stairway going up. She dashed up the stairs and immediately heard Rich come through the door below, heard his feet pounding on the stairs—she wasn't sure how near.

The stairs turned and turned again. Flying upward, she reached a landing and shouldered through another door. Cold air hit her face. She ran forward. She was on the roof, a vast flat expanse with a water tank at the far end.

Desperately she ran to the middle of the great flat black expanse and spun around. Beyond the roof on all sides sparkled the lights of Paterson. There was no way off.

Rich exploded through the door from the stairs, his chest heaving. He looked around, spotted her, and started toward her.

Chapter 21

"Give it up," he called to her. "You can either jump off the roof and splatter all over the road or I can give you a much nicer send-off. Why not go out smiling?"

She ran toward the edge of the roof, away from him, and reached the cistern she had seen from the distance. She backed up against it, heard the metal of the rod in her hand tap the metal of the great water tank. There she waited for him, her chest heaving, watching him slowly approach.

"Why're you playing so hard to get, baby?" He raised one eyebrow. "Hey, wanna be in my movie?" He burst out laughing and came closer.

She remained perfectly still, watching him. In the next instant he was upon her, nuzzling her neck. She felt his hot breath . . .

In a flash she spun around and, with the metal rod gripped firmly in her bound hands, brought her arms up with all her might, so hard she felt her shoulders strain at the sockets. She heard a soft grunt, an odd sound, and was afraid to turn around again, afraid of what she would find, but she did.

Rich was holding the rod now, but only its tip. The rest

of it was embedded in his belly. Staring at her blankly, dark blood sluicing down his hands and dripping onto the tar of the roof, he began to sink.

"*Please,*" he gasped in a thin, reedy voice.

She took a step toward him. Then she planted her right shoe firmly in the center of his chest and pushed him backward, until he lay collapsed before her.

She watched him for a moment, just to make sure he wasn't going anywhere. Then she ran to the edge of the roof, peered down at the cars racing by below, took a deep breath, and screamed, "Help!"

Chapter 22

"Thank you, missus," Florence said, wiping tears from her eyes. "I know my sister thanks you, too."

"You're welcome," Jane said, patting Florence's hand. They were in Jane's study. Jane had just explained everything to Florence, who now rose with an expression of sadness mixed with tranquility.

The door from the living room gave a little creak as Winky pushed her way in. She gave a short mew, then hopped into Jane's lap.

The doorbell rang. "Just one moment," Florence said, and went to answer it. A moment later she was back. "Missus, there's someone here to see you."

A fearful thrill went through her. She nodded. Florence turned and Stanley appeared behind her, a look of concern on his handsome face. Quickly Florence withdrew, softly closing the door.

Jane set Winky down gently on the carpet, then she was in Stanley's arms.

"I'm so sorry," she said.

"No, I'm sorry." He kissed her neck, buried his face there, breathing deeply. "I was such a fool."

"Now don't get me crying," she protested. "We're both

sorry, we were both fools . . . and I love you, Stanley Greenberg."

He took her in his arms again. "I love you, too, Jane Stuart. You know I do."

She burst into tears. "Now you've done it," she said with a laugh. "Come, let's sit."

They sat down in adjacent chairs and held hands. Winky popped right back into Jane's lap.

"Thank heavens you're all right," Stanley said. "Now, can you tell me what exactly happened last night? Start after you left me that phone message."

So she did. It took a while, but she explained everything, chronologically, from Roxanne Shaughnessy's disappearance a month earlier all the way up to Jane's confrontation with Rich Weldon on a rooftop in Paterson the previous night. "And if it hadn't been for Winky and Twinky and their blessed scratching," she said, lovingly stroking Winky's silky mottled head, "I would never have put it all together." She slumped in her chair. "I'm so tired."

"I'm sure the doctor has told you to rest. Shame on me for dragging you through it all again."

She waved away his concern. "I'm fine. Now, what do you have to tell me?"

"Mindy Carter has been arrested, of course. She's already ratting on her own son. These two make Sante and Kenneth Kimes look good."

"How is the dear boy?"

"He's at St. Joseph's Hospital in Paterson. The doctors tell me they expect a full recovery."

"Good." Her face grew troubled. "Now what about Roxanne and Keiko? Do you know where they are?"

"Yes, now we do."

She looked confused.

"Once we knew that Mindy Carter and Rich Weldon

were running a white slavery operation, we were able to make some connections and put together the whole picture. Mindy and Rich were, in fact, working for a much larger ring, with headquarters in Hilldale, Utah, and Colorado City, Arizona."

Jane frowned, then looked at him. "I know about those places. I've seen them on the news."

He nodded. "It's the renegade Mormon settlement—really one community with the state line running through it. These aren't mainstream Mormons, who gave up polygamy more than a hundred years ago. They call themselves the Fundamentalist Church of Jesus Christ of Latter-Day Saints."

"But polygamy is illegal."

"True, but it appears this part of the country is kind of a legal no-man's-land. Neither Utah nor Arizona is willing to deal with the polygamists who live there.

"These people will be the first to tell you they're in the business of making babies. The more wives and children a man has, the greater his stature in the community—and in heaven. So wives—women, girls—are a valuable commodity."

Jane slowly nodded. "So valuable they're willing to buy them."

"Right. And if you're going to buy a wife, she might as well be beautiful. This ring has been auctioning girls to the highest bidders."

"So that's where Roxanne and Keiko are?"

"We think Roxanne is there. Keiko is on her way there. As I said, we're plugged into the big picture on this one now, and we shouldn't have any trouble bringing these poor girls back home."

Jane lowered her head and whispered words of thanks.

"Jane?" Stanley said softly. "There's more."

She looked up, her eyes questioning.

"I've been thinking about our argument on Wednesday."

"I hope you've forgiven me."

"Yes, of course I have. I meant I've been thinking about what you said. I've been in denial. I didn't want to see what was right in front of me. Anyway, I think you're right. At the very least there's been an attempt at a cover-up, not to mention a serious conflict of interest. I'm going to see that charges are filed and that Eric Ward and Robert Bergman are removed from their jobs."

"Oh, Stanley," she said, and hugged him tightly.

A short time later, as he was leaving, he remembered something, and turned at the front door. "Some sad news, I'm afraid. Gabrielle Schraft—you know, the woman who runs that wonderful cat shelter up on Fremont Lane?"

"Yes?"

"Her beagle, Skipper, died."

"Oh, that is sad," she said, then looked at him cannily. "Why are you telling me this?"

At that moment, as if on cue, Alphonse galloped in from the family room, Winky and Twinky not far behind. Alphonse let out one bark and barreled up the stairs, the two cats in hot pursuit.

When Jane looked back at Stanley, he was smiling. "Just thought you'd want to know."

Epilogue

"I can't thank you enough," Gabrielle Schraft said to Jane and Stanley in her deep voice. They stood outside Paws for Love. Stanley held the end of Alphonse's leash. "Shall I get him now?" Gabrielle asked.

Jane and Stanley nodded. Gabrielle went into the building and returned a moment later with William. As soon as he saw Alphonse, he ran madly to the dog and threw his arms around it, nearly losing himself in the abundant white and light gold fur. Alphonse twisted around and began madly licking William's face.

"Mom," William said through his laughter, "can we have a dog like this someday?"

Gabrielle knelt down close to her son. "He's yours, darling."

The little boy's eyes grew immense and then he was hugging both his mother and his new dog.

Jane bit her lip to keep from crying. "Well, we'll be going," she said to Gabrielle.

Gabrielle rose and walked up to Jane. "Listen, I want to apologize for being so rude to you. Guess you hit a nerve."

"Not a problem," Jane said, putting out her hand, and the two women shook hands warmly.

"See you at the next reading group meeting?" Gabrielle asked.

"You bet."

When Jane and Stanley reached the far end of the lane leading back to Fremont Lane, they turned. Gabrielle and William were entering the house, Alphonse walking between them.

"You done good, Stanley Greenberg," Jane said with a firm nod. He smiled, put his arm around her, and they walked to his car.

It was another glorious Indian summer day. "Let's not go back yet," Stanley said, gazing out at the hills beyond the road. "It's Saturday. We're not working today. Let's take a ride."

He took her through her own neighborhood but past it, up Magnolia Lane and then way up to Magnolia Place, a cliffside cul-de-sac with a magnificent view of the village. They stood at the railing, quiet for a moment. Then Stanley turned to Jane, his face thoughtful and a little sad.

"So what have we learned from this?" he asked.

She didn't answer right away. Finally she spoke, concentrating as she formed her thoughts. "We've learned that it's not possible to love your children too much or to watch them too carefully . . . that meddling can get you into a lot of trouble . . ."

"And . . . ?" he prompted.

"And that it's a mistake to leave everything to the police," she finished with a mischievous grin.

He gave her a stern look and opened his mouth to speak, but instantly she was upon him, silencing him with a long, deep kiss.

Author's Note

Readers have asked me for more of Florence's wonderful Trinidadian recipes, so here is one of my favorites, Trinidad pelau.

Pelau is a dish famous in Florence's native Trinidad but also served throughout the Caribbean. Basically, pelau is a flavored, stewed rice. Caramelizing the meat is an African influence that became part of Creole cuisine. It's this process that gives pelau its trademark dark brown color.

People make pelau with vegetables, meat, poultry, and/or seafood, according to their preference. Recipes for this classic dish vary greatly. Florence's version uses chicken, but you can substitute beef, pork, shrimp, crab—even goat! If you can't find pigeon peas, you may substitute black-eyed peas. Butternut squash or pumpkin may be substituted for the Hubbard squash.

Florence's Best Trinidad Pelau

4–6 servings

3 tablespoons vegetable oil
¾ cup brown sugar

1 chicken (2½ to 3 pounds), cut up
1 onion, chopped
1 garlic clove, minced
1 celery stalk, chopped
1½ cups pigeon peas, drained
2 cups rice (not instant)
3 cups chicken broth
1 cup coconut milk
2 cups fresh Hubbard squash, cubed
2 carrots, chopped
¼ cup fresh parsley, chopped
1 teaspoon dried thyme
1 bunch scallions, chopped (including the greens)
¼ cup tomato ketchup
3 tablespoons butter

Heat oil in a heavy pot or skillet. With heat on high, add sugar and let it caramelize until it is nearly burned, stirring constantly. Add chicken and stir until all the pieces are covered with the sugar.

Reduce heat to medium and add onion, garlic, and celery, stirring constantly for 1 minute.

Add pigeon peas, rice, chicken broth, and coconut milk. Reduce heat and simmer, covered, for 30 minutes. Add remaining ingredients, mix well, cover, and cook until vegetables are tender, 20 to 30 minutes. At end of cooking time, pelau should be moist.

Serve with pepper sauce and chutney.

I always love hearing from my readers. If you have a comment about *Crushing Crystal* or any of my Jane Stuart and Winky mysteries, I invite you to e-mail me at evan marshall@TheNovelist.com, or write to me at Six Tristam Place, Pine Brook, New Jersey 07058-9445. I always respond to reader mail. For a free bookmark and auto-graphed bookplate, please send a business size (#10) self-addressed stamped envelope. Also, you can subscribe to my free newsletter at my Web site: www.TheNovelist.com.

Evan Marshall